Mom of the Chosen One

Magical Midlife Mom, Book #1

by

DM FIKE

Avalon Labs LLC

Copyright © 2022 DM Fike
All rights reserved

The characters and events portrayed in this book are fictitious. Any similarity to real persons, living or dead, is coincidental and not intended by the author.

No part of this book may be reproduced, or stored in a retrieval system, or transmitted in any form or by any means, electronic, mechanical, photocopying, recording, or otherwise, without express written permission of the publisher.

ISBN: 9798356895906

Cover design by: Avalon Labs LLC

For Eleanor. Always believe in dragons. I love you.

OTHER BOOKS BY DM FIKE

Magical Midlife Librarian Paranormal Series

Curse of the Fae Library
Secret of the Fae Library
Fate of the Fae Library

Magic of Nasci Nature Wizard Series

Chasing Lightning
Breathing Water
Running into Fire
Shattering Earth
Soaring in Air
Rising Scorn
Gathering Swarm
Howling Storm
Extending Branches

Legends of Llenwald YA Portal Fantasy Series

Magic Portal
Magic Curse
Magic Prophecy

CHAPTER 1

THE ONLY THING worse than getting woken up by an alarm is getting woken up by your kid.

The front screen door slammed shut. "Mom!" Regan yelled from down the hall. "Come quick!"

I jumped onto my bedroom floor in my cotton pajamas, adrenaline pumping. My teenage daughter's panicked voice was the only force besides caffeine that could have gotten me out of the warm covers and into the frigid morning air.

"Hurry!" she yelled as I stumbled down our narrow hallway toward the living room.

I found Regan panting in the entryway, wearing a form-fitting athletic jacket, her strawberry blond hair pulled back into a ponytail. She'd obviously just come back from her morning run. Her sapphire blue eyes were wide with fear, and she pointed toward the closed front door.

"There's a wolf outside!"

"What?" I marched into the living room and threw open the front window curtains to gaze across my mossy lawn. It was a typical start to a dreary March day in Salem, Oregon. Muted natural light flittered through the overcast clouds. A row of one-story houses, built in the 60s and in various states of repair, comprised our street. The neighborhood busybody, Nancy Tannen, still had her impeccable drapes drawn shut behind her neat yellow trim. It was too early even for her to begin a day of spying.

I searched everywhere, even the front steps, but there was no wolf.

"There's nothing out there," I said, my heart rate winding down.

Regan smashed her face against the panes, squinting. "I swear I saw a huge black wolf. It came out of the woods at the end of my run and followed me down our street."

I loved my kid more than anything. She was the complete opposite of the typical teenager: kind to a fault, way too smart for her own good, and rarely causes trouble. I counted myself lucky that somehow the universe decided to give me this child to raise instead of the one I probably deserved.

That didn't mean I never felt the urge to strangle her sometimes.

"It was probably just a stray," I grumbled, rubbing my bleary eyes. While we did live in a neighborhood not too far from the river, we were a far cry away from anywhere that housed wild wolves. "Or someone's lost pet."

"It wasn't a pet. I know it was a wolf."

"Well, I see no one huffing or puffing besides you." I turned away from the window. I'd been woken up too early to keep the sarcasm out of my voice.

Knowing she'd lost me completely at that point, Regan stomped past the counter. We had an open kitchen and living room combo divided only by our small dining table and tile flooring. Regan rummaged around in the refrigerator, muttering to herself.

I exaggerated slumping onto a stool at the kitchen bar. "The least you could do for waking me up so early is make coffee."

"You would've gotten up in ten minutes anyway."

I clutched at my heart. "Your screams almost broke my

old ticker. I may not survive without a shot of my morning medicine."

"I should just let you suffer," she said, but she did turn on the coffee machine.

Having gotten my way, I leaned forward as she prepared her own breakfast. "I've been telling you it's dangerous to go running alone. Maybe it's time we revise that particular policy."

"Did I say I saw a wolf?" she replied innocently. "I meant a stray dog. Probably somebody's lost pet."

"Har har. Don't play dumb this early in the morning."

"This is my best chance at fooling you. You're not thinking straight without coffee yet."

Heh. I couldn't refute that after my dramatic display, but I wouldn't let her change the subject. "Things can happen if you're in a secluded area by yourself."

"You want to wrap me in protective bubble wrap and throw me into a storage closet for good measure?"

"Is that an option?"

"Sure, but then I'd grow up all socially stunted and weird."

"You forget that I like weird people. You're only making my case."

"If you won't think of me, at least consider how much you'll have to spend on bubble wrap." She thrust a piece of toast in front of me.

"This isn't coffee."

"You need to eat."

"Who's the parent here again?"

"I've been asking myself that question since the fifth grade."

"Hey, I'm responsible." I swept my arms around the kitchen. "Look upon all I provide for you." Aging appliances surrounded us, along with sturdy but worn furniture and way too much kitschy bric-a-brac. I'd bought this house over a decade ago, and I still marveled that it was mine, mortgage notwithstanding. It had taken me years to get out of living paycheck-to-paycheck with a kid in tow, and even then, the down payment for the loan had almost broken my bank account. But owning my own home, despite its meager 1,100 square feet and outdated wood paneling, still filled me with pride.

Regan rubbed her hands over the chipped countertop. "This house is a time capsule. You should donate it to a museum."

"The Museum of Awesomeness." As a single mom, I'd struggled to build a stable life for Regan and me. I'd worked my butt off at several menial jobs before landing a full-time position at a local technology company. Even that wouldn't have dragged us out of abject poverty if the company's founder, Joshua Page, hadn't recognized my potential.

My chest heaved at the thought of the kooky old man.

Regan caught my mood shift. "Something wrong?"

"Just thinking about work," I said, not wanting to set her off. Even though it'd been months since Joshua's heart attack, I missed my former boss terribly. He'd become something like an uncle to me, always accommodating of the fact that I was raising a single daughter alone. I didn't want to dampen her day with my sudden grief.

"That's right," Regan said as she shoveled food into her mouth. I would have asked her to chew with her mouth closed, but I'd learned to pick and choose my battles carefully with a teenager. "You've got that presentation today, don't you?"

"Are you trying to remind me of my homework now?"

"You? The great and mighty office manager?" Mock shock flashed across her face. "Perish the thought."

I glared down my nose at her. "And best you not forget it, peasant."

We both maintained our ridiculous poses for a few more seconds before bursting into giggles.

I did miss my baby girl, the one who used to beg for walks to the playground and needed hugs when she scraped her knees, but I sure loved the banter with the young adult she'd become.

After we ate—and most importantly, I got sweet, sweet coffee in my system—we both retreated to our rooms to get ready for the day. The one luxury our house had was two bathrooms so we didn't have to fight each other in the morning. I threw on the pair of slacks and blouse I'd ironed just for today, then viewed myself in the mirror above the sink.

My tired green eyes gazed back at me. I'd been up late working on my laptop, and it showed. I plucked a few stray strands of gray hair from my frizzy chestnut-colored locks. I was inching ever closer to needing dye to cover them up. I'd gained more pounds than I wanted around the cheeks but still maintained an average weight to go along with my average height. I dabbed on some under eye concealer and pulled my hair into a tight French braid. Then I clipped on my employee badge, adjusting it so I could see my name "Melissa Hartley" printed in large letters next to a terrible mugshot of me.

On second thought, I flipped the picture toward my blouse. No point in anyone seeing me at my worst.

I met Regan back in the living room. She wore the same athletic clothes as before but had added a gym bag and a bulging backpack as accessories. Despite her lack of makeup, she looked fresh and beautiful. I did envy her youthful looks, but it was her metabolism I would have given my left kidney for.

"You ready to go?" It took me a second to push the front door open because it sometimes got jammed. I walked halfway down the driveway before I realized Regan wasn't right behind me. She was poking her head out the door, glancing in all directions.

I made a big show of scanning the street with my hand over my brow. "Coast be clear, Captain," I said in my best pirate voice. "There be no wolves in these waters."

Regan reddened, but she scooted outside. "You're

mixing metaphors."

"I'll think of a better pun next time."

"Please don't."

We entered the beat-up beige hatchback that Regan had nicknamed "Dirt Dash" as a joke on her favorite fictional toy pony. As I backed us out of the driveway, I yawned so big, my jaw popped.

"Ouch," I said, rubbing my cheek.

Regan tried to act casual by looking out the passenger side window. "You know, you could sleep in if you let me learn how to drive."

"Nice try, kiddo. You know I'm not ready for you to operate heavy machinery just yet. And besides, this may come as a shock to you, but I actually like seeing you once in a while. You're so ridiculously busy with track in the mornings and debate after school, I have to steal these precious moments together whenever I can."

Regan rolled her eyes. "Driving me around town is your idea of fun? You need to get out more. Why don't you try a dating app?"

I cringed as I threw on the wipers to get the morning dew off the windshield. "Ew. Why would you want me to date?"

"Because you're lonely, Mom."

"I've got friends."

"Not the same thing. And I know you're interested. Our Netflix queue has more romantic comedies on it than the Hallmark channel."

"That's pure fantasy. If I started watching more action movies, would you think I wanted to become a superhero?"

"I'm just saying, you're going to end up sad and alone at this rate."

I batted my eyes at her. "I'll always have you, right?"

She wrinkled her nose at me. "Love is not a zero-sum game. You can love more than one person."

I paused at a stop sign to stare at Regan. "You've been

talking to Jessie, haven't you?"

"Leah," Regan corrected, naming Jessie's daughter instead.

"Close enough." Jessie had been another crucial part of my village that had allowed me to raise such a wonderful kid. We'd been neighbors at the same apartment complex when Regan was a baby. Jessie had watched Regan with her own children while I worked all those odd jobs. Her husband Paul had been going to school back then, and they were barely able to make ends meet. I swapped babysitting duties with them. Her oldest daughter and mine were the same age and had remained close friends as they rose through the ranks of public education.

I took my turn through the intersection. "Just because Jessie and Paul love each other so much I want to vomit doesn't mean that's in the cards for everyone."

She gave me a patronizing pat on the shoulder. "You're scared of dating, aren't you?"

"I'm not scared. I don't date because all the good guys are taken. But don't worry about you," I added quickly. "Your soulmate's too young to be crushed by the void of despair that is adulthood. I'm sure you'll find the One."

Instead of coming back with a snarky response, she squirmed in her seat. "Yeah, whatever."

Her response set off my motherly warning system. "Do you already have a particular boy in mind?"

"There's no boy!" Her protest came with a furious blush.

"Oh, c'mon, you can't hold out on me. Tell me about him." Regan was always the levelheaded one among her peers. While others went through a string of failed angst-ridden romances, she remained the stoic shoulder to cry on. I was proud of her for that because I didn't want her to make the same stupid mistake that got me pregnant in the first place, but in the back of my mind, I was also worried she didn't take enough emotional chances.

Parenting is complicated and often contradictory.

Regan slunk in the car seat. "It's just a stupid crush. You and I both know it won't go any further than that. High school love never lasts."

"Sure, but that doesn't mean you shouldn't go for it. Tell me about him."

"What's there to tell? He's a new kid in a bunch of my classes, but he's also a troublemaker. He's perpetually late for school and always getting sent to the office. I shouldn't like him at all."

"Maybe it's an 'opposites attract' kind of thing?"

She snorted. "There's no attraction if he doesn't even notice me."

"How is that even possible? Everyone likes you. You've got friends from the chess club to the football team all the way through the goth musicians. You radiate charisma the way the rest of us breathe air."

Regan's cheeks reddened even deeper. "You're just saying that because you're my mom."

"Hmm. Maybe you have a point."

She curled up in the passenger seat. "I just wish you understood how I feel."

I squashed my sarcastic response. Teenagers have a way of thinking they are the first generation to experience all of life's problems. "I've done the unrequited love thing before."

"When?"

"When I was your age."

I was hedging, and she knew it. "Why don't you talk about your love life more? Maybe I could understand this better if you imparted some hard-earned wisdom."

"It's not like I have a string of guys chasing me," I said dryly. "Isn't that what started this conversation in the first place?"

"You obviously had something with my biological father, otherwise I wouldn't be here. Did he dump you at the altar? Or was it a one-night stand? I'm old enough to handle the truth."

I clenched the steering wheel. Regan and I generally talked about everything under the sun, but I refused to tell her anything about her father. She had so many questions, but I couldn't open up about him. I didn't want her to know I was scared of him.

And even more terrified of what would happen if he knew she existed.

"Your sperm donor has nothing to do with this conversation."

"As if I could argue otherwise."

A terse silence stretched between us. I turned on the radio to fill the void, settling on a station that was playing a classic hit from my own high school days. I mumbled along until it hit the chorus, then I belted out the lyrics at the top of my lungs.

Regan remained tight-lipped at first, but as I grew louder, she couldn't help herself. She knew most of my favorite songs by heart, so by the time the second verse hit "chica cherry cola," she was singing along with me.

We were mostly screaming off-tune as the song ended. Afterward, Regan fiddled with her phone, a mischievous grin on her face. It was one of our little in-jokes. Regan often changed her ringtone to match our latest impromptu karaoke session.

The glass-and-brick structure of her high school came into view. Located in the heart of the city's fastest growing neighborhood, the school had been built to impress the wealthy residents surrounding it. I drove past the main roadway to the smaller gym parking lot so Regan could exit closer to the track field.

After I pulled over, Regan leaned over to give me a hug. "Good luck today, Mom."

"Thanks. See for you dinner?"

"Probably not. Debate practice is going extra-long this week, remember? I need to prepare for the district qualifying round."

"Earning trophies by arguing with people sounds like

your version of nirvana."

"And your version is based on a grunge rock song about deodorant."

"Hey, that band was edgy back in the day. Seriously."

A gaggle of male track runners walking on the sidewalk noticed us and hovered, eager to talk to Regan.

"Gotta go." Regan skittered out of Dirt Dash. "I'll text you once I know when debate practice is going to end. Love ya. Bye."

"Love ya too. See you later, kiddo."

I lingered in the car, watching her chatter with her teammates as they walked away. Two boys rushed ahead, jostling for the privilege to open the gate for her. Maybe her crush hadn't noticed her, but she was far from socially outcast. I'd have to brush up on my witty one-liners for potential suitors soon.

CHAPTER 2

THE NUMBER OF cars increased after I crossed Center Street Bridge over the Willamette River, heading for the office. The morning commute had arrived in full swing. I thought I'd leave the main traffic artery and take a shortcut across State Street. Salem is the state capitol of Oregon, and the Capitol Building loomed in that direction.

I'd chosen poorly. A protest crowd had formed over the entire block of the Capitol. I had to wait three stop light changes before crawling forward. Media vans and camera crews had taken up all available street parking. Slogans like "Keep Our Public Lands Public" and "Forests Have the Right to Grow Old" sprawled over cardboard signs.

The signs explained the outrage of the day. Oregon maintains many "working forests," which meant they aren't just for hiking and camping. Some are harvested to provide timber revenue, and if the government cannot meet its economic goals, they sell the land to private companies. The environmentally minded come out in thick droves whenever that happened.

The roadways finally cleared, and the administrative buildings gave way to squat warehouses and offices. Long-haul trucks and pickups replaced sedans. I'd definitely crossed the invisible line into the commercial part of town.

I was among the first to arrive at the Cascade Vista office, not surprising since the younger programmers kept late hours. I parked in the wide lot of a single-story sandstone-colored building. I used my keycard to swipe in and got comfortable in the first room past the empty reception desk. The building had once housed several different businesses in the past, but as Joshua had expanded the software team over the years, we'd slowly taken over the entire building. My small room had once been an art co-op, which is why it had brightly painted yellow and pink walls with high ceilings and skylights. To me, it was a relaxing, if odd, mixture of comfy industrialism.

Cascade Vista was at a crossroads as a software development firm. Joshua had spent over two decades creating what he called a "lifestyle business," one where programmers could work 9-to-5 and maintain a real work-life balance. This was rare in the software industry, where 60+ hour weeks were standard. In order to maintain this goal, Joshua had only picked clients that aligned with his vision, generally cheaper state and local government projects no one else wanted to fulfill. They weren't as lucrative as the bigger, multimillion dollar contracts that ended up in bidding wars, but they paid everyone a livable salary plus benefits.

Over the years, his unusual strategy paid off. Many excellent software engineers who had burned out working in Silicon Valley or Seattle flocked to quiet Salem, Oregon to work for Cascade Vista. We eventually became a small powerhouse of talented, if laid-back, people. Everyone worked hard while they were in the office but then went home at a reasonable time to enjoy their families.

That all changed with Joshua's heart attack.

He'd just barely turned sixty last year, so no one had seen it coming. As the sole owner of the business with no real backup plan, the company had nearly gone under without its beloved founder. Some employees banded together and reached out to a San Francisco investment firm, Wrought Ventures, to buy out the company. We hoped they'd let us continue operating independently, but that was a pipe dream. Wrought had installed Lewis Sapien as the company's interim CEO. Sapien wanted to leverage our contacts with the state of Oregon and mold the firm into a premier governmental contractor and "realize the company's true potential."

Under his management, we'd taken on more lucrative software projects, many of them with bigger budgets. They required long hours and tight deadlines. Many of my favorite co-workers had already resigned, not willing to be chained to their desks for weeks on end.

Unfortunately, not every employee had the luxury of quitting, which led to my nail-biting presentation at the end of the day.

I couldn't look over my slides anymore without feeling physically ill, so I spent the morning reviewing office supply purchase orders. I loved playing fairy godmother to Cascade Vista employees. They enjoyed a fridge stocked with their favorite cold beverages, rarely complained about the snack selection, and never wondered why we always had the supplies they needed whenever they asked. I felt appreciated.

Well, I used to anyway. The older ranks had left notes with smiley faces on my desk or would drop by to chat. The younger crowd tended to complain more than anything else. I kept my door open so I could see them as they trickled in around ten o'clock. Most of them walked by without so much as replying to my friendly hellos.

When one kid, barely older than Regan, stuck his heavily gelled head in the door, I pushed my keyboard away. I slapped on my biggest smile, hoping to finally make some inroads with the new crew.

"Good morning. How are you?"

He waltzed right past any pleasantries. "Are you the secretary who orders stuff?" he asked bluntly.

"Well, yes, I'm the office manager and—"

"We ran out of teal post-it notes."

I rummaged in my desk. No teal. "I've got some other colors if you like. Regular blue, purple—"

"I need teal," he said.

"Hey!" a voice called from the hallway. "C'mon, man! We gotta prepare for that emergency Stronghold meeting."

"Be right there," he called over his shoulder. Then he looked me dead in the eyes and said, "Make it happen."

Then he slipped back into the hallway.

I clicked a pen in my hand furiously, having broken my stress ball earlier in the week. I wasn't some gofer intern. Not only did I manage this guy's payroll, I also oversaw all their HR issues. What that little turd didn't know was that Wrought Ventures planned to slash his and everyone else's health care benefits next month.

That's what my presentation was about today: fighting to keep those benefits for our employees. I couldn't just stand by and let Wrought screw over the people that I'd worked alongside for years. Mr. Teal Post-Its was just lucky all my hard work would benefit him too.

Around noon, a deliveryman rang to drop off a package. The receptionist had taken his typical long lunch, so I signed for it instead. I saw Howard's name on the box. His desk was just around the corner, so I decided to drop it off myself.

I leaned against the doorless frame of the cramped two-person office. By the window, Sam typed in front of her standing desk, a permanent smile on her face. From Thailand, she looked ten years younger than me although we were the same age. She sported a shiny black bob and always wore long sleeves no matter what the weather. Today she hadn't bothered to take her parka off.

On the opposite wall was Sam's physical opposite. With a bushy black beard down to his collarbone, Howard had blunt fingers that looked like he'd hammered them into squares to make them tougher. He leaned so far back in his chair that I wondered how he didn't fall over. He wore a thick T-shirt with a dragon scorching a knight in armor. Underneath it read, "Critical Failure."

"Delivery!" I announced.

Only Howard turned toward me, Sam still focused on her monitor full of rainbow-colored text.

Howard grunted, his equivalent of a greeting. "Is that my new RAM stick?"

"That's what it says." I handed it over to him.

"Why are you wasting time talking to me when you're facing the firing squad this afternoon?"

I never asked Howard how he'd found out about the benefit cuts or my plan to stop them. I'm sure it wasn't entirely legal. A self-proclaimed white hat, or ethical computer hacker, Howard tended to know things he shouldn't.

"Should I wear a bulletproof vest?"

"That's not the kind of firing I was referring to. Although it's not a bad idea, considering the kind of corporate shills you're up against."

Sam's smile widened even though she didn't take her eyes off her screen. Somehow, I knew she'd been listening.

Howard swiveled his chair closer to me. "I'm just telling it like it is. You're young and healthy. You don't need the full benefits. You're covered by the minimum plan."

Only a grizzled old fart like Howard would call me 'young.' He'd taught himself to program back when floppy disks were a thing.

"Our premiums will go up, so it's still a pay cut," I said. "Some of us are saving for college tuition."

"I don't want to see you get canned over this," he muttered into his beard.

I couldn't help but grin. For all his gruffness, Howard was a caring person. He stood to lose the most if we switched benefit plans. He'd confided in me recently he needed our current coverage for an upcoming surgery, one that he wasn't sure the proposed new medical plan would cover. He didn't know if he could afford the extra expense paying out of pocket without going into debt.

"They're not going to fire me for one proposal," I said. "Giving people severance pay is a big expense, and they need an office manager. The worst they could do is cut my pay and hope I'll quit on my own so they don't owe me anything."

"Don't be too sure they won't send you packing. You're not one of their bratty 'brogrammers' who stay in the office until ten at night before hitting the bars to drink."

"True, but I've got something they don't."

"What's that?"

I leaned in closer for a conspiratorial whisper. "I speak their language."

Howard frowned. "What language?"

"Dollar signs."

This time, Sam outright chuckled.

When Howard still looked confused, I explained myself. "I can prove that with my plan they'll make the most money. When you go into battle, you have to keep your eye on the objective, and we all know that the only thing Wrought cares about is the almighty dollar."

Howard broke out into a loud roar of laughter that shook his rounded belly. "I suppose if anyone can set 'em straight, it's you, Melissa. Good luck."

His confidence bolstered my spirits as I went to my meeting a few hours later, laptop in hand. I had to walk through the open warehouse room, where the rank-and-file developers worked. It had once been a bright cheery space with skylights, but the young programmers had turned it into a techno vampire den. They'd painted the walls black and boarded up the windows, the only lights coming from computer screens. Industrial fans lazily whirled above the huddled desks. Guys squinted in the gloom, pecking away at their keyboards with monstrous headphones on.

As I crossed the room, I wondered how anyone could work in this dismal environment, but they seemed to love it.

Sapien's solid oak office door created a stark border to the programmer's space. I pushed through it into the more traditional corner office he'd prioritized constructing when he took over the company. Upholstered chairs faced an elegant reception desk. Sapien's private meeting room beckoned behind a wall of frosted glass. Someone was already waiting inside.

Sapien's gorgeous young assistant of the week greeted me with perfect wavy hair and a stiff upper lip. "Who are *you?*"

She and Mr. Teal Post-Its apparently took attitude lessons from the same college. "I'm Mr. Sapien's four p.m. meeting."

"Are you sure?"

"One hundred percent." I'd had to schedule this meeting two weeks in advance, so yeah, pretty sure.

She squinted at her computer screen. "I guess it says to expect a few extra employees."

Wonderful. Sapien knew I was coming to talk about benefits. I bet that shadowy figure in the conference room had been sent from corporate headquarters to knock me down a peg. "The more, the merrier."

She waved me on.

My footsteps silenced on the carpet as I entered the meeting room. A long conference table cut the space in two, surrounded by leather swivel chairs and telecom equipment. Unlike the programming den, the windows here spilled glorious sunshine into the room. The view wasn't much, just some scraggly landscaping on the edge of an industrial park.

But I didn't need to look outside to get a good view.

A man in a work shirt with the sleeves rolled up to his elbows sat at the conference table, the black suit jacket that matched his pants slung over his chair. His muscles stretched the fabric taut along his chest, his biceps loudly declaring he often hit the gym. He heard me and glanced up from a stack of papers.

San Francisco had really sent some eye candy to quash my proposal.

I cleared my throat. "Hello, I'm Melissa Hartley, office manager for Cascade Vista."

"I'm Gabriel Alston." He did a slight double take, then stood up in greeting. "I didn't expect you."

He was so tall, I had to tilt my head back to meet his gaze. Dark brown hair with slightly graying temples framed his angular face. His steel blue-gray eyes made my heart do a flip. I suddenly imagined him lifting weights without any shirt impeding his movements.

Then I cursed myself. This was Regan's fault for putting the whole dating idea in my head. I didn't care how hot this guy was. I would not let him mess with my benefits speech.

He made a motion to extend his palm for a handshake, but I decided to jump right in. "Look, we both know why you're here. Let's cut to the chase, shall we?"

"I appreciate brutal honesty," he said, his hand falling back to his side. He looked at me warily.

Good. I wanted to keep him on his toes. I put my laptop on the conference table and patted it. "I have all the documentation I need to convince you not to go forward with your callous plan, even though you think you've crunched the numbers. You believe you're going to save money, don't you?"

He surveyed me from head to foot like a predator sizing up prey. "Cost is always a consideration of any venture."

I swallowed saliva that had gathered in my throat. "Well, I ran my own numbers too. You forgot to calculate long-term costs into your plan."

"Is that so?"

I nodded curtly. "Motivation is important to people. We here at Cascade Vista thrive on consistency, fairness, and most of all, mutual respect. Don't those things matter to you, Mr. Alston?"

He raised an eyebrow. "I'm not sure what any of this has to do with this meeting?"

That image of him straining a barbell over his head popped back in my mind, only this time, it fell on his thick skull. "They have everything to do with Cascade Vista."

Gabriel's eyebrows furrowed in confusion. "Did you say you were the office manager?"

Heat burned my cheeks. I'd had it with people thinking I was a mere secretary. "Do you find my position inferior?"

Gabriel held up a condescending hand. "Not at all. It's just that—"

I wasn't about to stand here and listen to him denigrate me any further. "I'll have you know that I've been managing our HR policies for years. I know the research. Turnover rates and employment happiness studies do not lie. Slashing health care benefits will destroy the morale of this company. Maybe you think you can just hire cheap college jerks to replace the good-working people of this firm, but I'm here to tell you that you're making a huge mistake."

At some point during my tirade, I'd inched closer to him. I didn't even realize it until Gabriel took a step back to give us more breathing room. "I think there's been a misunderstanding—"

I was too far gone to be placated now. "There is no misunderstanding. You're just another corporate flunky. You look at bottom lines and kiss behinds, but you don't care one wit about the real lives you're destroying. I will not stand here and let you tarnish what Joshua Page worked so hard to build."

"Ms. Hartley?" a voice asked from the doorway.

I flipped around to find Lewis Sapien standing in the doorway, his face bloated like a startled pufferfish. He'd gotten himself some sort of artificial tan, but he couldn't mask the wrinkles on his face. He wore two rings—a wedding band on one hand, an alumni ring on the other—and you got the feeling both were equally important to him.

His alumni ring hovered toward me now, pointed directly at my face. "What are you doing here?"

I knew I'd crossed too many lines already, but I didn't care. I had to win this fight. I folded my arms across my chest. "I'm discussing benefits with your corporate liaison."

His tan morphed into a mottled red. "That's not someone from Wrought Ventures. That's a potential client."

It took me a few seconds to absorb what he was telling me. Even then, I could only manage a single-syllable squeak. "What?"

Gabriel cleared his throat. "I'm here to discuss a potential contract between Cascade Vista and Stronghold Incorporated."

Every drop of blood in my circulatory system dribbled down into the bottom of my shoes. "B-but I had a meeting at four o'clock."

"I rescheduled it for tomorrow for obviously more important things," Sapien hissed. "Mr. Alston is quite busy. You must excuse us, Ms. Hartley."

I floated toward the door, coming to terms with what I'd just done. I'd just yelled at a client, and by the look on Sapien's face, a huge one.

"I'm so sorry," I tried to apologize. "I didn't know."

"We will discuss this tomorrow," Sapien said forcefully.

As if to emphasize my embarrassment, Gabriel called after me, "It was nice meeting you, Ms. Hartley."

I waved like an idiot as I backed toward the door. "Yes,

of course. Please excuse me." Once out of sight, I power walked as fast as I could, past the startled receptionist, through the den of drone-like programmers, and retreated into the safety of my office.

CHAPTER 3

AFTER BANGING MY forehead on my desk and nearly forming a bruise, I decided to do a web search for Stronghold Incorporated. I prayed it was a dinky firm with very little clout.

Of course, it wasn't. Stronghold was one of the US military's top defense contracting firms. As a privately held company, no one knew how much it was worth, but news articles stated they'd brokered multimillion dollar contracts before. And it got worse. Gabriel Alston wasn't just a rank-and-file employee. He was the freaking CEO.

It's times like these I counted my blessing of having a door so close to the exit. I managed to slip out of the office when no one else was looking, even the phone-entranced receptionist. I arrived back home within fifteen minutes. I thought about punishing myself by being productive. I had yard work, a week's worth of laundry, and vacuuming.

I opted to go for a run.

I pulled on a heather gray track jacket with matching pants, a Christmas gift from Jessie. Regan had inherited her love of running from me, even if I did skip exercising more often than I should nowadays. As I tightened the laces of my running shoes, the mental image of 10-year-old Regan in rainbow-colored athletic gear flashed in my mind. We used to warm up on our front steps together before we took off down our favorite river trail. I'd had to slow down for her back then, her little legs giving out after a mile or so. These days, she had to pause for me as she worked on her sprints.

Not that we ran much together anymore. Our mother-daughter runs had been relegated to school breaks and summer. She'd texted during my ill-fated meeting to pick her up at seven p.m. That meant a solo dinner for me after my run.

"Forget the kid," I told myself as I stretched my hamstrings on the bedroom floor. "Focus on what's really important, like the last bowl of chocolate peanut butter ice cream that I'll get to eat because Regan's not around to defend it."

With life goals ahead of me, I took off.

Unlike what I've heard from others, I've never experienced a runner's high. I basically have to push myself the first grueling ten minutes, when my lungs heaved and my limbs protested at shifting from sedentary to active mode. As my sneakers pounded away from our street, though, past the baseball fields of Wallace Marine Park and into the forested trails that hugged the river, my breathing steadied and my muscles adjusted to my rhythm. My body heat created a comfortable warmth as I settled into an easy pace my knees could maintain. Aching joints were no joke at my age.

I passed people walking their dogs, raising a hand in greeting but not hearing their replies as my 90s dance playlist blasted through my earbuds. I pushed all thoughts of Cascade Vista and my embarrassing meeting away as the quiet, mulched trail led to thickening trees.

All those jagged steps made me remember where I'd picked up my own running habit. Just as I had taught Regan how to run, so had my mother taught me.

Barbara Hartley and I had a complicated relationship, mostly because she was certifiably cuckoo. Despite never holding more than a temporary part-time job, she'd been an absent parent. I envied latchkey kids because they knew when their parents would come home. Barbara's schedule had no pattern. Even in the first grade I remember her being gone for days and expecting me to take care of myself.

Not surprisingly, she never did the normal mom stuff like show up for school performances or help me with math homework. Instead, she had a weird fixation on "magic." She read these creepy handwritten books that she refused to let me touch. She sometimes wore homemade jewelry she swore protected her from evil. I tried parroting her beliefs at school and got laughed at, so I quickly learned to ignore her superstitious nonsense.

I did, however, enjoy participating in her "training regimes." She'd taught me solid self-defense, which I can appreciate as a grown woman. I know how to escape out of someone's handhold and where to strike an opponent to maximize damage.

Basically, I accepted Barbara's weird absentee parenting style until it all came crashing down on my eighteenth birthday. Instead of a proper birthday party with too much junk food—not that anyone ever came over to our apartment—Barbara hauled me out into the middle of the Siuslaw National Forest. There, I met what could only be described as a cult, complete with a bonfire surrounded by chanting, robed people.

My mom announced me ready for the "Rite of Passage" to determine my "unique abilities." She donned her own formless cloak. I was asked to lie down on the ground and put on a blindfold. That's the last I remembered before a complete darkness came over me, as if I'd fallen into the middle of a black hole that I could never come out of. There was no light, no sound, nada.

It felt like death.

Whatever they were looking for, I did not pass their insane test. Afterwards, Barbara went a little ballistic. She pulled me out of my senior year in high school, saying it was distracting me from my real future. She tried to force me to read her once forbidden books, which I only pretended to do. She also upgraded my exercise schedule to Olympic proportions, complete with weight-training, swimming, and martial arts. I put up with it until she mentioned she wanted me to try her cult's insane ritual again in a year.

I couldn't bear the idea of going through that again, so I stole some cash, my birth certificate, and my social security card. Then I wrote her a goodbye note and left home, terrified and alone.

With my thoughts stuck in the past, I barely registered the woman dressed all in black coming toward me from around a curve in the trees. Lots of joggers use the river paths. Only when she refused to scoot over to the side did I really notice her.

She had an intricate Celtic knot pin stuck to her chest. It looked like it was made from green shoelaces with ribbon woven in it for good measure. It was pretty, but wearing jewelry was hardly appropriate running attire. Then I noticed she had something sticking out the back of her jacket. Were those costume dragonfly wings?

Most importantly, why was she wearing a ski mask?

I slowed to a dumbfounded halt.

She increased her speed, tilting ever so slightly in my direction. She was clearly gunning for me.

Instinct took over. I bolted back the way I came, scrambling through my pockets for the mace I always carried. My fingers trembled as I gripped the tiny cylinder in one hand. All those years of self-defense came back in a rush. Anything on you is a weapon. Aim for the eyes, the knees, the throat. Know where your opponent is at all times.

I couldn't hear much past my loud, shrill techno beats,

so I yanked my earbuds out. The external world's noises came whooshing in around me. Slapping sneakers. The river roaring in the distance. Someone's hoarse breathing growing ever closer.

She was gaining on me. I somehow strained my muscles to go faster. My pursuer's footsteps grew fainter.

Then nothing.

I risked lowering my speed to peer over my shoulder. I assumed I'd simply widened the gap between us, but the woman had completely disappeared.

I whipped around, frantically scanning the forest path, hoping to see movement. I was standing on a relatively flat stretch lined by trees. A steep incline to my left sloped down to the river.

My finger twitched on my mace. She couldn't have gone far.

I was so focused on finding my attacker from where I'd come from that the soft thud of something behind me took me by surprise. I twirled around to face this new threat.

The masked nutcase threw a handful of dust in my face.

Grit caked my eyes. My vision blurred to tears. I stumbled backward, clutching at my eyes, blind.

"Calm down," a voice growled somewhere in front of me.

"No!" I screamed. I tried to open my eyes, but it hurt too much.

"I said calm down!"

"And I said no!" I managed to pry an eyelid open, seeing a weird shimmering haze in front of me. "Stay back!"

"You need to listen to me."

My other eyelid opened a millimeter. Through the too-bright haze, I could just make out the outline of a person, her black clothing a blobby mirage.

"Listen to this!" I brought the mace up and sprayed her

face.

Her soprano scream told me I'd hit my target. She lashed out at me. I tried to dodge, but she landed a solid swipe across my chest. I jerked sideways and stepped onto the river embankment at an odd incline.

Losing my balance, I fell toward the mud and weeds below.

CHAPTER 4

I LOST MY mace and my dignity in the fall, rolling like a kid down a grassy hill until I reached the bottom. Only instead of nice soft grass, scratchy weeds poked me from all angles. I shielded my face with my arms, wincing at the cuts to any exposed skin. My bumpy ride ended in a mucky puddle at the bottom.

Heart pounding, I scrambled into a nearby copse of trees, letting tears clear my vision. A sore spot on my thighs reminded me I still had keys in my pocket. I retrieved them and adjusted them in one fist so that blunt metal daggers protruded between each finger. Then I put my back against a trunk and tried to calm my ragged breaths as I waited for the psycho to come down the embankment.

A minute ticked by. Then two. I couldn't see much of the trail above me from this angle. I carefully wiped away all the crud from my eyes until I could see clearly again.

No one seemed to be up there.

Finally, I scrambled back up the slope to the now deserted trail. My adrenaline-riddled mind tried to make sense of the entire scenario. The masked nutcase had smacked me around. She'd tried to grab me. Even after being maced, she couldn't have missed seeing me fall off the trail.

Where had she gone?

Something glinted all over my clothes. I ran an index finger over the shiny mess.

"Glitter?" The splatter on my jacket made a perfect sparkly splotch on my fingertip. More spots dotted my arms and legs. Shaking my hair, bits of glitter rained onto the bark chips.

Had it all been some sort of stupid prank? Was someone filming this for YouTube or something? In a weird way, it made perfect sense. I mean, my "attacker" had been wearing dragonfly wings.

Steps suddenly sounded on the trail. I tensed, but instead of the masked nutcase, a pair of bored teenagers with multiple piercings rounded the corner. They gaped as they scanned me from head to foot.

I opened my mouth to tell them to mind their own business, but then again, I couldn't blame them. Not only was I covered in yellow straw and mud, but I sparkled too. I casually brushed myself off, not that it helped with the mess. Then, with my chin held high, I ran past them in a runner's gait, acting like I normally looked like I'd just taken a nap on a preschool's arts and crafts table.

"Crazy old hag," I heard one snicker to his buddy.

"You don't know the half of it!" I yelled back behind my shoulder.

* * *

By the time I arrived home, I was full of rage. Not only had I endured an entire Little League's worth of snot-nosed stares as I rushed past the baseball fields, but I realized I'd have to throw away my entire beloved outfit. Washing the track suit would only clog up my laundry machine with glitter.

I stuffed the clothes into a garbage bag, sprinkling crud

all over the living room. I considered calling the cops to file a report, but then again, what was the point? Cosplay pranksters probably didn't rank high on their list of priorities. Plus, I'd maced her eyeballs out. Even if they did find her, knowing my luck, she'd countersue me for emotional damage. I figured I could cut my losses and hop into the shower to get squeaky clean.

Ha. I'm such a hopeless optimist.

Half an hour later, draped in my robe, glitter snowed down onto my terrycloth sleeves. I'd have sparkly dandruff for a month.

I sent Jessie a text that read, *AAHHHH!* followed by seven lines of crying emojis. She didn't respond right away, but I didn't expect her to. My bestie had a full schedule wrangling her own household this evening.

I ate a quiet dinner at the kitchen counter, scolding each glittery speck that fell from my hair. Then it was time to pick up Regan. I threw on the tattered clothes I used for yard work, not caring if they became permanently sparkly. The short sleeves wouldn't cut it for the cold weather, though. I reached for my jacket on its hook near the front door.

My fingers didn't quite snatch it. I'd just bought this jacket last fall. I didn't want to ruin it during one lousy car ride.

So that's how I ended up wearing my bathrobe over my clothes for my trip to the high school.

As I drove across town, I stabbed at the radio console until I found an 80s power ballad that reflected my terrible mood. I belted out "We're halfway there!" so loud that I startled a pedestrian at a red light. He gaped at me as I sped back into flowing traffic.

I parked next to the annex building where debate practice was held. After texting her I'd arrived, Regan hustled outside with three other debate team members. They all lugged backpacks so stuffed with books that I'm sure it would fuel some lucky chiropractor's business in the near future. Regan must have said something hilarious because the entire gang broke out into ear-splitting peals of laughter.

Ah, my little social butterfly. Track jocks in the morning, book nerds at night.

Regan broke off from them, waving enthusiastic goodbyes as they headed deeper into the parking lot. She was talking before she opened the car door, her face hidden by the roof of the car.

"Did you have a good—" she began as she slid into the car. Then she caught sight of me in my glittery bathrobe.

I lost the final bits of my composure. "Today blew chunks!"

"—day?" she finished lamely. She put a hand on my shoulder. "You need fries."

"I've already had my quota." French fries were my vice. If cruel fate hadn't given them the ability to give me love handles, I would eat them by the bucketful. Therefore, I limited myself to one medium fry per week.

Regan withdrew her hand and stared at the sparkling mess it made. "I think this qualifies for an emergency dose."

"You don't even know what happened yet."

"The evidence speaks clearly for itself."

I turned the key in the ignition. "You're not wrong. Fries it is."

I gave her a rundown of my harrowing run as we hit a local burger joint. I ordered their extra-large crinkle-cut fries with a huckleberry shake. Knowing I would not share without deadly retribution, Regan ordered her own medium fry, cheeseburger, and salted caramel shake. Regan munched on her food in the car, but I avoided eating on the drive home so I wouldn't end up further dazzling my robe.

As I pulled into our driveway, I asked, "Was I the victim of some sort of Internet fad?"

"I haven't heard of a rash of run-by glitter bombings."

"You're probably too busy practicing for district debate to notice."

"I'm pretty sure Leah would send me videos."

I pointed a stern finger at my child. "Tell Leah if she even thinks about it, I will end her. Jessie will totally back me up on this."

Regan raised her hands in defense. "Leah put eggnog in your coffee once in the sixth grade, and she's been in mortal fear of you ever since. Besides, some people like eggnog. It's festive."

"And some people just like to watch the world burn."

She gestured toward the greasy bags of food. "Can you bring dinner in? I'm going to check the mail."

"Don't worry. I already grabbed it this afternoon."

Regan's eyes went wide with shock.

I laughed at her outrage. "Just kidding. I didn't actually get the mail. I know it's your sacred self-appointed duty, and if I ever impinge on it, fate have mercy on my soul."

Instead of the eye roll I expected, Regan tersely slammed the car door shut and stalked down the driveway. Yeesh. Don't get between a teenager and their established routine.

While I separated our food on the kitchen counter, Regan came inside, put her backpack by the dining table, then fled to her room. I worried for a moment I'd seriously made her angry, but she reappeared as her normal, energetic self. She flung a few advertising envelopes into the recycling bin before joining me. With the dining table once again overflowing with random stuff, we ate at the counter.

Regan told me about her day, full of track practice, tests, school gossip, but most importantly, her unbridled focus on the upcoming debate tournament. Her childhood was so different than my own, completely by my design. I relished Regan thriving in a normal environment. Maybe some things didn't go as planned—cough, my job—but my kiddo was on the path to a bright future. I'd do anything to keep it that way.

Said kiddo retreated to her room immediately after dinner, unusual since she normally tackled homework in the living room. It must be one of those rare days that she'd gotten everything done at school. In any case, I was glad she'd forgotten to ask about my work proposal. One bad story per night was enough.

As bedtime approached, I got into an old T-shirt and, hoping I wouldn't ruin my favorite bedsheets with glitter, I snuggled under the covers. Jessie finally texted me back with a question mark, but I didn't have the energy for a chat. I wrote that I'd call her tomorrow so she wouldn't worry about me. The day's events had crushed me, but I honestly believed a new day would reset everything.

CHAPTER 5

HAVE I MENTIONED I'm a stupid optimist?

The next day lured me into a false sense of a security by starting out normal. Regan bribed me with coffee. Banter and bad singing accompanied her drop-off at school. The same protesters clogged up traffic at the Capitol Building. Everything felt good until I logged into my office computer and noticed my first meeting of the day.

The rescheduled benefits meeting with Sapien at ten o'clock.

I had no idea how to atone for my behavior. I could only hope he'd had a great meeting with Stronghold and he would be so thrilled imagining himself swimming in piles of future money that he'd forget about my outburst.

Plus, I still needed to convince him not to cut employee benefits.

I caught Howard in the hallway on the way to the meeting. "You got pushed back to this morning?" he asked.

"Yeah. Something came up yesterday."

He patted me on the shoulder. "Don't beat yourself up if you can't fight the man, Melissa. Many people have tried and failed."

On that gloomy note, I strode into Sapien's office suite.

This time I found someone I knew already in the conference room. A 20-something middle manager from Wrought Ventures, Bart Nilyard always wore a blazer that seemed out of place in our casual company. Not a single sandy hair was bent out of place on his carefully groomed head. He exuded lawyer-level sliminess as he shot me a smile that didn't even remotely reach his dull eyes.

"Hello, Melissa."

"Mr. Nilyard," I replied, willing them to call me by my last name out of respect like I did for them. "I have a meeting with Mr. Sapien."

"I know. He asked me to join you."

I stifled a sigh. Wherever Nilyard went, so did trouble. Newly minted from an Ivy League university, he'd made it clear as Sapien's right-hand man at Cascade Vista that his "business chops" far outweighed the combined experience of our veteran team. In his first month of management, he'd singlehandedly driven away a dozen of our best programmers by forcing them to adopt technology he felt was "up and coming" in our field. It turned out his college buddy had created the software package and needed clients. When the programmers complained that the software was too buggy to use, Sapien had just shrugged his shoulders and told them to follow Nilyard's orders.

Sapien strode in next, taking the seat next to Nilyard. "Good morning, Melissa."

"Good morning." I faced the inquisition by myself on one side of the long conference table. "Thank you for meeting with me today."

"What are you looking for?" Nilyard asked.

I patted the laptop in front of me. "I've prepared slides for you regarding my HR productivity research."

"No need, Melissa," Sapien said.

My heart slammed in my throat. "I thought that was the purpose of the meeting. I mentioned it several times in our email exchanges."

"Did you?" Sapien asked dismissively. "I don't recall."

My fingers itched to open my emails and show him where we'd specifically talked about my proposal. "If this is about my behavior yesterday, I would once again like to apologize."

"Don't worry about that." Sapien sounded so sincere, I almost believed him for a second. Then he waved to a chair opposite him. "Have a seat. This isn't going to be about general HR."

Stonewalled, I tried desperately not to betray my frazzled nerves.

Sapien's smile widened as he threaded his fingers on the tabletop. "Mr. Nilyard and I have had a discussion about your time at Cascade Vista. You've been here for a few years, yes?"

"Fourteen," I said, not willing to let them diminish my contribution to the company.

"And you were originally hired as a temporary assistant?"

"Yes," I said slowly, wondering what that had to do with anything, "but I got moved within months to the office manager position."

"Without any formal training," Nilyard said.

My face flushed. "I learned the ropes on the job like many people do."

"Did you?" Nilyard's tone went full-blown mansplaining as he clicked his own laptop, scrolling on the screen. "Because I'm looking at your workload, and you're kind of a jack-of-all trades, aren't you? It seems like mostly you just fulfill order requests and do light record keeping."

I couldn't believe what I was hearing. "That's the least of my duties. I manage payroll. I've been the HR liaison here for years. I even do events planning whenever the firm needs it for themselves or a client."

"Of course," Sapien said. "Very impressive." Although you could clearly tell by his tone he didn't care.

Nilyard folded his hands carefully in front of him. "The

truth is, Melissa, Wrought Ventures has its own team of HR employees. Everything that you can do, we can do from our office in San Francisco. It would save us a ton of money from a cost-efficiency perspective."

I focused on his smug face so the room wouldn't spin. "Corporate doesn't understand the employees of Cascade Vista like I do."

Sapien's face lost all congeniality. "I don't think you understand. The old Cascade Vista is gone. We're rebuilding a new one."

"That means restructuring, trimming down excess expenses for the sake of the company." Nilyard slid a manila envelope over to me.

My blood ran cold with dread as I asked, "What is that?"

Sapien sighed as if this was such a chore for him. "Your severance papers."

I shied away from it as if it were a snake. "If this about yesterday—"

Sapien's eyes flashed. "Your outburst had nothing to do with it. I have years of negotiation experience with people of Mr. Alston's position. I was easily able to smooth things over afterwards."

So, yeah. I'd blown it at the meeting.

A wave of despair washed over me, but I had to push it aside. This wasn't just about me. "I understand I screwed up," I said, trying to keep the desperation out of my voice, "but please don't take it out on the other employees. There are people in this building who depend on their entire compensation package. You can't reduce their benefits without harming them."

Nilyard glared at me. "I take offense to the idea that we're harming anyone. This is merely change, and as you know, young people love change."

I tried to hold on to my professionalism. I flipped open my laptop to show them the numbers I'd run on keeping the old benefits. "If you'd just browse my proposal—"

An alarm beeped. Sapien pulled out his phone. "I don't have time for this," he said to Nilyard as if I weren't right in front of him. "Can you finish this for me?"

"Of course," his toady replied.

I shoved my hands under my thighs as Sapien waltzed out of the room, saying, "Mr. Alston, so good to hear from you. How was your evening?"

As his voice drifted off, Nilyard faced me squarely, a judge handing down a sentence. "Once you have read all the papers, I'm sure you'll find your severance package quite generous. A month's pay for free, plus we'll keep you on our health insurance plan until the 31st."

"A month's pay?" I repeated. That seemed skimpy for such short notice.

Nilyard narrowed his eyes at me. "You'll need to sign it by tomorrow, which is coincidentally your last day with us. If you don't, we'll rescind our offer, and you will receive your last normal paystub."

"Is there a non-compete form I have to sign if I accept the terms?"

Nilyard blinked. "I'm not sure."

I'd caught him off guard. He hadn't expected an idiot like me to know about what forms to expect. His hedging was also a resounding 'yes,' and it meant even if I did sign the agreement, it would make it almost impossible for me to work for another technology firm for the next few years, shrinking my limited employment opportunities even further.

He stood and walked toward the door, expecting me to follow. "It'd be best if you took the evening to think about it. Go home. Get your stuff tomorrow. You'll feel better."

Nilyard blocked the door that led back into the office. Someone had grabbed my purse and coat from my office and had laid it on one of the plush chairs. I silently fumed at the personal intrusion.

But what could I say? I let Nilyard shuffle me out Sapien's special exit to the parking lot, where it had just begun to drizzle.

CHAPTER 6

I SAT SHELL-SHOCKED inside Dirt Dash, the rain spattering across my window. What should I do? Start an online search for my next job? Go home and bury myself under my bedspread? Find out where Sapien lived so I could put a flaming bag of dog poo on his porch?

In the end, I opted for what any sane woman would do: call my bestie.

I hit Jessie's number on my list of favorite contacts. As the third ring rang out, I sent out telepathic links to my incredibly busy BFF. *You need to answer the phone*, I thought as hard as I could. *This is an emergency.*

And like that, she picked up. "Melissa?" Her voice came in breathlessly, the sound of road noise in the background.

"Hey, what're you up to?"

"I'm on my way to Penny's school to drop her off." Penelope was Jessie's youngest child, the surprise baby of the family still in elementary school.

Tears stung my eyes. I hated asking for help, but I desperately needed it. "C-can we talk in person?"

Her tone shifted into mom-handling-a-crisis mode. "I've got some time before work. Meet at my house? Go for a walk? Maybe a coffee shop?"

"Coffee." I would need all the coffee today.

"Java Haus?"

"Yes, please."

"I'll be there as fast as I can."

I arrived first. Java Haus was a tiny manufactured home turned coffee shop, the outside painted light purple with brown trim. Decked out in faux hard wood throughout the structure, the walls had been knocked down to provide more space for seating. The place was jam-packed, but I got lucky and snagged a small table in the corner when an elderly man left.

Jessie appeared soon after and waved to me as she headed straight for the counter. She knew the drill. She'd order us both drinks and bring them so I could defend our territory.

Jessie's wavy black hair, tan skin, and slightly round shape accentuated her cute, bubbly personality. A neon floral ankle-length dress with a lemon-yellow jacket only added to her charm. Jessie loved flashy colors and patterns as much as Penelope. She joked with the college-age barista while he made our fancy drinks.

As she approached with cups in hand, I eyeballed the mocha-colored whip cream. "That looks rich."

"It's a new special, full of sugar."

"You should have gotten me straight black coffee to match my mood."

"There's melted chocolate chips in this."

"Why didn't you lead with that?" I took a tentative sip, and a mixture of milk chocolate and espresso warmed my throat. My taste buds did a happy dance.

Jessie took a sip from her identical drink. "Let's start from the beginning, shall we? The text I got from you yesterday indicated screaming."

"Ah, yesterday." I pressed the back of my hand to my forehead in an exaggerated sigh. "How young and naïve I was then."

"That bad, huh?"

"Worse. I chewed out a top client in front of Sapien."

Jessie smirked behind her coffee cup. "Guess you're fired now."

She meant it as a joke, but my heart sank. "Yeah. Just this morning."

Jessie sputtered on her coffee. "Are you serious?"

I cradled the paper cozy around my drink. "Unfortunately, yeah."

I told her about the whole mess at Cascade Vista. She knew I'd been preparing to fight for benefits, but she couldn't have anticipated my chance encounter with Gabriel Alston. Jessie cringed for me when I told her about misidentifying him. I finished by describing the awful severance meeting this morning.

"I know you want to blame yesterday for losing your job," Jessie said, "but if they had the papers already drawn up for you this morning, they were just looking for a way to get rid of you."

"You're just saying that to be nice."

"No, I'm serious. I've seen coworkers get canned at the bank." Jessie worked as a part-time teller. "I got a buddy in HR that once told me it takes a few weeks to get severance worked out. The corporate bigwigs are cutting costs at Cascade Vista."

"Even if that's true, it doesn't change the fact that I've got six weeks' pay to get my act together before money becomes an issue."

Jessie leaned over to put her hand over mine. "You know if you need anything, our family is there for you. It's not like you're going to be out on the street."

"I don't want a handout," I grumbled.

"And you won't get one, Ms. Grumpypants. It'll be a loan with exorbitant interest. The kind where I'll send Paul to break your knees if you don't pay up."

"Thanks." I laughed in spite of myself, which upset the delicate balance of my small bladder. I'd had one cup of coffee too many. "Gotta go to the bathroom."

Jessie leaned back into her metal chair, phone already in hand to scroll. "Okay."

After doing my business, I smiled at myself in the restroom mirror, relief clear in my reflection. It felt good to have Jessie's support, even if I'd do everything possible not to take her money. The Dunlaps weren't rolling in cash any more than I was.

I didn't know what I would do without Jessie and her family. I remembered the one time I'd tried to reconcile with my mom after I'd left home. I'd found out I was pregnant with Regan and decided to keep the baby. More afraid of the growing human inside me than my mom, I'd reached out to Barbara to ask for help.

She told me over the phone she had "bigger things to worry about than another ungrateful brat." Then she'd hung up on me. It was the last time we'd ever spoken.

Fortunately, the Dunlaps had become my de facto family after I became a parent.

But like any family, Jessie was extremely nosy. By the time I returned to the table, she'd pulled up a bunch of information on Gabriel Alston on her phone.

"You didn't tell me he was hot!" She flashed a professional headshot of him from his company's website.

I rolled my eyes. "The fact that he could grace fashion magazines didn't seem so important in the face of my imminent unemployment."

Jessie went on as if she hadn't heard me. "If Paul wasn't the sexiest man on the planet, this guy could visit my daydreams."

I refused to give her the satisfaction of knowing I'd also thought the same thing when I first met Gabriel. "Good to know you're focused on all the right things."

"You're darn skippy, I am." She glanced over at me. "You've got something on your face."

"What?" I licked my lips.

"No, not coffee. Something shiny, near your hairline."

She leaned over and patted my forehead with a fingertip. A teeny sparkle shone where she'd touched me.

I grimaced. "Ah, yes. The unfortunate glitter bomb incident." I'd forgotten to mention it in the angst of getting canned, so I filled Jessie in on that too.

By the end of my story, she was shaking her head. "I don't want to act like a crotchety old woman who's not with the times, but who throws glitter on random people?"

"I told Regan if Leah gets any ideas from this, I'll go ballistic."

"You have my permission to do whatever is necessary, even if Leah's my own flesh and blood."

"I knew you'd have my back."

We finished the rest of our conversation in pleasant banter. Tension eased out of my body. Talking with Jessie reminded me that although some things change, our friendship wouldn't. I would get through this.

Jessie had to leave fifteen minutes later to start her shift. She adjusted her purse over her shoulder as she stood.

"Hang in there, Melissa. You call if you need anything."

"Of course. I owe you."

"You don't owe me anything." Then she tilted her head to the side, hesitating. "Well, maybe some extra hands building a shed in our back yard this summer."

I made a face. "You know how much I hate physical labor, right?"

Jessie shrugged. "I'm just saying, it'll go faster if you help."

I laughed. The Dunlaps always had some project going on, and somehow, I always ended up offering free labor. "You know I won't turn you down."

"'Course you won't. I have you wrapped around my finger." She gave me a quick hug and left.

I sank back against the hard chair. Now that her radiant energy was gone, I felt a little deflated. What was I going to do with myself all day?

You know the saying, "Ask a stupid question . . .?" I got my stupid reply when my phone buzzed.

I glanced at the screen. It was the high school.

"Hello, this is Melissa Hartley."

"Am I speaking to the mother of Regan Hartley?" a nasally voice replied.

"Yes."

"I'm a secretary at your daughter's school. I have a Serena Fawcett here who wants permission to take your daughter home."

I frowned. "I don't know a Serena Fawcett."

Another female voice suddenly rose on the other line, clearly talking to the secretary. I couldn't make out any particular words.

"You're not on the release form," I heard the secretary tell her. "I can't just let anyone pick up a child without authorization."

More arguing ensued. A loud thud rang in my ear, as if someone had dropped the phone.

My heart raced. "Excuse me? Hello? Are you still there?"

The phone clicked and then the secretary came back on the line. "I'm sorry, Ms. Hartley. I shouldn't have bothered you. I can see everything is fine now. Regan will be released."

"Wait," I cried. "You're not going to—"

"Have a nice day," she said pleasantly.

The line went dead.

CHAPTER 7

I HAVE NO memory of leaving Java Haus and driving to the high school. I simply went into action, my mind reeling from that bizarre conversation.

Someone I didn't know was trying to pick up my daughter from school. Given that the school had called me for confirmation, it seemed odd the secretary would just suddenly change her mind. There was only one logical explanation I could think of, and it made my blood run cold.

What if John Moroz had finally learned he had a daughter?

The only good thing that had come out of my one-night stand with John Moroz had been Regan. I'd met him at a fancy holiday fundraiser where I'd served as part of the catering crew, long before I settled down to a real career at Cascade Vista. I'd found him charming, one of the few rich guests who treated me like a real person. I should have insisted on birth control, but he swore he had a medical condition that prevented him from having children. I thought it would be a wild night to remember.

And it was, for all the wrong reasons. I got the positive pregnancy test a few weeks later.

I decided early on to keep the baby. I did consider telling him at first. The child support payments certainly would have helped. After researching his personal life, though, I changed my mind. He lived a playboy lifestyle. He jokingly compared beautiful women to outfit accessories, saying he never liked to escort the same one twice. That alone gave me pause.

But what sealed my silence was his cutthroat business reputation. John was a great white among sharks. He'd built a lobbying empire by promoting sketchy practices like allowing corporations to donate money to political campaigns anonymously. He had ruined several business partners without any stated reason. He was also rumored to represent anonymous clients through dark web money. Because of this, many theorized his net worth had not been earned via legal means.

I didn't want my child anywhere near that creep. With a guy who didn't blink at screwing over everyone around him, how would he treat a daughter?

Fortunately, as one of his castoff conquests outside of his wealthy social circle, he didn't even remember I existed, so we'd never interacted again. I was happy remaining out of sight, out of mind.

I parked in a visitors-only spot near the school's main entrance, hustled up the walkway, and pressed a button on the front door intercom.

"Show your ID to the camera, please?" a meek voice responded.

Huh. I'd never had to do that before. I flashed my driver's license.

"Ms. Hartley," the voice answered in a strangely apologetic tone. "Of course. Come right on in."

I strode through the double glass doors into the school's administrative office. The place had been thrown into a panic. A plastic cup on the receiving desk had been knocked over, spilling pens all over the chest-high countertop. A stack of papers had half-slid to the floor, scattered like leaves around my feet. In a far corner of the room, a group of women with matching shirts sporting the high school's colors huddled around one of their own, who sobbed into a damp wad of tissues. I couldn't quite hear her over the angry male voice yelling behind one of the closed office doors.

The ladies all glanced over at me simultaneously, like a herd of herbivores on the lookout for a predator. The crying woman burst into fresh tears. "I'm so sorry, Ms. Hartley!" she wailed.

A younger woman with purple glasses pulled away from the comforting mass. "Let me inform Mr. Spencer you're here." She'd been the voice on the intercom.

I somehow managed to keep my cool as Purple Glasses knocked on the office door generating all the noise. The man stopped his shouts to yell, "What?"

She opened the door the tiniest crack to stick her face inside. She whispered something unintelligible.

"Here?" he roared, stunned. "Now?"

She nodded frantically.

"Send her in." As Purple Glasses scooted away, he said to someone else, "And you, take a seat out there and wait for me. I'm not done with you yet."

Purple Glasses gestured me around the counter and toward the door.

I threw my hands up in the air. "I just want to see my daughter. The school called and—"

The crying woman sobbed yet again.

"Mr. Spencer will take care of you," Purple Glasses said over her shoulder as she went to soothe the hysterical woman.

With no other options, I walked toward the office of doom as a teenager sauntered out. He had curly jet-black hair and wore a leather jacket and jeans, the poster child for disillusioned teenagers immemorial. He took one lingering look at me with his bright brown eyes before deciding I wasn't interesting. He stuffed a maroon and gray duffel bag he'd been carrying underneath a nearby bank of uncomfortable-looking plastic chairs before manspreading himself over them.

A plump man wearing a polo shirt and slacks greeted me inside the office. He extended a meaty hand. "Ms. Hartley," he said through a handshake. "I'm Mr. Spencer, the assistant principal."

He motioned for me to sit, but I willfully ignored the gesture. "I'm very concerned about my daughter, Mr. Spencer. I received a call from the school that someone I don't know tried to pick her up."

He shut the door behind me. "I am incredibly sorry about the confusion, Ms. Hartley. Rest assured, your daughter is safe and sound in class as we speak."

"How can you be sure?"

"I'm having our resource officer check in on her now. He's a member of our local police force who assesses threats against students."

I bristled. "Is my daughter in danger?"

"Of course not. I merely mentioned our highly qualified staff to comfort you." His reassuring tone contradicted his mottled face, still red from yelling. "There seems to be a bit of a misunderstanding."

"I distinctly heard your secretary on the phone say she was willing to release my child into the custody of a stranger."

Spencer pulled on his collar. "That was before she was reminded of official protocol. We are only allowed to release students to their direct guardians and other adults whom those guardians have previously authorized. I checked Regan's form, and she's only allowed to leave the premises early with you or a Ms. Jessie Dunlap."

"Can I see your records?" I wanted to make triple sure of what they had on file, given the circumstances.

"Certainly." This time I did sit down as he pulled the keyboard closer to his chest and began typing. Once he'd found what he was looking for, he spun the monitor around so I could see a photocopy of Regan's latest release forms. It was the one I'd signed her freshman year, and it indeed only listed Jessica and me as contacts.

At least that all checked out. I decided to throw him a bone. "Thank you. Forgive my concern. That phone call really rattled me."

"No need for explanations, Ms. Hartley. We take care of students in all kinds of familial situations. That's why you were called in the first place."

I doubted he had many kids who were secretly related to one of the most influential lobbyists in the United States. "Do you know if Serena Fawcett was acting on anyone else's behalf?"

"Not that I know of. She simply asked Regan to be released into her company, and we refused."

Maybe my instincts were wrong and this had nothing to do with John Moroz. "Is it common for something like this to happen?"

"Kids sometimes convince their older friends to impersonate responsible adults to help play hooky, but your daughter has a stellar attendance record and grades. I only know her name because I've seen it on the Honor Roll so many times. She doesn't seem like the type to pull this kind of stunt."

"Perhaps this was a mix-up with another kid," I said, more thinking aloud than to the assistant principal. "Or someone wanting to get Regan into trouble?"

"Perhaps," he replied, although he didn't sound convinced.

Now that the danger had passed, I suddenly felt very tired. All I wanted to do was get my daughter and go home.

I caved to self-indulgence. "If you don't mind, I would actually like to pull Regan from class and take her home right now."

Mr. Spencer didn't look happy. "As I said before, she is perfectly safe here with us. We would never let a stranger take a child off school grounds."

"I'm sure you wouldn't, especially given the potential lawsuits." He flinched at the last word, but I continued. "I'm not angry at the school. It's just that I've had a really rough morning. I think it's best if I take Regan home."

"It's your right," he said, clearly not happy with my decision. "Let me call our resource officer to escort her to the office. I'll print out the paperwork." He made a quick phone call, then asked me to wait back in the larger office area until Regan could be retrieved.

With the surly teenager still slumped over the seats and the group of women huddled in the corner, I had nowhere to sit in the open office. I ended up leaning awkwardly against the countertop as I waited.

The slouching teenager straightened. He sniffed the air, a dark expression crossing his face. He zeroed in on me.

"What happened to you?" he demanded.

I frowned at him. "Excuse me?"

He got off his seat and was next to me before I could skirt away. He ran a finger down my shoulder and showed me the results.

Glitter.

"Who did this to you?" he asked.

"Lucas Valera!" Purple Glasses snapped. "Get away from Ms. Hartley."

He glowered at her. "Or what? You'll allow another random stranger off the street to drag her daughter off campus?"

The crying woman hiccupped in her handkerchief.

"Now see here—" Purple Glasses began.

"Don't lecture me," Lucas cut her off. "If it wasn't for me, you'd have let Regan get kidnapped."

"What?" I gasped.

He smiled, showing his teeth. "Didn't Mr. High and Mighty Spencer tell you? They almost let Regan leave with that woman."

Purple Glasses bore down on him. "We would never

do that."

"Oh really?" He whipped out his phone and showed me a video. Although it was hard to hear with the office staff yelling at Lucas to put the phone away, I could clearly see a woman talking to the now distraught secretary.

I expected Serena Fawcett to look like a criminal, but honestly, she was gorgeous. She'd styled her silky auburn hair into an artful bun with loose strands falling in waves on either side of her face. Her makeup accentuated all the right features—full lips, slender cheeks, and flawless skin. She could have been a model except she had a slight hunchback under her jacket.

The video showed Serena talking sweetly to the secretary, who put down the phone in a daze, then began to nod at everything the beautiful woman told her. The clip suddenly went blurry and out of focus before abruptly ending.

Lucas put his phone away. "That's when I tackled her before the idiot secretary called for Regan to come to the office."

"I didn't mean to!" the crying secretary wailed. "I don't know what came over me!" The other women formed a tighter ring to console her.

Purple Glasses fumed at Lucas. "Now look what you've done!"

A new voice butted into the conversation. "Mom?"

A confused-looking Regan entered the office, a tiny man in uniform behind her. Clutching a thick textbook to her chest, she had that crinkle above her brow that indicated she was upset but holding it in. The little officer poked his head in the room, saw the secretary crying, and fled. So much for campus security.

"What's going on?" Regan asked.

I decided not to poke the gaggle of hysterical women further. "I'll explain in the car."

Lucas snorted. "Good luck with that."

At the sound of his voice, Regan jumped as if touched

by a hot poker. "What are you doing here?"

"Keeping you out of trouble," Lucas said.

"I'm not in trouble," she said, although she didn't sound so sure.

"Sure, you're not."

I tapped Regan's shoulder. "Just ignore him."

Regan did the opposite by stomping toward him. "Why are you always up in my business?"

Lucas shrugged. "Someone needs to be."

She poked him in the chest. "No, no one needs to be."

He grabbed her finger. "Says who?"

I was about to yell at Lucas's audacity, but my kid had me covered. She jerked her hand away from him and shoved him so hard he stumbled backward into the bank of seats.

Behind me, Purple Glasses sucked in a breath. She opened her mouth to say something.

Regan was faster. "What is your problem?" she pressed a stunned Lucas.

He glowered up at her. "You just shoved me. I'm not the one with the problem."

"Oh really?" She leaned over him, a fraction of his mass but all of his ferocity. "Because you're the one acting like you have a right to my private life. Don't think I haven't noticed you following me around. Funny, coming from the jerk who pretends I'm not alive. Remember blowing me off when I offered to walk you to gym class? Or how you 'didn't hear' me ask you three times if you wanted to be my lab partner?"

Lucas actually shrank under her simmering rage. "I, uh—"

"So now you're suddenly interested? Why? Is there juicy gossip involved? Need to satiate your morbid curiosity, Mr. Cool?"

Lucas stared at her as if she'd sprouted horns.

Mr. Spencer's office door suddenly swung open. "Mr. Valera. Are you stirring things up yet again?"

His arrival broke up the teenagers. Regan backed away to stand next to me at the counter. Lucas looked like he wanted to say something but thought better of it. He grumbled in his seat.

We suffered a few tense minutes filling out papers to release Regan from school. As I wrapped up my signature, Mr. Spencer said to Regan, "I hope to see you back at school tomorrow."

"You will," I answered, thrusting the papers at him. "Here you go."

"Goodbye, Ms. Hartley, Regan," he said in a pleasant voice. Then his demeanor changed as he shifted to face Lucas. "It's your turn back in my office, Mr. Valera."

Regan glared at Lucas. "Looks like you've got places to go."

Lucas ignored the assistant principal as he called him a second time, instead staring after Regan with calculating eyes. As we made for the exit, he shifted his intense gaze to me, his expression grim.

"Take care, Ms. Hartley," he said.

I didn't reply. It was a common enough phrase. I tried not to read too much into it, since Lucas clearly was a juvenile delinquent.

So why did those words send a shiver up my spine?

CHAPTER 8

REGAN WAS STILL fuming about Lucas as we drove away from the high school. Given her outsized reaction, I felt confident I'd stumbled onto her mysterious crush. However, we had enough problems on our hands that I decided not to provoke any more teenage drama. I diverted her attention by giving her a rundown of my ill-fated morning, starting with my firing.

Regan's irritation faded as I told her what I knew about the weird woman who'd tried to pick her up at school. She was appropriately freaked out by the time I pulled into a discount department store parking lot.

"Who is Serena Fawcett?" she asked.

"I don't know, but that's why we're shopping for one of those fancy video camera doorbells."

"I thought you said those things spy on the homeowners as much as protecting them."

"They do, but desperate times call for desperate measures. I'll trade some privacy right now for peace of mind."

As we browsed the electronics section, Regan couldn't get her mind off the fact that someone had wanted to take her from school. "Who'd want to take me? Do you think

Barbara wants to reconnect after all these years?"

Regan knew my history with my mom, including the 'ungrateful brat' comment. "She's never cared before."

"Then maybe my father?" She glanced at me with eager expectation.

"Doubtful," I hedged. "Okay, I think we're going with this doorbell. You want to pick out the color?"

"You're distracting me so we won't talk about my dad." She pouted.

"Absolutely true. Can I sweeten the deal by letting you choose where we eat lunch?"

"You'll let me get sushi?" she asked excitedly. I didn't care for raw fish, while she loved it.

I grimaced but said, "Sure, as long as you drop the subject."

"Deal!"

I let her call in an order while I got a sandwich at the deli counter. Then we bought our loot, picked up her salmonella spread, and headed for home.

"I haven't had a rainbow roll in ages!" Regan exclaimed on the couch as she broke the wooden chopsticks apart. Before she could delve in, though, a look of dejection crashed over her face.

"What's the matter?"

"You just lost your job." She pointed at the receipt for the sushi restaurant with her chopsticks. "Maybe I shouldn't have ordered this."

Although I loved my empathetic kid, I hated that reality had already come crashing down on her. "It's okay for a final splurge," I said. "We'll work out a budget later."

"I'll be more responsible from now on, I promise." Regan kicked her backpack at her heels. "I probably should get math homework done for tomorrow."

"And I should start my job search."

Then we both looked at the blank TV screen in front of us.

"It's been a really bad day," I said.

"A few bad days really," Regan added.

Without further prompting, Regan grabbed the remote and started up a Christmas rom-com. I ran back to the kitchen to make us hot cocoa.

"It's March." I pointed out as fake snow filled the screen.

"And this doesn't go with Japanese food at all." She sipped on her cocoa.

Our observations went unchallenged. We both snuggled up under blankets and let ourselves get lost in bad acting, empty calories, and good company. The banter between us swelled as we ogled the handsome lead and groaned at the heroine's terrible dialogue.

I tried not to get misty-eyed, not because of the film, which was cheesy, but because we hadn't enjoyed a movie night together in a long time. They had once been a staple of our relationship. Even when money was tight because of an emergency household repair, we could always pop in a DVD and watch a favorite show together.

The minutes ticked by with a ridiculous meet-cute, contrived reasons not to fall in love, and a series of huge mishaps which somehow still brought our dashing couple together. As the upbeat music swelled over the credit rolls, we stretched and yawned, ready for bed.

Only it was two in the afternoon.

You can only put off the inevitable for so long. "I'd better see how difficult it is to install this new doorbell," I said.

"Yeah. These trig questions aren't going to answer themselves."

"Guess it's back to the old grindstone."

We sighed in stereo.

I patted Regan's kneecap. "Thanks. The movie was a nice little ray of sunshine."

"The only kind you get in Oregon this time of year," Regan agreed, reaching for her backpack.

We plodded our separate ways, Regan cracking a

textbook and me attacking the almost impenetrable plastic shell that housed the doorbell camera. Maybe we'd get lucky and I'd bought the camera for nothing. Then I could return it and use that money in my new post-employment budget.

***

The camera did catch something while we slept that night, just not the mysterious Serena Fawcett.

It recorded the wolf.

I studied the furry black monstrosity. It looked like it could snap our mailbox in half with its jaws. It didn't just wander down the street either. It came right up the walkway onto our front stoop, sniffing around the door. It paused when it noticed the camera, obscuring the view for a few seconds. Although there was no sound, I could see the wolf growling as it took a step back. Then it bounded back up to the street and out of sight.

That had been around eleven p.m., right after we'd both gone to bed. I wondered if I should tell Regan.

"Nopity, nope, nope," I muttered. There was too much going on. I certainly wasn't going to add the wolf to Regan's list of worries.

The camera went off several more times during the night when a car drove by. Our quiet street didn't warrant the amount of traffic I recorded. That's when I noticed it was mostly the same blue Honda Civic cruising by.

I grimaced. I'd given Jessie a rundown of the weird high school situation before going to bed the night before.

Did Paul suddenly develop insomnia? I texted her. *I have video of him driving by the house at all hours.*

She replied immediately. *We just wanted to make sure you were okay. You should have stayed with us last night.*

I told you we'd be fine.

You're also way too stubborn for your own good.

I texted an emoji with its tongue stuck out. She

responded with the middle finger.

That's me and my bestie. The height of maturity.

I relished the chuckle. I wouldn't be laughing while turning in my severance papers before the end of the day. We needed the extra money to tide us over, so I couldn't turn it down, not even if it meant tying my hands for the next job.

At least Regan didn't have track practice this morning, and given everything going on, she agreed not to go on a morning run by herself. That meant we both got to sleep in an extra hour before I dropped her off.

"If I knew a place where you'd be safe, I'd put you there," I said as we waited at a stoplight near the high school.

"You could always send me away on vacation. I hear rural Scotland is nice."

"Yeah, I'll cash a check from my fat bank account and get right on that."

Regan patted my arm. "It'll be okay, Mom. The school's not going to let me go anywhere after yesterday, and I'm certainly not walking off with any stranger."

"I trust you but not the school. That ridiculous secretary would have shoved you out the door without a second thought."

"It is really odd she'd do that," Regan admitted. We'd pulled up into the drop-off lanes behind a line of other cars. "Oh, and remember, I'm leaving with Leah after school today."

"Don't you distract her while she drives," I yelled as Regan slipped out of the car. "She just barely got her permit. Her brain isn't used to defensive driving yet."

"I promise I'll get her to drive five miles per hour all the way home, and I'll wear double safety belts."

"You're joking with me, right? Because if not, I love the double safety belt idea. Maybe a five-point harness like a baby car seat."

"Bye, Mom," Regan said with emphasis as she slammed

the door shut, but I could tell she wasn't really annoyed because of her bright smile.

My stomach twisted as I prayed that my baby girl would stay safe.

Then I was off to another kind of gut punch. I stopped at Java Haus to prepare myself. I wanted to arrive at the office during lunchtime, when most of the younger programmers left to eat. Then I'd whisk into Sapien's office and hand in my severance. I might as well leave Cascade Vista with as much dignity as possible.

Just as I was throwing my coffee cup away, my phone buzzed on silent. I checked the screen, an unknown local number.

"Thanks, spammers," I said while sending them to voicemail. The phone buzzed again as I eased back onto the road to work. Persistent little buggers.

Unfortunately, I didn't count on the protesters being in full swing and outside their normal zone. They'd spilled all the way to the parkway, several blocks from the Capitol. I inched through downtown Salem among three lanes of barely moving traffic, surrounded on one side by an impatient soccer mom and on the other by a rich dude in a sports car. Vehicles squeezed in tight to discourage the crowd from getting through.

It didn't work. The sports car almost ran over a jaywalker who suddenly jumped out in front of him. A stocky guy with a salt and pepper buzzcut dodged the bumper. He wore a long, black trench coat and had a cross-shaped scar on his chin.

Mr. Sports Car leaned on his horn as the jaywalker attempted to walk away. The jaywalker responded by smacking the guy's hood with both palms. I cringed, shrinking in my seat. I did not want to get involved in a road rage incident.

The jaywalker won their chest-thumping contest. Sports Car sulked low in his seat, completely cowed. The jaywalker strolled back to the sidewalk and traffic moved forward. Finally, the flow resumed to a reasonable speed so I could head toward the commercial district.

When I arrived at the Cascade Vista parking lot, the first thing I noticed was the sleek black SUV. It looked like it belonged in the President's motorcade, complete with fully tinted windows and polished chrome. To top it off, it had taken Sapien's personal spot right next to his entrance.

Who could possibly be visiting our dinky office that warranted an armored vehicle? I shrugged, going through the main office entrance. Not my problem anymore.

The sleepy receptionist near the front looked excited for a change. In his early twenties, he dressed in T-shirts, shorts, and sandals despite the chilly weather. He was whisper-talking to Mr. Teal Post-Its, their heads close together. Birds of a feather, I supposed.

"Sapien's about to lose his mind," the receptionist was saying. "The guy just showed up out of the blue and—"

Mr. Teal Post-Its tapped him on the shoulder, and the two acted as if they'd never seen a middle-aged woman before. "Where have you been?" the receptionist asked.

"None of your business," I shot back. I supposed everyone would know soon enough I'd been fired, but I wasn't going to break it to these two.

"Sapien's been calling you all morning."

"What?" I grabbed my cell phone and played one of the many messages now left in my inbox.

Sapien's voice rang through loud and clear. "Melissa, I need you at the office before—"

I paused it before the two office gossips overheard anything more. "Oops. I didn't recognize his number. He never calls me."

"Well, he wants to see you. Now. In his office.

I held up my hands in surrender. "Yeesh. Okay." Sapien must have really wanted me to sign those severance papers and be gone. Maybe he got some corporate bonus if I left before five p.m. or something. I just hoped whatever tizzy Sapien had worked himself up to, he'd give me time to clean out my desk before booting me out the door.

As I left, clutching the severance packet, the receptionist picked up his office phone and dialed a number. "Melissa's on her way, Mr. Sapien," he said behind me.

Howard stuck his head out into the hallway as I passed. "What's going on? Those two idiots at reception are so wound up, I'm worried they might hit puberty again."

"I'm not sure," I lied, not wanting to tell Howard about my firing as a drive-by, "but I'm about to find out."

"Maybe it's about your proposal," he called after me.

I hoped Howard didn't see my expression. The one time he didn't already know office news would be the one time it affected him the most. Poor Howard.

I trekked through the dank den of programmers. Unlike last time, they all cast furtive glances at me. Apparently, the rumor mill had reached all the young employees. Wonderful. They remained quiet until I opened Sapien's suite door, then conversations resumed in whispered hushes.

Sapien's gorgeous assistant nodded at me the moment I stepped inside. "They're waiting for you."

Sapien and Nilyard had taken their usual seats on one side of the conference room table, but I wasn't the only one facing the firing squad this time.

Gabriel Alston sat across from them.

The C-level executives looked more harried than usual, Nilyard's face grim and Sapien jerking to his feet in a strange lurch. "Melissa, glad you could join us," Sapien's relief was palpable, "Won't you—"

"Ms. Hartley," Gabriel interrupted.

A shiver went up my spine at his deep voice pronouncing my name.

Sapien sputtered. "E-Excuse me?"

Gabriel gestured at Nilyard. "You didn't introduce him as Bart. Therefore, I assumed you addressed all your employees by their last names."

I managed to keep a neutral expression while Gabriel pointed out this misogyny. Inside, though, I gave him a high five.

Sapien's jaw tightened. "Ms. Hartley," he said with a hint of strain. "You remember Mr. Gabriel Alston, CEO of Stronghold Incorporated."

"Of course." *How could I forget?* I silently added.

Gabriel stood up to shake my hand. I didn't refuse the gesture this time. His palm felt rough but warm, sending a pleasant shock through my spine. I couldn't tell if I was happy or disappointed when he let go to hold out a chair for me.

I cleared my throat as he sat down next to me. "May I reiterate how sorry I am for my behavior the other day, Mr. Alston."

Gabriel waved my nervousness aside. "All water under the bridge. We have more important things to discuss."

"We do?" I couldn't imagine why I'd been summoned to this meeting besides apologizing profusely for my actions.

Sapien's hands clenched in front of him so tightly on the table, I worried he'd break a finger. "Mr. Alston wants to consider Cascade Vista for a Stronghold consultation project, but only if you take charge."

"Me?" I couldn't hide my surprise. "I'm just an office manager. I don't work directly with the software engineers."

"That's what we've been trying to tell him," Nilyard said under his breath.

Sapien glowered at his minion. "We're excited for any opportunity to work with Stronghold." Nilyard withered under the scrutiny.

Gabriel fixed me with an intense stare that made all my nerves stand on end. "After our conversation the other day, I did a little digging into your history."

"That can't be good," I said before I could stop myself.

Sapien flipped his head to scorch me with his beady eyes.

Gabriel continued. "I assure you, everything I heard was positive. You have a stellar reputation for managing an office with diverse personalities. Your longtime colleagues rated you as fair, very competent, and someone they trust."

"How could you possibly know that?"

"Employee interviews," Nilyard said, a hint of disapproval in his voice. "Mr. Alston asked to speak with many of the staff yesterday. We didn't realize at the time it was to get a better sense of your character."

Well, it was nice to know all the original employees still valued my contribution to the office. Then I snorted. "What did the more recent hires say?"

Gabriel flashed me an unexpected grin. "They grumble about inconsequential details, as many their age do, but even then, if you read between the lines of their answers, I can see their respect for you."

I clenched the manila envelope in my lap, out of sight. "This is all very flattering, of course, but I'm not sure what this has to do with Stronghold Incorporated."

Gabriel straightened, his incredible height unavoidable even while sitting at the conference table. "I'm looking for someone who can help me set up a new office. Stronghold is considering opening a branch in Salem. We just signed a rental agreement for a temporary space earlier this week."

Sapien spoke up. "If Stronghold decides to make the office permanent, he will likely require the help of local software developers."

Ah, that's why this was important to Cascade Vista. Having a juggernaut like Stronghold in town could open up doors for lucrative contracts. The look Sapien was boring into my skull screamed at me to make this happen.

"I foresee one problem," I announced.

Gabriel frowned. "And that is?"

I lifted the manila envelope and slapped it on the desk in front of me. "Today is my last day at Cascade Vista."

I will never forget the look on the executives' faces, the

whites of their eyes, that bright flush of concealed fury. They really hadn't thought I would reveal my looming unemployment.

"That is a problem," Gabriel said, steepling his fingers in front of him.

"Easy to rectify," Sapien announced. "We no longer accept your resignation."

Oh no. I wasn't letting him get away with lies. "You know I didn't resign. You fired me."

"Really?" Gabriel asked. "On what grounds?"

"Unfortunate redundancy," Nilyard interjected smoothly. "Wrought Ventures already has a robust HR department."

"But aren't they all based out of San Francisco?" Gabriel asked. "Don't you still need an onsite office manager?"

Nilyard squirmed, losing his confident expression. "I suppose we didn't think it through."

I knew this would put the nail in the coffin on my job here, but I didn't care. "You thought it through just fine." I turned to Gabriel. "Wrought Ventures is cutting corners to save money, starting with my position. They also plan to reduce employee benefits, which will harm our older employees who need, and I daresay earned, the more robust health care plan they currently enjoy."

Sapien relaxed, letting out a derisive chuckle that came from his belly. "This is precisely the reason why I warned you against considering Mel—Ms. Hartley for this consultation position. She has a very hard time understanding how corporations must maintain their bottom line."

Gabriel nodded in agreement. "You're right, Mr. Sapien. Corporations must turn a profit or they will go out of business. Good leaders, such as you and I, must show them the way."

My heart sank. So much for my knight in shining armor.

"Yes, yes," Sapien said. Nilyard flashed me a victorious grin. I shrank farther in my seat.

"So tell me, Mr. Sapien," Gabriel leaned forward. "What benefits of yours did Wrought Ventures slash?"

Sapien's smile faltered. "I beg your pardon?"

"I asked what kind of personal loss will you endure due to flailing bottom lines? Surely if you are taking away health care benefits from older employees, you're also giving up something. Your own bonuses, perhaps? A pay cut? Reduced time off?"

"I'm not taking any reductions," he said indignantly. "Why would I? I'm management. Without me, nothing gets done."

Gabriel's eyes narrowed. "The same can easily be said for rank-and-file employees."

Sapien's composure slipped. "That's absurd!"

Gabriel eased back into his chair, his eyes darkening. "I guess we have two very different ideas about leadership, which is very unfortunate for the potential relationship between our two firms."

Sapien must have seen dollars signs slipping away because he slapped on a salesman smile. "No need for hasty judgments. We can still work things out. Perhaps we should discuss this at a later time, when cooler heads prevail."

"That won't be necessary. I've found what I'm looking for." He turned his attention back on me. "Ms. Hartley, I would be happy to offer you a job coordinating my new Salem office."

My head spun. "Are you serious?" I asked, hating how I sounded more like Regan than my professional self.

"It may only be temporary if we ultimately decide not to make the branch permanent," he warned, "but I would love to have you on my crew."

"You can't hire her!" Nilyard spat. "She has to sign a non-compete clause to get her severance."

Nilyard reached for the manila envelope, but Gabriel

scooped it up before he could snatch it away.

Gabriel looked to me for permission. "May I read these documents? They are legally yours."

"Of course," I said.

He pulled forth the packet and began skimming the dense legalese.

"This is outrageous," Sapien fumed. "You call yourself an honest businessman and poach one of our most senior employees out from under us."

I snorted. "Really? You were going to fire me, and now you're worried I'm getting 'poached?'"

Sapien and Nilyard both looked like they wanted to strangle me. I suddenly felt glad that I sat next to a guy who looked like he could bench-press them at the same time without breaking a sweat.

Gabriel sealed my gratitude with his next words. "'Poach' is a very strong term given these papers. Your non-compete clause will not likely hold up in court the way it's written. If you're not willing to honor her severance payment for her years of service at Cascade Vista, I'm more than happy to help Ms. Hartley hire an attorney."

"A-attorney?" Sapien turned green.

Gabriel flashed him a wicked smile. "I'm sure my lawyers will have a field day tearing not only into this flimsy legal document, but any others Ms. Hartley may have signed for you in the past."

"There's no need for any of that," Sapien huffed. "We'll honor the severance agreement regardless of where she works next."

Gabriel turned back to me. "What's your verdict? Will you come work for me?"

I sat there, completely stunned. Not only had a job landed in my lap, but it appeared I'd still get my final payout.

"Ms. Hartley?" Gabriel prodded.

"Yes," I said. I probably would have agreed to anything he asked at that point.

"Excellent." Gabriel stood up. He put the papers back in the envelope and tossed it in front of Sapien. It landed with a satisfying smack. "I believe our work is done here. I will escort Ms. Hartley back to her desk where she can gather her things, and we will be on our way."

Sapien and Nilyard said nothing as we sauntered out of the conference room.

CHAPTER 9

IT TOOK ME several hours to gather fourteen years of personal effects out of my office. I could have done it in half the time except word spread like wildfire about what had happened. Older employees came flocking to give me a tearful goodbye, many of them asking if the rumors about cut benefits were true. I told them I couldn't officially say anything without breaking confidentiality, which they understood as a resounding "yes."

A few of them helped me load up the car, including Howard. "You fought the good fight, Melissa," he said as I slammed Dirt Dash's trunk shut. "I guess it's up to us now."

I gave him, and Sam beside him, big hugs. "It will be okay. Jobs come and jobs go. Promise we'll see each other again?"

"Of course. You always need coffee," Howard replied. There were tears in his eyes, but I ignored them to help him save face.

Gabriel stood guard just outside my office door the entire time, making sure no one entered that I didn't give express permission to. It was a good thing because Nilyard sent some of his more ambitious brogrammers to try to grab some of my personal files. One stone-eyed glare from Gabriel Alston, though, sent them all packing.

"Don't you have better things to do as CEO of a mega million-dollar defense firm?" I asked him.

"I cleared my morning," he said. "Besides, this is fun."

By the twinkle in his eye as he sent Mr. Teal Post-Its scurrying back to the warehouse, I believed him.

Finally, I slammed my trunk full of all my office belongings. I glanced back at the sandstone building one last time, a few familiar faces waving. I couldn't meet their eyes without choking up.

Gabriel ushered me toward his bulletproof SUV. He'd been the one to park it in Sapien's sacred spot. He got a tissue from out of the glove compartment and handed it to me.

"You must think me overly emotional, getting worked up about this," I said, dabbing my eyes.

Gabriel shrugged. "There's nothing wrong with tears during a final farewell."

And it really was that. A goodbye to the place that had gotten me through raising my fabulous kid. A goodbye to the job where I'd made so many friends and managed to save money for a house. But most of all, a goodbye to Joshua Page himself, the only boss who had ever recognized my true potential.

Now I stood next to this new employer. Besides my wildly inappropriate physical attraction to him, which I'd have to curb, I didn't know much about him.

"So . . ." I drawled the word out. "When do I start at Stronghold?"

"As soon as I can draw up the paperwork."

"Okay." I interpreted that to mean next week, or even the week after. The wheels of bureaucracy always turned slowly, especially with anyone who worked for the government. I felt even more glad he'd gotten me my severance pay.

He reached inside his vehicle again, this time retrieving

something larger.

"Here. This is for you."

"A pager?" I hadn't seen one of these in years.

"I want you to keep it on you at all times."

I palmed the outdated plastic brick. The display screen was pixelated and probably wouldn't have color. "Wouldn't you rather just have my cell number? That would be a lot more convenient."

"I must insist on this, Ms. Hartley. Keep it on you at all times. It will give you instructions on how to reach me. I will expect a response within minutes when it goes off."

"Within minutes?" This all seemed way over the top for a new hire.

"We are a security company, and we take a quick response very seriously." His voice had grown stern. "Do not disappoint me."

* * *

"He just put you on a pager leash and drove away?" Jessie asked, wrinkling her nose.

"Yeah." I took a sip from the mug she had given me, letting the bitter coffee ease down my throat. Normally I would have sweetened up my java this late in the evening, but after breaking so many calorie laws this week, I decided to cut back.

I was sitting in Jessie's living room which also doubled as her creative workspace. Besides a large sectional couch and huge flat screen TV for Paul's weekend sportsball viewing, a sewing machine on a modified dining table huddled in the corner. Dolls of various sizes lay strewn across the cutting mat and in a wicker basket on the floor. Some were old dolls that first Leah and then Penny had outgrown, but Jessie had bought half of them herself over the last few months.

While Jessie worked part-time as a bank teller, her real passion was sewing. She'd set up an online shop a few years ago, hoping to sell her unique maxi dresses with oversized fabric belts in blindingly bright colors. She'd only garnered enough sales to cover her costs.

When a customer asked her to make the dresses as doll clothes, she'd complained at first. However, the first order led to five more, and the numbers continued to pour in. Her unique style of doll clothes went viral and became a viable side hustle. Jessie had even used last year's profits to take the family to Hawaii.

I'd come over to the Dunlaps' after Jessie got off work and caught her up on the latest twist in my ridiculous life. All the kids were holed up elsewhere, including Regan in Leah's room. Most Friday nights we ate dinner together, an old holdover from our apartment days. The smell of delicious pot roast simmered throughout the house, just waiting for Paul to arrive so we could dig in.

Jessie let out a long whistle. "Monday morning's going to be fun when you get more details from pager boy."

"Until then, TGIF." I raised my mug in mock salute and took a long swig.

Regan and Leah waltzed into the adjacent kitchen, heading straight for the pantry. Even though Jessie's back was to them, she didn't turn around as she yelled, "You better not be snacking before dinner."

"Just getting some juice," Leah replied. She was one of those mini-me kids, a smaller version of Jessie right down to the wavy black hair and round face. The biggest difference was the black-framed glasses she wore and her more subdued T-shirt and jeans.

I noticed a thick binder in Regan's hands. "Are you hauling your debate research around like a security blanket?"

She lifted her chin in self-defense. "I'm testing some of my arguments out on Leah. She doesn't mind."

"It's really interesting," Leah agreed in all seriousness. "I'm learning so much about how to structure a good rebuttal."

"You should join the debate team next year," Regan said. "It'd be a lot of fun."

Leah's eyes glazed over. "Yeah. That could be fun."

Jessie snorted. "That's rich. Voluntary public speaking for Leah? She doesn't like to order food at restaurants by herself."

Leah laughed. "It's true. Debate is never going to be my thing."

Regan retrieved two tumblers from the cupboards. "Well, you should at least volunteer to monitor the debates. We need a few extra hands, and you could watch one of my matches."

"I could do that," Leah said. "As long as I'm just setting up the classrooms and not actually arguing with people."

"I didn't think I'd like it either, but it's been so fun this year. And the team has a real shot of going to state."

"That's because you're the master of talking people into agreeing with you."

"I am not."

"Oh, please." Leah gave Regan the juice carton. "Remember how you convinced Mrs. Ives to let you do a book report on *The Hobbit*? She never lets any kid read fantasy books for credit. She says it rots our brains."

"Well, maybe she changed her mind."

"Or how about today when Jake let you have the last garden burger in the cafeteria? He's a vegetarian for crying out loud. He ate lettuce and tomato on the side for you!"

Regan pursed her lips. "Oh, come on. I'm not that pushy."

"Yeah, she's not that pushy," I said with mock outrage. "She can't get that Lucas kid to do what she wants."

"Mom!" Regan snapped, clearly betrayed.

"It's not like I don't already know what's going on there," Leah said matter-of-factly. "Speaking of Mr. Bad Boy, did you hear what happened to him today? He apparently ran out of English class in the middle of a test."

"I know." Regan glowered. "I'm in his English class."

"Why didn't you tell me earlier?" Leah exclaimed. "You gotta give me details."

Regan shrugged as she poured herself a glass. "The dude's nuttier than a fruit bar. One minute he's scribbling away, and the next he's fixated on something outside, like a dog that's spotted a squirrel. Then he just ran off."

"The teacher didn't stop him?" I asked.

"Lucas was gone before Mrs. Bickle could do anything about it. Then he came back a few minutes later covered in glitter. He claimed someone threw it on him on the way to the bathroom. Mrs. Bickle wasn't hearing any of it and sent him straight to the office."

"There's sure a lot of glitter stories going on this week." Leah smiled slyly at me.

I pointed at Regan. "See, you don't have any right getting mad about me blabbing about your embarrassing secrets if you're broadcasting mine."

Regan at least looked a little chagrined. "I know the whole glitter thing really sucked at the time, but you gotta admit, in hindsight, it's pretty funny."

The girls tittered to themselves.

Jessie sighed. "Is there some sort of teenage reasoning behind glitter that I'm too old to understand?"

I shrugged. "That's what I thought, but I've been reassured by the whippersnappers that glitter bombing is not a thing, despite the fact that Lucas went ballistic when he found some on me in the school office."

Regan stopped laughing. "He did?"

"Didn't I tell you? That's why Lucas went all aggressive on me."

"He must be allergic to glitter," Leah joked.

The front door opened, halting our conversation. Paul walked into the house, dressed in a dark green collared shirt and gray pants rumpled after a long day of accounting work. A wiry guy of medium build, he had a receding ash-blond buzzcut with matching soul patch.

Setting his bag in the corner and inhaling a long breath, his expression brightened. "Something smells great!" He crossed over into the living room to plant a kiss on his wife's forehead. Then he immediately rolled up his sleeves and headed into the kitchen.

I envied Jessie's and Paul's easy marriage. They meshed so well together. They split household chores effortlessly between them. They enjoyed creating things with their hands, Jessie with her sewing and Paul in his corner garage woodshop. They never went to bed angry, were on the same disciplinary page as parents, and worked hard on mutual financial goals like saving up for the kids' college or a new car.

They were relationship goals, as the kids say.

Ten-year-old Penny came inside after hearing her father return home. She'd been in the back yard looking for slugs and had one caught inside a plastic cage. Lanky like her dad, she had her mother's dark hair and a bright smile all her own, a perfect blend of her Ortega mom and her Dunlap dad. Jessie shooed her to the bathroom to strip out of her muddy clothes.

"At least she took her boots off before stomping her way in," Jessie grumbled.

Blake also appeared to set the table without being asked. A quiet middle schooler with caramel-colored hair and a kind soul, he slid around the chatty crowd like a ghost. Jessie yelled at the older girls to help him get drinks on the table while we rinsed our mugs in the sink.

In no time, all seven of us were seated around the long dining table, plates of food passing between us. We all offered generalities about our day, even quiet Blake, often breaking out into smaller side conversations filled with banter. Having spent my life as part of a duo—first as an only child and then raising one—I never took these boisterous meals for granted. As I watched Regan laughing with Penny about some fart joke that Paul unsuccessfully tried to ban from the table, my heart swelled. I loved that my daughter had these experiences, so different from the solo dinners I scrounged up myself growing up.

After dinner, the four kids did the dishes and then wandered to the TV to play a racing video game. The adults took seats around the now clean dining table, partaking in a little post-meal alcohol. Paul kept yawning.

I clucked my tongue at him. "You'd sleep better if you didn't go on night patrol in my neighborhood."

"He had to check on you," Jessie replied irritably. "Especially since you're a stubborn idiot and wouldn't stay with us last night."

"Hey, I bought a video doorbell. That should be enough."

"And if it shows even the slightest hint of something fishy, you'll come over here, right?"

I made a vague affirmative noise as I took a sip of wine. I loved Jessie to death, but she'd force Regan and me to sleep on her couch permanently. As much as I appreciated her having my back, I didn't want to live in constant fear. My daughter deserved better than that.

Besides, the wolf was just nature, and Serena Fawcett was a random whacko. I couldn't imagine anything serious would actually come of either incident, strange as they were.

CHAPTER 10

REGAN HAD AN out-of-town track meet over the weekend. At first, I asked her to skip it, but she begged me to let her go. Deciding not to give in to fear, I called her track coach and told him about the Serena Fawcett incident. He assured me upside down and sideways he'd keep a close eye on her. Her coach even reassured me again when I dropped her off at school. I reminded myself life had risks and watched the bus drive off with Regan on it late Saturday morning.

That left me with a deliciously empty weekend to decompress. I had no looming work meeting, no big deadlines to meet. Although I worried about what would happen to my colleagues at Cascade Vista, I no longer had any control over that. A weight had lifted from my shoulders. For the first time in weeks, I had free time.

Normally, this is when I would go for a long run, but Regan and I had made a promise not to run alone anymore. I could have hit one of the school tracks to run around in circles with a bunch of strangers, but that didn't appeal at all.

So, even though I was tempted to just lounge around on the couch watching TV, I decided to be productive. I went outside to do yard work.

Lots of women find comfort in gardening. Jessie has a vegetable garden that produces way too much zucchini in the summer. I, however, hadn't gotten the green thumb gene.

In my defense, I'm pretty sure plants hated me. Moss had long since taken over much of the front yard, thriving after Oregon's rainy winter. That meant the remaining grass was green and tall but getting choked out. I mowed that down first, then used a seed spreader to put moss control on the lawn. It would turn the yard black for a few days before hopefully giving the grass room to grow.

Next, I decided to tackle the weeds that had sprung up in the bark mulch alongside the house. As I got down on my hands and knees, I reminded myself for the hundredth time I should just tear the whole front lawn out and replace it with a bunch of waterless features like rocks and native bushes. I knew I'd never do it, though, because I didn't have the patience to do it myself nor the money to pay a landscaper.

I yanked at stubborn weeds with a vengeance.

"You think that's really going to help?" a familiar voice drifted at me from the sidewalk.

I had my back to my neighbor when she made that statement. That allowed me to make a face before plastering on a fake smile.

"Good morning, Ms. Tannen."

The impeccably dressed senior citizen with smart red glasses actually looked tall since I was viewing her from the ground. Nancy Tannen's sleek designer jacket had no wrinkles, her pumps shiny without a smudge of dirt, every dyed-black hair firmly in place within her layered haircut. She was the only Oregonian I knew who carried an umbrella if there was even the hint of rain, the rest of us resigning ourselves to damp hair.

She must have seen me from her front window and came to scold me for a supposed home infraction, one of her favorite pastimes. She was a retired home economics teacher and could have been bosom buddies with 50s-era TV show moms. I'm sure she would have rather lived in a neighborhood with a homeowner's association, but she'd inherited her current house after her elderly parents died. If someone granted her one magical wish, I'm sure she'd ask for the world to remain entrenched in the "good old days."

Nancy gestured toward the clump of dandelions in my hands. "You should have removed those earlier. They've already sprouted seeds and spread across the road into my lawn."

I glanced at the pristine carpet of grass that spread in front of her perfect house. Her roses and hydrangeas were artfully trimmed back, prepped for gorgeous blooms in a few months. Not a single lingering dead leaf lingered from her two-story maple tree.

"I'm pretty sure any dandelion seeds that dared to cross the road would have withered at the thought of touching your grass," I told her pleasantly.

"Is that one of your jokes?"

"You know me." I said, standing so she'd at least have to look up her nose at me. "Always good for a laugh."

"This isn't a laughing matter. Your house is an important asset. You don't have many of those as a single mother."

I chewed the inside of my mouth to stop a sarcastic response about her own spinsterhood. This is how things always were with Nancy Tannen. Rarely pleasant, always demanding, and insulting you as a way to encourage you to make the "proper" life choices.

Since I didn't enjoy living next to neighbors who hated my guts, I generally either joked with her or let it go, often a combination of the two. "I'll keep that in mind the next time I meet with my estate planner."

She squinted at me. I must have successfully ridden the fine line between making fun of her and acting serious because she nodded in agreement. "It's good to have all your affairs in order. I just made some modifications to my own will recently. I'm prepared to meet my Maker."

I kinda wished I could see Nancy interact with her god. I didn't know a person she couldn't critique.

"Life is full of unpleasant business," she continued. "One should always be prepared."

I thought of my messy prior week and snorted. "There are some things you just can't prepare for."

"Nonsense. That's defeatist talk. If I thought like that, I wouldn't have led the fulfilling life I have lived."

It was hard not to laugh. I couldn't imagine how keeping an impeccable house and nitpicking your neighbors was the ultimate life dream, but to each her own, I guess.

A large vehicle drove up our quiet street. The gleaming SUV pulled up right behind Nancy. I recognized it from the day before.

The engine cut and the driver's window rolled down. "Ms. Hartley?" a deep voice called out to me. I hated the anticipatory goosebumps that formed on my arms at the mere sound of Gabriel Alston's voice.

Nancy flinched but managed to demurely turn around. She could not, however, maintain an aura of calm when she met Gabriel's intense gaze. She took a few steps back, dirtying her pristine shoes on a patch of moss.

I couldn't judge Nancy's appearance, given that I was covered in grass stains with my hair falling out of a ponytail. I straightened, pretending we were all at a business mixer rather than my weedy front lawn.

"How did you find out where I live, Mr. Alston?"

"Your address is public information, Ms. Hartley." He frowned, a tinge of irritation in his voice. "I thought I made it clear that you should have my pager with you at all times. I've been trying to reach you for the last hour."

I folded my arms across my dirty shirt. "In case you haven't noticed, it's Saturday."

"The day of the week is irrelevant now that you work for me."

"I don't recall signing any employment papers."

"Why do you think I'm here?"

My shoulders went slack. "Really? It can't wait until Monday?"

"No, it can't."

Nancy had been watching us with wide eyes, head bouncing back and forth between us. She finally recovered enough to clear her throat. "Excuse me. It's rude not to introduce me to your new boss."

Either I did what Nancy wanted now, or she'd corner me for information later. Better to get it over with.

"Ms. Tannen, meet Gabriel Alston of Stronghold Incorporated. Mr. Alston, meet Nancy Tannen, my neighbor."

"Former high school educator," she corrected with a snap. "And Ms. Hartley's confidant."

I couldn't stop myself from rolling my eyes. Nancy didn't catch it, but Gabriel did. He might have smiled, but it was hard to tell since he was enshrouded in a vehicle that sucked the light out of the atmosphere.

Gabriel surprised us both by exiting the car. He wore a black overcoat over his expensive suit. Nancy squeaked as she realized just how massive he was. He looked like he could reach down and flip the reinforced vehicle over if he wanted to.

Instead, he extended a large hand to her. "Ms. Tannen."

She recovered and gave him a firm shake. "Pleased to meet you, Mr. Alston."

"I apologize if I'm interrupting your conversation, but I really must speak to Ms. Hartley in private."

I snorted. Nancy never retreated. She'd argued with police officers last year during a house fire on our street, demanding that she deserved a closer look.

To my utter amazement, though, she nodded curtly.

"Of course." She released his hand and peered over at me. "I'll see you later." She gave Gabriel a final "Good day" and then skirted around the SUV to her side of the street.

I gaped at her retreating back, and yet I understood how she felt as Gabriel stalked toward me, not caring at all about moss killer or dirt clods. There was nothing gentle about this giant.

I mentally pinched myself back to reality. I'd definitely been watching too many cheesy rom-coms. He was just a guy, a rich one perhaps, but human like the rest of us.

"Come on." I motioned toward the front door. "If you want privacy, we'd better go inside. Otherwise, Nancy's going to smudge her makeup plastering herself to her front window watching us."

He had to duck under the doorframe to enter my house, but at least my ceilings were high enough he didn't have to hunch over in the living room.

I crossed over into the kitchen. "Coffee?"

"No thanks."

"Straight to business then." I grabbed the lukewarm mug on the counter and took a sip. It was better than nothing. "Okay, let's sign some papers."

He shook his head. "Not here."

"Why not?"

"It's a large contract. It will take some time for you to read through. I'd prefer not to wait in your private residence while you go over it."

"Maybe I'll just sign it without reading."

He raised an eyebrow. "I thought you weren't stupid."

I nearly spat out my coffee.

"Is something wrong?" Gabriel asked.

"I'm not used to being called stupid to my face," I said around a cough.

"I said quite clearly that I didn't think you were stupid."

"And you're apparently unable to recognize a joke."

"I'm a busy jet-setting executive. When do I have time for jokes?"

Well, now he had me confused because I could have sworn he was teasing me, but he looked so serious.

I decided to test him. "Maybe you're the stupid one here. It's to your advantage if I don't read through the contract. I could sign away anything, even my soul."

He leaned forward, casting an eerie shadow over his face since his height completely blocked the ceiling light. "Do you think I'm the devil, Ms. Hartley?"

I stifled a shiver. "Well, you are the CEO of a security firm that works closely with the US military. Can we compromise and say 'Satan adjacent?'"

His perfect composure finally crumpled. A smile spread across his face, changing his entire persona from that of an aloof businessman to a drop-dead gorgeous flirt.

My heart did a little flutter.

Then he tucked the smile away. "As amusing as this all is, I'd rather not conduct business inside your private residence."

"And I don't like to conduct business looking like I slept in grass clippings. If you give me ten minutes to change out of my yard clothes, I'll come with you."

"Sounds like a plan."

I swigged down the last of my coffee, then headed for the hallway. "Make yourself comfortable," I called over my shoulder.

I wished I had time for a shower but settled for scrubbing my face and arms with copious amounts of soap. I put on a mostly wrinkle-free blouse and slacks. I gave my reflection in the mirror a critical eye. It wasn't my best look, but it would do. I should have done laundry instead of working on the lawn.

I quickly gathered all my scattered belongings around the room: keys, purse, and phone. I found the pager next to my bedstand and noticed it only had two messages, one from an hour ago and one just before Gabriel arrived. Grimacing, I shoved it into my shoulder bag. As charming as he could be, he clearly would be one of those employers who believed his subordinates were always on the clock. Suddenly, I was glad this was a temp job.

Gabriel had wandered to the fireplace by the time I returned. He seemed so out of place, not exactly a bull in a china shop, more like a warhorse in a secondhand store. Nestled amongst various ceramic knickknacks, he'd picked up a framed photo of Regan from her kindergarten play. She was dressed as a princess firefighter, complete with crown on top of her bright red helmet.

He pointed to her goofy expression as she spread her arms out wide to the audience to deliver her line. "Who's this?"

I suppressed a giggle as I relived the memory of that moment. It was a long story that didn't bear repeating at this moment. "My daughter, Regan." I grabbed a jacket off the coat rack and shoved my arms through it. "You have kids?"

"No." He placed the photo back in its dust-free spot. "Can her father take care of her while we conduct business?"

"There is no dad."

"Divorce?"

"He was never around," I said, unable to keep the irritation out of my voice. I did not want to go down this road.

"My apologies. I've been rude."

"No worries," I waved it off. "Besides, Regan's in high school now and off at a track meet. She's past the babysitting days."

He assessed me from head to toe. "You don't look old enough to have a teenager."

"Ah, single mom flattery." I wouldn't admit it was working. I opened the door for him. "Shall we?"

He ushered me into his tank of a vehicle, and we were off.

Gabriel drove into the heart of downtown where a lot of the fancier firms had their offices. We had to maneuver through a gaggle of protesters, a lot thinner on a weekend, but still in clusters asking motorists to honk for their cause. Their ruckus slowed down traffic around the State Capitol.

I gestured at Gabriel. "Aren't you going to lay on the horn?"

"I try not to get involved in politics."

I gave him a sideways glance. "You're a defense contractor."

"Let me rephrase that: legislation is not my area of expertise."

I didn't press the issue as we slid through the crowd.

After passing a beautiful wooded park with a stream running through it, we entered the underground parking lot of a squat brick building with a fancy glass facade. Gabriel eased the car close to the elevator, which we entered with a swipe of his keycard. Given how the cables in the dingy space jerked us upward, I imagined the upstairs to be equally drab and spartan.

Instead, the first-floor lobby resembled a posh hotel. A few comfy chairs faced each other on top of an expensive plush rug in front of a gas fireplace. The floor-to-ceiling windows allowed light in from the outside, but with enough shade that it didn't make the area seem overly bright. A tall reception desk stood in one corner, the guard tower for a heavy metal door that led to the inner offices.

A woman about my age with tight curly hair framing her dark face manned the desk. She wore the same conservative suit as Gabriel, although cut to accentuate her feminine frame. She approached us with a baton in her hands, her stride more soldier than secretary.

"Sir," she greeted Gabriel. Her spine straightened, but she did not go as far as to salute him.

"Ms. Hartley, this is Vanessa Sinclair. She's my head of security and will conduct a basic scan before you enter our office."

"A scan?" I asked dubiously.

She showed me the baton in her hand. Up close, I could see that it actually had a bumpy texture and had been painted over in what appeared to be shiny metallic paint. "Think of this like a metal detector wand. Can you stand with legs and arms apart, please?"

"Sure thing, TSA agent."

Vanessa's eyes narrowed at my quip, but she maintained her professionalism, waving the wand over my limbs and torso. She always kept at least four inches away from touching my skin and clothes. The wand made no noise, although I swear I felt a strange buzzing in my bones now and again.

I thought I was out of the woods until she did a quick swipe over my head and the baton chirped. And when I mean chirped, I'm not exaggerating. It sounded like baby birds peeping in their nest.

"I swear I don't have metal plates in my head," I said.

I was still spread out with Vanessa behind me, which is why I flinched when the baton tapped the top of my head. It didn't hurt, just startled me. The chirping noise increased to an unpleasant squawk.

"Hey!" I exclaimed, whipping around.

"Is something wrong?" Gabriel asked.

Vanessa scrutinized the tip of the wand. "Shiny dust in her hair is setting it off."

I blushed. "Yeah, that's glitter. I guess it's metallic." It was still embedded deep in my scalp. I had no idea how long it would take for it all to shake out. Maybe I'd be buried with it.

Gabriel leaned forward and Vanessa let him see the glimmering spots on the tip of the baton. "Glitter?" he asked incredulously.

I didn't know how else to explain it, so I just went for the truth. "Some punk threw it on me while I was jogging the other day."

Gabriel's eyes widened. "Were you recently assaulted, Ms. Hartley?"

"No, nothing like that. Just a harmless prank."

"Your attacker didn't hurt you?"

I tried to steer the conversation away from the entire embarrassing incident. "It was just a teenager, I'm sure of it. Something similar happened at my daughter's school too. Really, I'm fine."

Gabriel didn't look convinced, but he let it go. "Come this way."

Vanessa stayed in the lobby examining the glitter on the wand as Gabriel opened the heavy metal door with his keycard, leading me into the back offices. Unlike the upscale lobby, this area was bare. As we crisscrossed down a few corridors, I saw nothing in any of the handful of office spaces we passed. The sterile smell of recent disinfectant blended with an air of musty disuse. The whole ambiance felt even more bleak given there were no windows to bring in natural light.

Gabriel led me to a large room with a modest conference desk and two surprisingly comfortable swivel chairs. He set me down on one of them and said he'd return with the contract. When he returned with a stack of papers that took him both hands to keep balanced, my stomach fell.

"That's the contract?" I asked.

"Half of it. Plus applications and questionnaires." He plopped the stack in front of me.

"I signed less paperback when I mortgaged my house," I complained.

Gabriel shrugged. "We're thorough in our line of work. You may be exposed to confidential, or even classified, information. We take every necessary precaution to ensure you're a good fit for our company."

"In other words, drown in red tape." Suddenly, I understood why he wanted to get started on this. It might take me all day to get through everything. I reached for the pen he offered and then craned my neck side-to-side to loosen up.

"You won't get cell service back here, so the top sheet has information on how to log into our local computer network."

"Wonderful," I muttered.

He ignored my sarcasm. "I'll be down the hall in the first office near the front doors if you need me." Gabriel then disappeared, leaving me to my bureaucratic nightmare.

CHAPTER 11

I WAS WRONG. Signing the papers wouldn't take all day. It would take all weekend.

In some ways, it was for the best that I was sequestered in a room with no way to tell time. Otherwise, I might have gone mad, shuffling through form after form, answering lengthy questionnaires about my employment eligibility and struggling to remember details about my education. The monotony of filling in boxes was only broken by long stretches of legal text that I didn't dare skip, both because Gabriel wanted me to be detail-oriented, and I was scared to sign my firstborn child away. I even took the time to look up some terms on their sluggish network connection.

Gabriel did check on me at regular intervals. First, he asked me about lunch. I jokingly told him I wanted steak, and he actually brought me one, along with a salad with the best dressing I'd ever tasted. He tried to make small talk with me, but I'd been too happy eating to do more than grunt at him.

Several hours later, I was only 75% through the initial stack of papers, and I'd had it. My phone said it was only 3:30, too early for dinner, but I needed a break. I decided to stretch my legs for a bit.

Rather than return to the exit, I went deeper into the building. I knew about the bathroom across the hall but found an unused kitchen. Other than that, I didn't expect much more than empty office rooms, which is why I was surprised to find myself inside a super long hallway with no doors on either side. It curved to yet another long hallway, this one with a set of plain metal doors at the end.

Curious, I approached them for a closer look. They appeared similar to the solid metal ones in the lobby, only the doorframe had been made with cube-shaped rocks in a variety of soft blue and gray shades. The carefully crafted masonry stood in sharp contrast to the modern drywall around it.

I didn't see any sort of keycard. I pushed tentatively on the doors, but they were locked.

"What are you doing here?"

I hadn't heard Vanessa approach and yelped when she called to me from down the hall.

"Sorry," I said. "I was just looking around."

"Well, you can't be down here. This is a restricted area."

I folded my arms across my chest. "I didn't see any signs."

Vanessa pointed to printout taped to the wall. Sure enough, it said "Warning: Restricted Area. Authorized Personnel Only."

"Okay, I stand corrected."

Vanessa glared at me. "I'll put up bigger signs so you won't make the same mistake again." Then she motioned for me to exit the hallway.

Vanessa followed me back to the conference room. We found Gabriel coming toward us. He'd taken off his suit jacket and rolled up his shirt sleeves, leaving his muscular arms bare. Having worked mostly with software engineers the last decade, I hadn't run into any guys with this kind of physique outside my TV screen. I'm pretty sure his sinew had sinew.

I shook that ridiculous thought out of my head. I, of all people, should know better than to be attracted to rich and powerful men by now.

Gabriel seemed surprised to see Vanessa and me together. "Something amiss?"

"I found her near the end of the hall," Vanessa said with all the authority of a prison guard.

I threw my hands up in the air. "I'm sorry! I just got stir-crazy and went for a walk."

He regarded me for a few seconds, then said to Vanessa. "I'll take it from here." She left but not without throwing me several suspicious glances, as if leaving a thief in a bank vault.

Gabriel didn't seem nearly so put out after she'd gone. "If you needed a walk, you should have said something. I'm happy to go with you."

As much as my hormones said 'yes,' I felt a bit mortified at pulling the CEO into my impromptu break. "Oh no, you don't have to bother. I'm happy to see myself out."

"Actually, you can't. We don't have an extra keycard for you yet. Besides, I need the fresh air too." He started walking away but then paused to look back at me. "Unless you have some sort of objection."

"No good ones."

"What bad ones are you holding back?"

"Clearly none since I'm running off my mouth again."

We returned to the lobby doors. I confirmed that this doorframe was made of the same stuff as the door itself, no fancy masonry. Gabriel used his keycard to open them.

I grumbled at the metal doors as they shut behind me. "It's like a jail in here."

"It's secure," Gabriel corrected. "I told you we take security seriously."

"So seriously you can't afford windows in the main office?"

"Windows are notoriously hard to protect."

"Should we even be taking a walk?" I asked, dripping with sarcasm. "Who knows what big bad monsters are lurking outside."

"You'll be safe enough with me." That infuriating monotone did not betray whether he was teasing me again.

"Pardon me if I skip the swoon."

Past the lobby, we emerged into glorious sunshine, rare for this time of year in Salem. Vitamin D hit my skin, immediately improving my mood. If I'd had running shoes on, I would have sprinted down the street. As it was, Gabriel had to take longer strides to keep up with me.

"You're looking quite refreshed already," he said as I steered us toward a nearby park.

"It's amazing how much better a person feels not being chained to a desk with paperwork on Saturday."

"I know the work is tedious, but I appreciate your diligence on the matter."

His praise lifted my spirits. "I'm sorry if I seem ungrateful. I do appreciate the opportunity to work for you."

"Despite the mountains of paperwork?" he asked, a grin threatening to form.

"It's a necessary evil. I'll get to dive into some real work soon enough." I paused as I realized I didn't know many specifics about my new job. "Whatever that is."

"You're an experienced office manager. I'm happy to let you take the reins on whatever you deem necessary. It's been a while since we spun up a new office. I assume you know what needs to be done to get it up and running."

I made a mental list of tasks. Find out who would work in the office at what times and with what duties. How best to organize all those people in that labyrinth of an office. Get all the furniture set up in the rooms. Unpack the office supplies. Stock that kitchen I'd found…I could think of a million things that needed to be done, just off the top of my head.

"I'll find something to do," I said confidently.

"Excellent."

We followed a creek that wound through the secluded park. Road noise faded away as the foliage surrounded us. My steps became lighter, and I took a deep breath.

Next to me, Gabriel seemed to feel it too. His shoulders slowly relaxed as he threw his thick arms out in front of him in a stretch.

"This park is fantastic," I said.

Gabriel regarded the lush trees and bushes surrounding us. "I always try to locate our offices near a natural area, even in a city. I've found it lifts employee morale."

I nodded. "This would be a great place for your employees to go for a midday run."

His eyebrows furrowed. "You're thinking about running alone even though you were recently attacked?"

"You're still worried about that?" I managed not to make a face. "Look, you don't have kids, so let me spell this out for you. It was a teenage prank. The kid was wearing dragonfly wings of all things."

What I believed would calm him down actually made him more agitated. "What?"

"*Fake* wings," I said. "Like she was doing cosplay. She dumped all that glitter on me and then ran off."

"You never experienced any adverse side effects?" He stopped me in the middle of a small wooden bridge so he could scrutinize the part in my hair. "No flu-like symptoms? Any periods of time you can't account for."

This time I couldn't help but roll my eyes. "She dosed me with glitter, not hallucinogens. Nothing bad happened to me afterward."

He scowled. "I'll have you make a sketch of the perpetrator for me."

"She wore a mask." This was getting to be too much. I needed to distract him. I struggled to think of any good topic. I found a worry rattling around in my brain and latched onto it.

"Why would you hire me of all people?" I clamped my mouth shut. Why did I have to choose my insecurity of all things as my great distraction?

Gabriel tilted his head, puzzled. "Come again?"

Well, he wasn't thinking about my glitter bombing anymore. "Not to downplay myself, but I'm a nobody to you. Your company must have the resources to hire almost anyone you want. Why choose an office manager that chewed you out during a chance encounter?"

"Maybe it's because you chewed me out that I hired you," Gabriel said.

Now I was confused. "Why would that make a difference?"

Gabriel clasped his hands behind his back. "You don't get to be in business as long as me and not recognize red flags. I knew Cascade Vista had recently been acquired by Wrought Ventures. There's been big changes at the office, haven't there?"

"Yeah," I said bitterly.

"It's very common for the acquiring firm to squeeze out the best parts of the original company. Things like encouraging senior employees to quit because they cost more than younger ones. Cutting wages and benefits, which lowers morale. Any of this ring a bell?"

"All the bells," I admitted, "but those tactics are common for a reason, right? They save the parent company money over time."

"Not really," Gabriel said, surprising me. "A company's best assets are almost always its people. From what I've heard, Cascade Vista's founder Joshua Page understood that."

My heart twisted, remembering the old man.

Gabriel noticed. "You miss him, don't you?"

"Every day. He was the best."

His expression softened. "You're like Joshua Page. You understand what makes a firm great: taking care of talented people. It showed in your fight for employee benefits.

That's the kind of company I've built at Stronghold. The Sapiens and Nilyards of this world will never understand."

"Are you trying to tell me," I said slowly, "you hired me exactly because I was fighting for employee benefits, even if it meant a hit to the company's immediate bottom line?"

"That and because you were about to be fired. Your needs and mine aligned. Those are the best types of relationships."

I tried not to fixate on the word "relationship." "What you're saying makes sense, but I can't help the feeling it's not the whole truth. You're keeping secrets."

His sudden smile made my toes curl. "My business is secrets. They're my currency and my livelihood."

"Then that's where we diverge, Mr. Alston. I don't keep secrets."

"Really? Then if I were to dig into your past, I wouldn't find any skeletons?"

I paused. I'd never told anyone, not even Jessie, who Regan's father was.

"Not a single one," I said with what I hoped was convincing gusto. "Well, since you decided to hire me, I'll make my first major recommendation."

"And that is?"

"You need coffee for your office kitchen. Good stuff, not the cheap kind. State law says it's illegal to labor under unsafe conditions, and nothing is more dangerous than bad office coffee."

In a complete deadpan, he said, "I've also heard coffee stunts your growth." He pointed at my smaller frame.

"Then you should drink more! You're freakishly huge. I can't even imagine what it's like finding a bed in your size."

As soon as the word "bed" came out of my mouth, impure thoughts of him raced through my head. I flushed. Why couldn't I control my stupid thoughts about this guy?

Thankfully, Gabriel steered the conversation away from

the bedroom. "I'll put coffee at the top of my priority list tomorrow."

"See that you do," I said as we approached the end of the looped path, heading back into the urban jungle of sidewalks and cars.

CHAPTER 12

GABRIEL LISTENED. The next morning at the Stronghold office, there was not only a coffee machine but several flavors of delicious, expensive java. He'd even bought extra-large mugs that could have moonlighted as soup bowls.

I would have thanked him, except Vanessa informed me that Gabriel had left town early that morning and planned on returning Monday. Besides mumbling about setting off her security wand again with my glitter hair, she left me to my own devices. Devoid of any human contact, I spent my early Sunday in a windowless room, eyes crossed as I finished the second half of the Leaning Tower of Paperwork. Well, almost everything. There'd been a questionnaire in the middle that had asked specific questions about my family history. I filled the entire sheet out as "unknown." If Stronghold wouldn't hire me based on my evasive answers, so be it. The job wasn't worth my mom's wrath, since she hated when I listed her on anything.

I finished around two o'clock and drove home. At least I had a half hour to grab a late lunch from my favorite Mexican restaurant before picking Regan up.

I got to the high school just before the school bus, pulling into a nearby parking lot as it rolled to a stop in front of the main entrance. Reaching over to snag a chip from the food bag, I almost missed seeing the first kid who disembarked from the bus.

Lucas. He glanced around in all directions with his maroon and gray duffel bag thrown over his shoulder. His eyes settled on me for a second, but I'm not sure if he actually recognized me before I lost him in a sea of track suits.

Regan was one of the last kids off, wearing her favorite hoodie with the rainbow heart patch and chatting with a boy with teal locks. She broke away from him once she spotted Dirt Dash.

"Good track meet?" I asked as she threw her sports bag in the back seat. It landed in a pile of discarded receipts with a crunch. I'd get around to cleaning that right around the time I figured out how to add a twenty-fifth hour to my day.

She strapped herself in. "Not so great. I didn't place in a single race."

"Sorry to hear that."

She shrugged. "Meh, they weren't my best events. Coach'll shuffle me around for the meet after next."

I raised an eyebrow. "You bombed so bad you're not even participating in the next meet? At least when you fail, you do so spectacularly."

She bonked me lightly on the head. "No, Mom. I've got district debate, remember? I can't miss it."

"Of course. How could I forget? You're the Princess of Persuasion. The Diva of Depositions. The Queen of Quotations."

"And you're the Theologian with a Thesaurus, apparently."

I waited for a group of teenagers to ease out of their parking spot before I did the same. Better to keep the reckless drivers ahead of me than riding my bumper.

"How'd the rest of the team do?"

"Not bad. A handful really killed it."

I couldn't help myself. "You mean like Lucas?"

Regan acted like I'd poked her with a cattle prod. "Why are you asking about him?"

"He was the first guy off the bus. I didn't even know he was on the track team."

"He wasn't," Regan said darkly. "He hasn't attended a single practice, but Coach announced him as a new addition right before we left Saturday. Apparently, he did a demo run, and Coach was so impressed, he put him on the team as a substitute."

I glanced over at her, arms across her chest. "Why are you so mad?"

"Because he didn't try out like the rest of us."

"He's a new kid. He missed tryouts. If he's just a sub, it seems fair enough."

"It's just weird, that's all. Lucas is truant all the time. He shouldn't be allowed to do athletics until he straightens out."

"Maybe they're hoping sports will do the trick."

"I guess. Look, Mom, I know you're super curious about him and all, especially after our little encounter at the school office, but can we just not talk about him?"

As much as I was dying to ask more questions, I let it drop. "Sure. Can you guess what I bought for dinner?"

She inhaled slowly. "Do I smell enchiladas?"

"And chips and salsa, although I doubt you can smell that."

"Yes!" She reached for the bag behind my seat.

I smacked her shoulder before she could retrieve it. "Wait until we get home."

"I'm starving!"

"You'll get crumbs in the car."

"You're kidding, right?" She pointed out the various coffee drippings on the dash and unvacuumed floor at her feet.

"Okay, fine. I'm more worried you'll eat all the chips before I get any."

"I wouldn't do that," she said, knowing full well that's exactly what happened the last time I'd ordered Mexican.

We made it home a few minutes later. Not bothering to grab her belongings, she fled into the house without checking the mail this time. By the time I walked in, she'd already poured both of us two huge glasses of milk to help with salsa burn.

"Hey, Hungry Pants," I said. "You left your stuff in the car."

"I can get it after I eat."

"I left the car door open so you could grab it."

"Why didn't you grab it?"

I shoved the greasy bag onto the counter, hoping I hadn't gotten any on my shirt. "I hauled in our delicious, but leaking, bounty."

"Argh!" she declared, huffing it out the door. She reemerged before I could lay plates down next to the food. She hurtled her sports bag into the living room. It must have been partially unzipped because clothes and papers spilled onto the rug.

Regan gave me the highlights of the competition, names of her swift teammates rushing past me so fast I'd never remember who won or lost each race. To be fair, she looked about as interested in me when I told her I'd spent my weekend filling out forms for my new job.

We considered watching a movie afterward, but Regan began receiving a series of texts from Leah. Her fingers flew over the screen as the two replied in rapid fire.

"It'd be quicker if you two just called each other," I said. "Probably have better grammar too."

"How do I convey my feelings without emojis?"

"I don't know. Voice inflection?"

She didn't respond as she wandered down the hall to her room, still typing furiously. From past experience, I knew that meant the conversation with Leah had gone private. She wouldn't return for at least a half hour.

I hoped that only delayed movie night instead of canceled it. I'd been really looking forward to some quiet time with my kid after a mind-numbing weekend.

With time on my hands, I tackled dirty dishes, annoyed at how difficult it was to rinse out the deeper stains. Then I wiped the counter and swept the kitchen floor. Go me.

With the kitchen and dining area taken care of, I almost plopped down onto the couch but snagged my toe on Regan's sports bag. More clothes and papers came spilling out of it in a cascade.

Bending with a grimace—why do human backs give out around middle age?—I thrust the clothes back into the bag. I was gentler with the papers because I figured it was her homework for tomorrow.

Except for one stiff, official-looking envelope.

Curious, I read the return address label. I recognized it instantly as one of those DNA testing companies where you send in your spit, and they tell you a bunch of stuff about your ancestry.

It was addressed to Regan Hartley.

I went numb. Surely Regan hadn't given away her genetic profile to some random company without discussing it with me. I didn't exactly approve, but she had to know I wouldn't forbid her. We could have talked about it and come to a compromise. My daughter and I discussed everything.

So why not about this?

Confused, I pulled out the creased papers and immediately understood why. The headline "We can connect you to family" popped out at me. A list of potential relatives, mostly distant cousins, appeared with their names blotted out, from which she would have to pay an additional fee to gain access.

The one that made my blood ran cold said "Possible father."

A bedroom door opened down the hall, followed by

approaching footsteps. "You still want to watch something?" Regan asked as she stepped back into the living room.

Then she saw me holding the letter and let out an audible gasp.

We both stared at each other in horrified shock.

I recovered first. "You went looking for your father?"

"I just . . ." she couldn't quite finish her thought.

I thrust the envelope toward her. "You have no idea what you're messing with!"

My anger fueled Regan's. "Because you won't tell me who he is!"

"He doesn't care about you!"

She balled her hands into fists. "Then why hide him from me?"

"Because he could take you away from me!"

She glowered. "Sounds more like you just want to keep me to yourself."

My jaw dropped. "What?"

"What's that saying . . . 'The apple doesn't fall far from the tree?' Don't you realize you're acting exactly like your own mother?"

I flushed. "This has nothing to do with Barbara Hartley."

"Then what is it about?"

"Privacy. Am I not allowed to have one private part of my life that you don't know about?"

"No, not when it affects me too."

"It doesn't."

"Oh really? What if his family has some rare medical condition I should know about? Or what if one of his family members starts looking for me?"

My defenses cracked a little. Maybe she had a point, but I knew deep down that she needed to steer clear of John Moroz until he couldn't use parental rights to force her to live with him.

"What if I told you he was the worst kind of person?" I

asked. "Would you still want to meet him?"

Regan glowered. "I should be the judge of his character."

"You'd be too clouded by curiosity to make the right call. Your father terrifies me. He could tear you apart before you even knew he meant to hurt you."

She narrowed her eyes at me. "It sounds like you're trying to poison me against him."

My jaw hurt from clenching my teeth so tightly. "How can I convince you not to go looking for him?"

She clamped her mouth shut, refusing to respond.

There was my answer. I couldn't convince her. Regan had that stubborn Hartley streak, and I knew she wouldn't budge. She wanted to meet her father and decide for herself. The moment she did, she'd be shark bait.

There was no way she could be legally safe from him until she turned eighteen. Even then, with all his power and money, he might destroy her beautiful spirit forever.

"It's too late anyway," Regan finally said. "I already paid for the family report."

"You what?" My blood boiled so close to the surface, it was amazing lava didn't shoot out my ears.

"It should get here in a few days. I'll find out his name when it arrives."

I slapped the letter in my palm, making her flinch. "Then I'll just have to check the mail before you and make sure you never see it."

She lost her victorious smirk. "You wouldn't."

"I come home before you almost every day. How are you going to stop me?"

Her face twisted into an ugly frown. "It's mine! I ordered it. You don't have any legal right to take it."

"Don't I? You're a minor. I'm sure if I look into this company's fine print, they weren't even supposed to send you a report like this without parental permission. Or did you forge my signature on the original form?"

She turned away, refusing to look me in the eye.

"That's what I thought." I walked across to the kitchen to shove the envelope into my purse. "Sorry, but I can't let you see that report."

Regan's face splotched as she screamed, "Why? I'll just go look him up in two years anyway."

"Because then you'll be an adult, and he can't force you to do anything you won't want to do."

She heaved hard enough that her shoulders bobbed up and down. "You mean like you're doing to me right now?"

I held out a pleading hand to her. "There are just some things you aren't ready for yet."

Tears formed at the corners of her eyes, but she hadn't lost her fury. "If I ever do find him and he gives me a choice, I'll leave you in a heartbeat."

"Regan . . ." I called, but she'd fled into her room, slamming the door shut so hard it rattled the pictures on the walls.

CHAPTER 13

THAT CONVERSATION HADN'T ended well.

Why is it that when one thing goes wrong, everything does? I had expected to get lambasted at work, but I didn't think I'd end the week being on the wrong end of a glitter prank and possibly needing to call animal control for a stray wolf. Joking aside, having some weirdo try to remove my child from school had launched my stress levels into orbit.

On top of all that, if Regan found out John Moroz was her biological father, she'd definitely reach out to him. The outcome would be catastrophic. Nobodies like me don't take on the one percent and win.

Deep down, I knew this battle I'd been waging to keep Regan from John was over. Somebody in a lab had already connected the dots, so it was only a matter of time before it became public knowledge. My heart lurched as I realized it may have been the DNA test that sparked the stranger to contact Regan in the first place. John must have been notified somehow. I didn't have any proof, but it couldn't be coincidence that this was all happening at the same time.

I'd have to tell Regan. She'd either hear it from me or

someone else, but it was literally the last thing I wanted to do.

I pulled into the underground parking garage at the same time as Gabriel. He gave me a concerned look as he exited his SUV. "Are you feeling well, Ms. Hartley?"

I slapped on a smile. No need to bring my personal business to work. "It's just morning sluggishness. I'll feel better after a round of coffee."

Vanessa once again greeted us in the lobby with her fancy wand. The chirping noise sounded almost immediately. I was now three-for-three with the stupid wand.

"I'm sorry," I said. "It's really hard to get the glitter out."

"I suppose she's clear to go," Vanessa told Gabriel, giving him a pointed look. "May I remind you that the restricted area is completely off-limits. Don't even go down that hallway."

"I wouldn't dream of it," I said. Then Gabriel ushered me inside the metal doors.

Given that I'd just been here yesterday, I expected to find the office in the same half moved-in quality I'd become accustomed to over the weekend, but someone had clearly been busy overnight. The spartan walls had been filled with tasteful framed photographs of mountains and waterfalls. There were real potted plants by each of the doors, although how they could survive with no sunlight was beyond me. Even the air smelled pleasant, a soothing blend of some flowery fragrance replacing the stale musk from before.

"Wow," I said. "You really spruced up the place."

"Wait until you see the kitchen."

Gabriel wasn't kidding. In the span of a single evening, the kitchen had been transformed. Someone had set up several stylish tables with matching chairs, like you might see inside Java Haus. A ring of plush chairs surrounded one end table. There was even a full standing fridge, and I opened it to find milk, cream, and various cans of pop.

"Do you have elves or something?" I asked.

He stilled. "Excuse me?"

I gestured at a pantry I'd opened, filled to the brim with dry snacks. "None of this stuff was here yesterday."

"My moving crew finished office setup last night."

"That's an understatement. Whatever you paid them, they deserve double." I took a deep inhale of roasting beans. "Especially if they're the ones that started the coffee."

Gabriel smiled. "That was me earlier this morning. I like to keep the people who work for me happy."

The fact he wanted me happy made me giddier than it should have. I poured myself a cup of coffee before he ushered me back out of the comforting kitchen.

Gabriel didn't lead me back to the previous conference room but instead across the hall to a tidy office. He held the door open for me, so I slid inside first, noting the modern work desk, high-backed leather chair, and sleek new computer with double monitors connected to a small printer. I didn't like the drab beige walls with no outside window, but other than that, it was a very nice space.

"Our IT guy connected your computer to the network, including programming his number into your landline phone. That should be all you need."

I walked over to the desk and laid my shoulder bag on top. "Great," I said, turning back toward the door. "What do you want me to—"

Gabriel had disappeared.

"—do?" I finished lamely. I jogged back to the hall, finding Gabriel just about to round the corner back to his own office.

"Wait!" I called.

He turned around, tilting his head at me thoughtfully.

"I don't know where to begin. What are your priorities?"

He shrugged nonchalantly. "That's your job, Ms.

Hartley. You are the office manager. I'm sure you can figure it out." Then he left.

"Guess they're big on self-starters here," I grumbled. Well, I had made that mental list over the weekend of what I wanted to tackle first. A good office needed everything in its place. Sure, the kitchen looked great, but I doubted the rest of the rooms had been put together. I could begin there.

Or so I thought. I ended up going through every room. There were four more small offices, very much like mine, and all seemed in good working order even if no one currently occupied them. The conference room had gotten an upgrade with a projector, phone line, and an entire cabinet of office supplies. I found more office supplies in a neat and tidy closet next door. Even the restrooms had seen minor upgrades, such as feminine products in a tasteful wire basket in every stall.

When I spotted a plunger inside a sleek white canister, I nervously tapped my shoes. "They really thought of everything."

Okay, so the office had been put together, but Gabriel himself had said Stronghold's real assets were its people. I needed to get to know them if I wanted to meet their needs.

The only problem was I couldn't find anyone else. Gabriel had holed up in his office, and Vanessa sat in the front lobby past a door I couldn't open without triggering an alarm. The only noises I heard came from down the restricted hallway sporadically. Huge warning signs had been taped down the adjacent hall for my benefit, so I didn't dare head that way.

I passed the time by checking my computer, hoping software might yield some clues as to how I could be useful. However, the thing looked pre-installed with basic word processing and spreadsheet software. No unique files sat in any of my personal folders. I couldn't connect to any open company network drives.

I appeared to be stuck in an office-themed Twilight Zone.

As late morning dragged on, I drank the last dregs of my fourth cup of coffee, knowing full well my bladder would demand action soon. Who cared if I had to run to the bathroom multiple times? It's not like I had anything to do. Why had I wasted a weekend filling out a mountain of paperwork for a job that didn't seem to need me?

That's when I saw the number that had been preprogrammed into my landline phone. It had been labeled "Patrick Kelly, IT." He had to be housed behind those ridiculous restricted doors, where I couldn't reach him.

I perked up. Maybe he could come to me. I picked up the phone and hit his number.

"Hello?" a pleasant voice with a slight Irish accent answered.

"Is this Mr. Patrick Kelly?"

"Aye, it is. You must be our new, ah, manager. How can I help you?"

"It's difficult to explain over the phone. Could you come down to my office?"

"Right now?" he asked, surprised.

"It would be extremely helpful."

"I s'pose." He didn't sound all that enthusiastic, but at that point, I didn't care.

"Great! See you soon." I hung up before he could change his mind. Finally, I would meet one of these elusive Stronghold employees.

A half hour went by without him showing, which should have tipped me off the meeting would not go well. I considered giving up on him to take a bathroom break, the ghost of the morning's coffee creating an increasingly urgent situation.

The overhead lights suddenly flickered. As I wondered if we were experiencing some sort of power surge, I heard the restricted area doors open and shut down the hall. The lights stabilized as footsteps came toward my office. Finally, the little bugger had decided to come.

I didn't realize how prophetic my internal monologue would be.

Patrick was short, maybe the height of an average middle schooler. He wore a dark vest over a button-up shirt and black slacks, an outfit more suited to a wedding than work. He had tousled blond hair and orangish fuzz that was attempting to coalesce into a goatee. With all those combined elements, I honestly couldn't tell if he was in his late twenties or early forties.

"Ms. Hartley." He nodded his head instead of extending a hand for a shake. "How can I help ya?"

"Please have a seat, Mr. Kelly." I motioned to the chair I'd stolen from the kitchen and placed on the other side of my desk. The furniture clashed, but I had to use what was available.

His thick eyebrow furrowed in confusion. "I thought you had a software problem."

"I wanted you to come down to speak to me," I corrected. "I'm the office manager of this location, at least temporarily, and I'd like to meet everyone who works here."

"I'm rather busy." He shuffled toward the door.

"This won't take long."

"I don't know . . ."

I couldn't let the only Stronghold employee I'd found get away. "Mr. Alston gave me authority to conduct employee interviews." Well, he hadn't explicitly done so, but how was I supposed to do my job without talking to people?

My half-truth worked. Patrick stiffened but took the seat across from me. "As long as you're quick."

I pulled out the legal pad where I'd written sample questions. "What's your official job title?"

"IT guy."

I gave him an incredulous look. "That's your official

title? Not IT Manager or something like that?"

"We're pretty informal around here."

An informal defense contracting company that had secret restricted areas. That made no sense. Well, I guess his title didn't really matter.

"How long have you been employed with Stronghold?"

"A few decades."

So, he was in his forties. "Is that typical for the company?"

"People tend to stick around."

Low turnover. That was good. "Do you enjoy your work?"

He shrugged.

"Would you say you're happy here?"

"Sure." He didn't sound sure.

I put the pad aside to give him my full attention. "It would help if you expanded on your answers, Mr. Kelly. I'm trying to gauge employee satisfaction."

"Okay." I thought he might say more, so an awkward silence fell between us.

I sighed. "I hope you're not implying that Stronghold would retaliate against you if you said bad things about the company. I assure you I will keep any answer you provide in complete confidence, off the record."

"Sounds great," he said in the same monotone.

I tried a different tactic. "Do you have any suggestions for how to improve the new Salem office?"

"Nope."

I gestured at the walls. "Not even asking for windows or natural light?"

"I'm good with whatever." He stood up. "I really should get going. Is that all?"

I'd have better luck getting Vanessa to let me into the restricted area. "Just one more question. Can you get me in contact with another employee so I can do an interview?"

I expected a negative response, but Patrick actually perked up. "Absolutely. You should talk to Ida Funar."

I wrote the name down, asking for the correct spelling. "And what does she do?"

"She repairs things."

I didn't quite understand. "Like a building manager?"

"Yes," he said. "I can program her number into your phone."

"Can you also provide her email address?"

"Stronghold isn't so big on emails."

That seemed odd, given how far we'd come into the 21st century. I thought all companies used email at this point, but whatever, a phone number would work.

I moved aside so he could fiddle with the landline handset, doing Kegels as I prayed for him to finish quickly. Despite his lackluster interview, I caught his obvious enthusiasm for me to talk to Ida. Every building manager I had ever met was pretty chatty. I hoped she wouldn't disappoint.

Once finished, he fled for the door. "Thanks for the tip," I called after him, but he didn't so much as say goodbye. I heard him leave back through the restricted area, the lights once again flickering on and off for a few brief seconds.

After emptying my stupid teaspoon-sized bladder, I called Ida's number. It went to a generic voicemail box, so I left a message.

Gabriel poked his head in not long after to ask if I wanted to go with him to lunch.

"Nope. I'm waiting on a call."

"You are?" He seemed surprised but not necessarily in a bad way.

"Yep. My second employee interview."

"Who was the first?"

"Patrick Kelly."

His lips twitched. "How did that go?"

"Fine," I lied. In my defense, it was my first day on the job. I wanted to make a great impression.

"Well, should I bring you back something then?"

"No need." I pulled out a Tupperware container with enchilada leftovers. "I always come prepared."

"I'm learning that." He smiled. "Who are you waiting to talk to now?"

"Ida Funar."

He cocked his head at me. "You met her in the office?"

"No, Patrick told me I should talk to her."

"Did he now?" Gabriel's bemusement intensified.

I stiffened. "Should I not talk to her?"

"Of course not. It's an office manager's job to get to know people onsite." Still, he looked a little distracted as he wandered back in the hall.

"Have a good lunch!" I yelled after him.

I spent a lonely lunch hour wishing I had taken Gabriel up on his offer. Literally no one besides me seemed to use this wing of the office. I even saw Gabriel head off to the restricted area later after lunch.

What was the point of being an office manager of an empty building?

As if to contradict my sour mood, my desk phone rang around two o'clock.

I answered like a fisherman reeling in a prize haul. "Hello, Melissa Hartley, office manager."

"I'm Ida Funar," a tired voice replied. "Gabriel said I needed to talk to you."

"Oh," I said, worried that Gabriel had intervened on my behalf. What did that mean? "I didn't mean to bother you."

"No bother at all," she said, but her yawn said otherwise. "I'll be in your office in seven minutes. Will you be there?"

"Absolutely." I hung up with a smile. Seven minutes seemed like an oddly specific time.

True to her word, though, Ida arrived exactly seven minutes after our phone call. She looked like she led a motorcycle gang, the kind that got into violent brawls. She wore a denim jacket that did nothing to hide her beefy arms, wild brown hair scattered around her broad face. She may not have been tall like Gabriel, but she sure looked like she could arm wrestle him just fine. She stomped her heavily booted feet over to the chair across from me and plopped down so hard, I worried it would break.

"Whadya need me for?"

I tried to keep the surprise out of my voice and failed. "You're the building manager?"

She rounded on me in a heartbeat. "Who told you that?"

I cowered. "Patrick Kelly."

Her eyes flashed. "Is that why you want to talk to me? Because of something that little punk said?"

I held my hands up in futile self-defense. "No, I want to talk to everyone. I'm the new office manager and—"

Ida was talking to herself now. "I can't believe this. I've been pulling overnights every day this week, and that little pea brain, who just snaps his fingers around computers a few times a day, thinks he can just waste my time?"

"Ms. Funar," I said, trying to grab her attention. "I assure you—"

"I ain't got time for this." She leaped back to her feet. "I've been working overtime. I deserve a break. I won't sit here and be the butt of that smelly hedgehog's jokes."

She stormed out of the room, down to the restricted area. The walls shook as the door slammed shut. I almost didn't notice the lights flickering this time as I cringed.

That should have been the gloomy ending to an otherwise pointless workday. I didn't intend to get much more work done, sitting alone in my office. I flipped through an outdated employee handbook someone had left inside my desk. The rules seemed about as relevant as I felt.

I did have a glimmer of hope close to quitting time. I heard the lobby doors open and a trio of people walked past my office. They wore shell jackets and had damp hair, indicating they'd been out in the rain.

I wanted to redeem myself after Ida's interview. I ran after them, coming up to the gruff-looking guy at the rear of the group before they turned down the off-limits hallway. He had sideburns, a massive five o'clock shadow, and hair coming out of the collar and sleeves of his plaid shirt, an excessive amount of body hair. He had enough muscle mass in his upper torso that he could have worked as a bouncer. He looked about as friendly as one too.

"Hello?" I tried to catch his attention.

Instead of slowing down to talk to me, the man sped up, never once looking back at me. He pushed past the guy in front of him, someone several decades his junior.

"Hey! Watch it, Henry!" the younger guy protested. He looked fresh out of college, wearing cargo pants to go with his navy jacket. Freckles dotted his skin, even the palms of his hands. He had long blond hair down almost to his waistband.

I hate to admit that the younger guy didn't intimidate me nearly as much as Henry the grumpy baby boomer. I slapped on a forced smile, determined to make this work.

"Hello," I said loudly, startling the poor kid. "My name's Melissa."

He froze with wide eyes, as if he'd just been caught by a monster.

"I'm the new office manager." I motioned for him to walk toward me. "You work for Stronghold?"

"Yeah," he said, frozen in place.

"What do you do for the company? Where have you been all day?"

"Uh, the Capitol?"

"Why would you be there?"

A feminine voice interrupted us. "Noah?"

A female version of the kid in front of me waited at the bend in the hallway. She'd been the last member of the trio. She and Noah must have been brother and sister, having the same flowing hair, patchwork freckles, and slightly below average height.

She glared daggers at Noah. "What are you doing?"

"Sorry, Naomi," he muttered.

The young lady turned to me. "Noah's got other things to do. C'mon."

Her exaggerated wave put Noah back in motion, and I watched the duo disappear into the restricted hallway. Returning to my office in defeat, I bit my lip so the telltale flickering lights didn't make me scream.

CHAPTER 14

BY THE TIME I returned home, I'd rationalized my frustration away. I needed the job. I had to find a way to make it work, at least until I could find another job that would pay the bills. I couldn't pull from savings, not when college loomed so close on the horizon.

Regan's sour mood that evening did nothing to uplift mine. I tried to win her over with Chinese takeout after debate practice, but she tried to grab her meal and haul it into her room.

I snatched the cardboard container from the counter before she could reach it. "C'mon, you don't have to act this way."

"You're the one being an overcontrolling mom. Why can't I fulfill my stereotype and be the moping teenager?"

"You can't keep it up forever."

"You're trying to keep my dad's identity a secret forever. What's the difference?"

I flushed. "You're on the debate team. They ever teach you about false equivalence?"

"They taught me to speak for myself." She dismissed the chow mein with a wave. "Never mind. You eat it. I'm not hungry."

Turns out I wasn't either. I put all the food in the refrigerator, every inch of my body exhausted. As I finished cleaning up, I called Jessie. She answered breathlessly that they were late to Penny's school play. A selfish part of me wanted to ask her to skip it so I could vent, but I held my tongue and said I'd catch her later.

I ended up huddled under a mound of blankets on the couch, endlessly scrolling my streaming services. Nothing fit my mood, so I eventually gave up. I'd never turned on the overhead lights, so as the sun set, it slowly left me alone in the dark.

I must have fallen asleep on the couch because the next thing I recall, I was jolted awake by a loud thud.

The room was pitch dark, the mantle clock reading 2:30 a.m. I got up and glanced down the hallway, but Regan's bedroom door was still shut.

Had she made the noise trying to leave the house?

Given my recent track record for disaster, I had to check on Regan. I hated invading her privacy. We had a clear rule not to encroach on each other's bedrooms without permission, but given everything that had happened in the last few days, I needed to know my baby was okay. I'd just take a peek.

I quietly opened her bedroom door. Through the faint light streaming via the half-open window, I saw her hair spread over the pillow, the rest of her body submerged in blankets. Her bedsheets rose and fell in a comforting rhythm. Regan was in bed and sound asleep.

I relaxed. I'd probably just heard some random street noise. I should just try to calm my frazzled nerves and go to bed. I inched the door to close it.

That's when the snarls erupted.

I squealed. It sounded so close that it made me lurch back into the hallway to protect myself. Regan's door banged on its frame and bounced.

The snarls didn't fade away. They morphed into a series of sharp barks and scuffling, originating from the back yard. I approached Regan's window cautiously, heart leaping in my throat.

"Mom?" Regan's head wobbled up from the pillow.

"Shh." I stood next to the window, unable to see much from the thin slice where the two navy curtains didn't meet. I could barely make out a bush against the side of the house.

Something clattered to the ground outside. I took an involuntary step back.

Regan crawled out of bed to stand behind me. "What's going on? Is it a cat in heat?"

Deep growls cut through the end of her question.

"That ain't no kitty."

"What is it then?" Before I knew what she was doing, Regan flung both ends of the curtain wide open, exposing our back yard.

Looking back, I would identify this as the exact moment that my understanding of the world changed forever.

A massive black wolf crouched next to Regan's ancient swing set, hackles raised and tail end toward us. It snapped powerful jaws in a clear warning, the noise making my bone marrow vibrate.

Regan sucked in a sharp breath. "It's the wolf from the running trail."

The terrifying wolf faced off against something even more bizarre near the far side of our fence line. A shimmering fog covered the head of what appeared to be a woman in a midthigh dress over long black boots. Delicate dragonfly wings sprung from her back.

My heart raced. Those were the wings of my glitter bomb attacker. The Celtic knot pinned to her shirt confirmed it, but why was she fighting the black wolf in my back yard?

The wolf's growls increased in volume, a warning before it surged forward to attack.

The woman made a swooping motion across her chest

with her hand. The glittery haze coalesced, concentrating into a barrier so thick that she became a mere silhouette behind it.

The wolf stopped just short of touching the fog, skittering back to create distance between them.

The pair kept this dance up for a few more rounds, the wolf looking for a way to attack and the woman somehow moving the glittery fog to block it.

"What are they doing?" My voice sounded too high-pitched to my own ears.

As the wolf jerked in another retreat, the fog abruptly changed directions, suddenly not content with merely blocking the wolf's advances. A basketball-sized chunk of mist broke off from the rest, glowing bright red.

The wolf noticed the odd change with a split second to spare. It leaped behind my wheelbarrow as the red fog exploded in a fiery blaze. It singed the patch of grass where the wolf had been standing mere moments before.

The woman took a step forward out of the fog to examine her explosive handiwork. A sliver of weak light coming from our back porch caught her face. I gasped as I recognized her instantly.

It was Serena Fawcett, the woman who'd tried to take Regan out of school.

She wasn't the runway model version of Serena I'd seen in Lucas's video. Her crazed eyes blinked rapidly, cheeks gaunt, skin flushed. She tilted her head toward the house, and we locked gazes.

Serena cracked a broken smile worthy of any unhinged clown. She splayed her fingers toward us gawkers at the window. Incredibly, the Celtic knot shifted colors into a luminescent, fiery red.

My instincts kicked in. I grabbed Regan by the shoulder and yanked her backward as a second globe of fiery red dust headed our way.

The bedroom window exploded in a shower of glass. I must have gone immediately into shock because I felt no heat and no pain besides a piece of stray glass that made a shallow cut on my arm. I lost my grip on my daughter and fell into a heap onto the floor.

In a daze, I felt something rustle next to me. "Are you okay?" I called to Regan, reaching out into the dusty air for her.

Something slammed down on my hand, crushing my fingers.

I screamed, managing to pull my injured hand to my chest as I glanced upward.

Serena towered over me, her wings a horrible halo behind her. "Stay out of this," she hissed as she kicked me in the chest.

Wracked with pain, I curled into a ball. Squinting, I watched Serena saunter over to a cowering Regan. The intruder reached into a pouch and threw glitter all over Regan.

"You're coming with me," the lunatic declared.

Regan moved as if to comply at first, but then ducked back down. "No! I won't!"

Serena's face twisted in anger. "You will obey me!" she screamed, grabbing Regan by the arm.

"Let go of me!"

Serena let out a bellow that made my skin crawl, her face contorted in an ugly grimace that contrasted with her feminine features. "Why won't you listen?" She pulled a blade out of an ankle sheath near her boot and pointed it at Regan.

Despite the throbs coursing through my core, I couldn't just sit there and watch my daughter get murdered before my eyes. Gathering up all my strength, I lurched forward, smacking against Serena's knees, forcing her to rebalance.

"I said, stay out!" she yelled at me, the blade now aimed at me.

I winced, preparing myself for the stab.

Instead, the wolf charged through the broken window,

its teeth finding a mouthful of her leg.

Serena cried out, twisting at the last minute to engage the wolf. The blade sunk in a few inches near its neck. The animal whimpered but held on, maneuvering so that Serena lost her grip on the weapon.

Serena wasn't going down without a fight. She punched the wolf several times around the face, finally landing a blow to an eye. The wolf's jaw loosened in a snarl, and she escaped his grasp.

Her eyes flashed with rage as her hand summoned another sphere of red mist, the Celtic knot once again flashing neon. She lobbed it at the wolf and flung herself outside for cover.

I acted on pure motherly instinct. The blast wouldn't just hit the wolf, not with Regan right there next to him. Some of us were going to die.

But maybe I could save my daughter.

I intercepted the red-hot orb, then enveloped myself around it. My stomach covered most of it, my arms and legs sealing in the sides.

The detonation rocked me backward. The air around me contracted and expanded in a whiplashing burst. I expected searing heat. I expected pain. I expected to close my eyes and die.

None of that happened. I simply held on tight as if playing bucking bronco with the world's most violent, runaway balloon as it ran out of air.

A shaky hand touched my shoulder. "M-mom?"

I slowly unclenched all my muscles and glanced down at my shaking body. My clothes had melted away, bits of smoldering cloth falling off me, but my skin remained unburned, only bruised from Serena's kick to my chest.

CHAPTER 15

REGAN GAPED AT my intact skin. "How are you still alive?"

"I have no idea," I said as I covered my bare chest with my arms. "More importantly, where'd that lunatic go?"

"The wolf went after her."

Sure enough, in the aftermath of my heroic rescue, the wolf had vanished. All that was left of its presence was the splotch of splattered blood where it had bled from its neck injury.

Regan and I both peered toward the busted window, the thin slice of night we could see eerily normal. I expected more animal growls or, heaven forbid, Serena's nightmare-inducing face.

Nothing outside stirred.

My brain lurched, trying to make sense of the attack. "I can't believe she showed up again."

"Who showed up again?"

"That woman." My hands shook as I grabbed Regan by the shoulders. "She's the same woman who tried to take you from school the other day."

"What?!?"

I pulled Regan into an embrace so tight, it hurt where

Serena had kicked me, but I didn't care. "Don't worry, honey. I won't let her take you. I promise."

Regan latched onto me with the same fierceness. "I don't understand what's going on."

"Me neither."

We squeezed each other tight until an exceptionally loud knock at our front door startled us. "Melissa?" Nancy's voice drifted down to us.

Regan groaned. "Are you freaking kidding me?"

"She must have heard the racket."

"Maybe if we ignore her, she'll go away."

As if in response, Nancy's knocking grew more insistent. "Hello? Is anyone home?"

"Right, because Nancy Tannen is known for letting things go." I looked for something to cover my torso with and spotted Regan's bathrobe draped over her desk chair. She was a few sizes smaller than me, but fortunately it had enough bulk to hide my tattered clothes.

"What're you gonna say to her?" Regan asked.

"I don't know. I'll wing it." I smiled in spite of myself. "Ha. 'Wing' it. Get it?"

"Ugh, Mom, no puns. Too soon."

"Sorry." All humor left my voice. "Go into my room. There's a baseball bat under my bed if you need it. Stay there while I handle Nancy."

Regan disappeared into my bedroom as I unlocked the front door. Nancy was talking before I'd fully opened it. "What in the world is going on in your back yard?" She gave off an air of superiority even though she wore a long overcoat over satin pajamas. Behind her, she'd switched on every single outdoor light on her property, making our little chat seem like a police interrogation.

I slapped on an embarrassed smile. "Oh, I'm sorry. Did we wake you?"

"Wake me? You woke up the entire neighborhood."

I nervously glanced up and down the street, but no one else had turned on any lights. Everyone seemed hunkered down for the night.

Unfortunately, Nancy was the most formidable foe on the block. "I thought I heard snarls and screams."

"Oh that?" I laughed weakly. "A stray dog wandered into our back yard."

"A dog?" Nancy asked. "It didn't sound like a dog."

"The dog cornered a possum." We lived close enough to the river that wildlife would appear on our road. Nancy often complained about possums in particular, since they looked like oversized rats. "The two got into a terrible fight. I had to shoo them off with a broom."

"No wonder you look so awful." Her gaze scorched me from top to bottom. I hated presenting myself as a disheveled mess to the gossip queen of my street, but at least she appeared to buy my story.

"I'm really sorry to wake you, Ms. Tannen," I said, inching the door to close it, "but everything is fine now."

She surprised me by sticking her foot onto the door sill, preventing me from making a full retreat. "Everything is not fine. We have two mongrels loose in the neighborhood. We should call the police."

I tried to imagine what the police would think if they came and saw the busted wall in Regan's room. I doubted they'd believe my possum story. Telling them the truth, that a fairy and the Big Bad Wolf had duked it out on my property, probably wouldn't go over well either.

I needed to convince Nancy not to report anything, so I appealed to her nostalgia for the good ol' days. I leaned dramatically against the door and sighed.

"What's the point?" I said, mustering every last bit of suburban martyrdom I could. "You know how it is with crime in this city. The police have too much to do. They'll never respond."

Nancy puffed up, feeding off my performance. "We should at least try."

"And risk getting put on," I paused for dramatic effect, "the blacklist?"

Nancy leaned forward conspiratorially. "What blacklist?"

"The one they use to mark the people who make too much of a fuss." I shook my head sadly. "Haven't you noticed how the cops don't seem to take you seriously?"

She nodded sagely, since she made this complaint to me verbatim roughly every other month. "I have noticed. They dismiss everything I say."

Because you make a huge deal out of everything, I said in my head. Aloud, I said, "It's because you're on the list."

Her eyes bulged. "No."

"Yes," I nodded gravely. "I didn't want to burden you with this before, but it's why I don't often call the police about every little thing." And totally not because there was honestly very little to call the police about.

Nancy's foot slipped out of my doorway as she wrung her hands. "I never knew."

"I'm sorry you had to find out this way. I wish you'd never known."

"No, it's best I did know." I could almost hear the gears turning in her head. "Do you think the police use the same list as Animal Control? Because they don't return my calls often either."

"It's possible," I said, slowly inching the door closed. "In any case, good night."

Thankfully she didn't try to stop me. "Good night," she muttered as she shuffled back down the walkway.

I exhaled as the door shut. One crisis averted.

"That's not going to bite you in the butt later," Regan said loudly somewhere behind me.

I jumped, not realizing she'd been lingering in the hallway. "I thought I told you to wait in my room."

"We have a problem."

"Another one?" I quipped, but my pulse quickened as I scurried after her toward her bedroom.

At first it was hard to make out anything in the dark, but then I saw something move underneath the broken window. The black wolf had returned, curled up tight with forelegs tucked under its chin.

Fury and fear mixed in my gut as I stepped between Regan and the wolf. "What is it doing here?"

The wolf opened one eye into a slit and growled in response.

Regan pulled me back. "He does that whenever I get too near."

"Well, it needs to go. Now." I looked around the room for a weapon. "Where's the baseball bat?"

"Mom!" Regan used her exasperated teen voice. "You can't move him. He's healing!"

"What?"

"Look behind his neck. See the wound in his fur?"

I could see matted blood behind its ears. "So?"

"There was a gaping wound there when he first crawled back into the room, right after you went to talk to Nancy. I've been watching him the whole time, and his flesh repaired itself before my eyes."

Great. More freaky stuff. "Then we need to get it out of here before it recovers and decides to attack us."

"He's not going to attack us," Regan insisted. "He protected us from that freaky lady. I think he's guarding us."

As if to prove her point, the wolf raised its head and sniffed the air. Satisfied with whatever it had sensed—or hadn't sensed—it dropped its head back between its paws.

"Regan, it's not a stray puppy," I tried to reason. "We can't just let it stay in our house."

She shook her head violently. "No, you're not listening. If it weren't for the wolf, that psycho would have kidnapped me. That's what she came for. He saved me."

"We can't really know the wolf's intent. You're just projecting your emotions onto it."

"And you're letting your fears get in the way of the truth. Again." To my surprise, Regan put herself between me and the limp wolf. "The wolf has never attacked us, not once. He only went after the person trying to harm me."

"So, you just want to let one of nature's apex predators lounge around in your bedroom?"

"Yes!" Regan exclaimed. "Unless you have a better idea of how to protect us tonight. That woman could come back."

My blood chilled as I realized Regan was right. "We shouldn't stay here tonight. Maybe I'll call Jessie . . . but no, that could put her family in danger." I hated how I was rambling, but I sometimes thought better out loud. "The cops will never believe us, so they're no good. And we've only got a couple of hours before dawn. It's too late for a hotel."

"Well, you've just gone through all our options. We have nowhere else to go."

I couldn't believe staying in our home with a wild animal was our best option. "Fine. The wolf can stay, but you're not sleeping in here with it. We'll share the bed in my room tonight."

"Deal. Just let me get some food and water for the poor boy."

I remained with the wolf as Regan rummaged around in the kitchen. I inched closer to the wolf, flinching only a little when it let out a simmering growl.

"Make all the noise you want," I hissed. "I don't trust you, and I swear, if you try any funny business tonight, I will bash your skull in and use your corpse as a throw rug. You understand?"

To my surprise, the wolf stopped growling. Then it sniffed the air before settling down.

Regan returned with a bowl of water and a plate of sliced deli turkey. She laid both near the wolf's head.

"There you go," she said softly.

The wolf whined, took a few licks of water, then closed its eyes.

Regan and I left the wolf and barricaded ourselves in

my bedroom by pushing the dresser partway over the door. After throwing on a clean T-shirt and yoga pants, I settled down into the queen bed with my daughter, the baseball bat leaning against my nightstand for easy access.

Regan yawned. I gawked at her. "Are you really going to sleep after all this?"

"I'm exhausted. Aren't you?"

"Not enough to overcome the post-adrenaline rush."

She snuggled under the covers. "What is it you're always trying to tell me? 'Don't worry about things outside of your control?'"

"I changed my mind. You can worry about fairy kidnappers even if you can't do anything about them."

"Good to know the exception to the rule." Her eyelids fluttered shut. Her breathing evened. I thought she'd fallen asleep, but then she spoke with a shudder in her voice.

"I'm sorry I said I'd leave you for my bio-dad. I didn't mean it."

"Oh, Regan." I scooped her up into my arms. "Don't even think about that."

Regan buried her face underneath my chin. "I guess we have bigger problems to worry about now."

"Yeah," I agreed grimly. I didn't think it possible, but we'd found something scarier than John Moroz.

Regan said nothing more, quieting down for good this time. I envied her. There was no way I could join her in slumber. My heart pounded at every slight noise outside. I kept brushing my fingers along the metal bat for comfort.

It was going to be a long night.

CHAPTER 16

A HALF HOUR before my alarm went off, I finally gave up all pretense of sleep and pushed the dresser away from the door. Regan grumbled at the noise but didn't leave the bed.

I went to check on old wolfie first, but when I glanced into Regan's bedroom, the wolf had vanished. It'd consumed all the water and turkey, leaving only broken glass and blood splotches on the floor.

A chill breeze drifted through the broken window, and I shivered. There wasn't any rain in the forecast, but given we were in Oregon March, the drizzle would return sooner or later. I wondered whether I should call my normal handyman or an actual window company to have it fixed.

Then I realized the only fix I needed was coffee.

Once I had caffeine in my system, I surveyed the kitchen and considered all my options. None of them were good. I considered talking to my security-crazed boss, but we'd only known each other for a week. I had no idea if he'd label me a looney and fire me. Next, I thought about calling Jessie and asking if we could stay with her, but the thought of that nutcase attacking her family made me physically ill.

That left me with absolutely no solution.

My fingers trembled as I took another long swig of coffee.

"Mom?" Regan stumbled into the kitchen, looking about as awful as I felt.

"Heya."

Regan made her way over to the coffee pot and poured herself a cup. Even loading it up with sugar and milk, she grimaced when she swallowed. She always said she loved the smell of coffee because it reminded her of me, but she rarely drank it.

Apparently, she needed the extra jolt today as much as I did.

We were eerily quiet as we sipped from our mugs. I finally broke the silence. "We can't tell anyone about what happened."

"So, we just go about our day as normal?"

"That seems safest. We'll be around lots of people, you at school and me at my job. You promise not to go anywhere alone off campus?"

"Of course." Regan wrapped her arms around herself. "Maybe you should get in touch with Barbara. She believes in magic."

I made a face at the mention of my delusional mother. "She believes in New Age mumbo-jumbo. It'd be like getting a conspiracy theorist to teach your AP science class."

"Then what about tonight?"

"I don't know. I'll think of something."

The doorbell rang, the electronic sound shrill. We both flinched. Regan spilled a little coffee on herself.

Regan patted her now stained sleep shirt. "Speaking of conspiracy theories, how much you wanna bet that's Nancy coming back to haunt you?"

"You really think it's her?" I wished we had at least a peephole on our front door, but we didn't.

"Who else would be bothering us this early in the

morning?"

"Good point." I marched to the doorway, not caring that I had bedhead to rival Medusa's. Nancy had already seen me at my worst last night anyway.

"We're not calling Animal Control, Ms. Tannen!" I said before I'd fully opened the door.

Gabriel's massive bulk slid into view. "Why would you need to call them?"

I stared, momentarily dumbfounded at seeing his piercing steel gray eyes. I was suddenly very aware that I looked like I crawled out of a ditch. The last thing I should have cared about was my appearance, but sometimes, when you're stressed out to the max, you do stupid things.

At least, that's how I rationalized slamming the door shut in his face.

"Uh . . . ?" Regan said as I hyperventilated. "Who was that?"

"My new boss."

"Then why did you shut the door on him?"

"I don't know!"

Gabriel's muffled voice drifted over us. "Maybe we should try this again, Ms. Hartley?"

I reopened the door and went straight on the defensive. Jamming a finger into his designer suit, I demanded, "What are you doing at my house at seven in the morning?"

He folded his arms across his chest, which knocked my finger aside. "Picking you up for work. You'd know this if you checked your pager."

That stupid pager! I'd forgotten all about it during the frantic night's events. I scrambled through my purse on the couch, and sure enough, there was a message sent at 6:30 a.m. I must not have heard the beeping through my barricaded bedroom door.

"Why can't you plan ahead like a normal human being?"

Gabriel ducked to come inside. Regan's eyes grew wide

when she realized how big he was.

"That's not the terms of our contract. You are to make yourself available 24/7, remember?"

I rubbed my temples. "Look, it's been a really rough night. Can't I just meet you at work in an hour, just this once?"

To my chagrin, he shook his head. "No. I insist on escorting you."

I looked for a way out. "Then I'll take a sick day."

"You haven't accrued any."

Regan, who had been watching us bicker, suddenly straightened. "Excuse me. School's starting soon. I've got to get ready."

Gabriel's stance relaxed. "My apologies for interrupting your morning routine." He extended his hand. "My name's Gabriel Alston."

She timidly accepted it. "Regan," she whispered as he executed a firm handshake.

"Feel free to get ready for school, Regan," he said. "I'm happy to drop you off on the way to driving your mother to work."

Regan looked to me for approval. I motioned toward the hallway. She scampered off in relief.

I took a few deep breaths until she was out of earshot, then focused back on Gabriel. There was really no talking my way out of this. I'd signed a contract and was botching it up royally.

"I'm sorry about missing the pager twice. It won't happen again."

To my surprise, Gabriel laid a comforting hand on my shoulder. His touch made me irrationally want to melt against him.

"I understand I'm asking a lot of you. I'm not offended in the least."

"Why not? Haven't you noticed I live to offend people?"

"You're clearly under a lot of stress."

I snorted. "You don't know the half of it."

"Anything I can help you with?"

The words came out of my mouth before I could stop them. "Not unless you can fight off fairies."

His fingers tightened on my shoulder. "Excuse me?"

I faked a laugh, brushing his hand away. "Sorry, I've got a particular brand of humor, if you haven't noticed."

"I've noticed." He took a step back from me. "Do you also need some time to get dressed?"

"What?" I did a twirl on my heels to showcase my rumpled clothes. "You don't like this?"

Something in his eyes shifted, a sort of longing, causing me to curl my toes into the living room rug. "I suppose I don't mind at all."

I flipped around, unable to meet his gaze. "I'll be right back," I said as I retreated.

I scuttled into my own room. By the time I'd thrown on some work clothes and battled my hair straight again, I'd convinced myself I'd imagined Gabriel's sensual look. Regan and I ended up emerging from our rooms at the same time.

"Sorry you keep having to wait in my living room for me," I said to Gabriel as we returned. He'd been standing very still in the center of his room with his hands clasped in front of him and his eyes closed.

They fluttered open at my declaration. "Do you still need to call Animal Control?"

My mouth hung open. I couldn't think of a sensible reply.

Regan saved me. "It's just an inside joke between us and our neighbor," Regan offered. Then she turned to me, hiding a snicker. "Get it? Like 'inside' my bedroom?"

"Don't even go there," I said. The last thing I needed was Gabriel seeing the destruction in Regan's room. "Come on, let's get out of this house before it gets me into any more trouble."

If Gabriel was confused at our rambling, he didn't ask

as he followed us outside.

We all climbed into Gabriel's massive SUV. We enjoyed a thankfully uneventful trip to the high school, where Gabriel pulled into the bus lanes despite numerous signs saying it wasn't a parental drop-off point. I exited from the car with Regan. I threw my arms around her in a fierce hug, not caring if it made her look uncool. For Regan's part, she returned my embrace with the same intensity.

"Be careful," I whispered into her ear. "Don't go anywhere with anyone."

"Are you still going to pick me up?"

"Absolutely." We withdrew from each other. "Right after school?"

She shook her head. "After debate practice. I don't want to miss it."

I hesitated, but school was probably safe enough. "Just stay inside the building until I call you from the car."

"Of course. Love you, Mom."

I trembled as she disappeared into the crowd of teenagers gawking at Gabriel's illegally parked tank of a vehicle.

Gabriel gave me a worried glance as I buckled back into the passenger seat. "Is everything all right with you, Melissa?"

I thought again about telling him everything that had happened. He seemed like exactly the kind of person you turned to during a crisis. It's probably what made him so successful in the security business.

But he was my boss, and now more than ever, I needed this job. I suddenly appreciated all the ridiculous protocols and windowless rooms at the office. At least I wouldn't worry about Serena blowing me up during my lunch break.

So instead, I tried to make light of the situation. "'Melissa,' huh? Whatever happened to calling all your employees by last name?"

"That was a norm at Cascade Vista. We tend to be

more informal at Stronghold, but I'm happy to be formal, if that makes you more comfortable."

"Definitely call me Melissa. 'Ms. Hartley' makes me feel old, like I should be hosting bunko nights."

"What's bunko?"

"See? You're too young to understand."

His chuckle made my heart race. "If I call you Melissa, then you must call me Gabriel."

"Not 'Gabe?'"

"Not unless you go by 'Mel.'"

"Nope, I'm with you. Why give someone a name just to cut it off at the knees?"

Gabriel's smile turned serious. "You know if you need anything, you can trust me, right?"

My hands wrung each other in my lap. "Do you trust me too?"

"No."

My fingers balled up into fists. "Please, don't pull any punches."

Gabriel sighed. "I don't trust anyone easily. It's not smart to do so, but as far as I can tell, you are as benign as they come. All records indicate you've lived a very honest, quiet life."

"No one wants to be told their life is boring."

"I apologize. I didn't mean to imply that your life's boring."

"It's fine." Besides, a little boring would have been great right now.

Silence widened between us. I thought he'd decided to ditch the conversation when he added, "You should consider it a compliment. You've raised a wonderful daughter, all on your own. You should be proud of that."

Warmth flooded my body. "Thanks," I said, and I meant it. Most bachelors didn't examine the plight of the single mother, nor did they attempt to try. It made me disproportionately happy that Gabriel broke the mold.

Maybe I was judging Gabriel too harshly. Maybe he did

understand me better than I gave him credit for.

CHAPTER 17

NOPE, I WAS wrong. Gabriel was a complete jerk of a boss.

Why he'd cared at all to pick me up at 7:30 in the morning was a complete mystery because I had literally nothing to do. Yesterday, I'd had a million questions for him based on the cold welcome I'd received from the Stronghold crew, but given the panic of last night, I'd forgotten to ask him a single one on the ride over. Now, when I thought to ask him about it, he shut himself into his office all day.

I should have been grateful for the lack of tasks because I spent most of my morning doing Google searches on Serena Fawcett. It was slow going given how awful Stronghold's network was. I made a mental note to talk to Patrick about it as I searched for any sight of her—a social media profile, some reference to her full name, anything—but came up empty.

"It might not even be her real name," I finally admitted as I turned off my monitor. I'd forgotten to pack a lunch, so at noon I wandered into the kitchen to scrounge. That's where I ran into Ida.

Or rather, I walked in on Ida's nap. She was fast asleep

in one of the comfy chairs, her hands folded neatly on her belly like a gruff Sleeping Beauty. Her breathing came out slow and even. The circles under her eyes had deepened from when I'd seen her last.

Even though my stomach growled, I didn't want to accidentally wake her. I tried to tiptoe away quietly.

"I'm awake," she announced before I could make to the door. "I could hear you coming from a mile away with your stomping feet."

I looked down at my soft-soled flats. "I'm sorry. I didn't realize I made noise."

"You could wake the dead." She cricked her neck in both directions, making a cringeworthy popping sound.

I didn't know what to say, given how we'd parted after our disastrous interview. I finally settled on apologetic. "I didn't mean to say anything offensive yesterday."

"You didn't have to mean anything. Just repeating Patrick's garbage is offensive enough."

"I'm sure he means well."

"He means to make everything a joke, including my contribution to Stronghold."

I furrowed my eyebrows. "I don't understand."

"I ain't no building manager," Ida ground out. "I'm an engineer. I build things, things that Patrick could only dream about while typing on his dinky keyboard."

Ah, so I'd stumbled onto an office feud. I'd discovered over the years that it was best not to get involved when two employees hated each other. I tried to gently steer the conversation away from Patrick.

"I'd still like to conduct a proper interview with you, if you wouldn't mind. Not if you're busy," I added quickly when she narrowed her eyes at me. "You look like you're just getting off shift."

She stretched her thick legs one at a time and then stood. "If you mean I look like I've been working all morning fixing disasters, then you're right. I have been. That's what I do."

"Maybe I could help," I offered.

She threw back her head and laughed. "Ah, that's a good one."

I swallowed the anger rising in my chest. "I don't see how my offer is so funny."

"That's because you don't know much about Stronghold, do you? And you never will. You're a temp, here today, gone tomorrow."

I couldn't stop my defensive retort. "Gabriel…I mean, Mr. Alston said he'd consider me for a full-time position."

"Of course, he would say that." She paused by the door. "But what exactly do you offer us?"

"I'm an office manager," I said, although even I thought my voice was weak.

"Then find something to manage."

"What do you think I'm trying to do?"

To my surprise, her face softened. "I get that you're doing the best you can. You're not meant to stay here, that's all. You'll never be one of us."

On that gloomy note, she sauntered off.

* * *

It would have been easier to dismiss Ida's prediction if she'd continued to insult me. Her sympathy hurt worse than her criticism. She had the confidence of someone stating facts, not a bully out to hurt people.

The words stung because they were true. At Cascade Vista, I'd had a sense of purpose. I made my fellow coworkers' lives easier by running the building and getting them the supplies they needed. I went to bat for them on HR issues. I managed payroll issues. Here at Stronghold, I had done absolutely nothing and had no idea how to make any sort of meaningful contribution.

That's why I gave up working for the remainder of my sad day. I focused instead on researching fairies, still struggling with the painfully slow Internet connection. I barely looked up from my desk later that afternoon when Henry, Noah, and Naomi trudged down the hall at four o'clock. They passed by my open office door, as tired as the day before. Henry strode past first, not even bothering to look my way. Noah gave me a nervous glance, but I pretended not to see him. He blew a sigh of relief and scurried after his sister. I heard them enter the restricted area, and after the lights flickered, all went quiet.

I wished I could say ignoring my nonexistent work at Stronghold was worth it, but the only thing I learned about fairies was that some seriously delusional people will post anything on the Internet. Nothing I read sounded even remotely credible.

Vanessa took me home that night, which was just as well because I probably would've quit if it had been Gabriel. Tired of our awkward silences, I tried to turn on the radio. I reached for the center console.

Vanessa shooed my hand away before I could get to the power button. "What are you doing?"

That was the most syllables she'd said all afternoon. "Looking for a song to listen to."

"Why?" she asked, her expression deadly serious.

Because that's what normal people do, I almost said. Instead, I attempted diplomacy. "Because I like music."

She wrinkled her nose. "Radio stations are so tinny and contrived. It makes me want to vomit."

Wow, okay, Ms. Dramatic. "Not a fan of pop music, I take it?"

"Any recorded music. Why would anyone want to listen to some pale version of an instrument or a voice? It sounds like death itself."

I decided to let the music snob have her way and just let road noise buzz around us.

After Vanessa dropped me off at the house, I realized I'd never called anyone to fix the window. All those hours of doing nothing, and I couldn't even get that right. Not wanting to hang around in case Serena came back, I ate dinner at a crowded fast food restaurant, ordered a burger and fries to go for Regan, then went to pick her up from debate practice.

The rest of my life had imploded, but at least Regan seemed to have forgiven me. She launched herself into Dirt Dash and gave me a fierce hug. "How did today go?"

I didn't want to burden her with my stupid work problems, so I said. "Great. You?"

"Awesome. They set the schedule for the district tournament. I've got some of the best time slots. Coach wants me focused because she believes I'm the one who will earn enough points to qualify the whole team for the state competition."

"I'm so excited for you." I changed the subject to our plan for the evening as we drove toward the house. "I didn't call anyone to get your window fixed, so we probably should stay in a hotel tonight."

"Why not go to the Dunlaps?"

"We can't get them involved, remember? They're not any more equipped to handle fireball-flinging fairies than we are."

"Yeah. I know."

After arriving home, Regan went to her bedroom while I stayed in the kitchen, grabbing snack food for our overnight stay. I figured once we hit the hotel, we should try to lock ourselves in all night.

"Mom!" Regan suddenly screamed from down the hall.

I dropped a bag of chips in terror. Then I raced down the hall. Had the fairy returned? Had some new horror crept into Regan's room?

I rounded the corner and smacked into her back.

"Oof," she breathed, somehow keeping her balance.

She certainly looked okay. "Why did you yell?" I demanded.

Regan pointed across the room. "Look."

It took me a second to process the room. Everything looked normal. There was no glass on the floor. The window had returned to its rightful place on the wall, good as new. Even the same navy-colored curtains hung from the rods with no signs of fire damage.

"I thought you didn't call a repairman?" Regan whispered.

I couldn't find my voice, so I simply shook my head no.

It was as if last night had never happened at all.

CHAPTER 18

REGAN AND I both thoroughly examined the entire wall. Whomever had fixed it was a professional. They'd even painted the walls the right color. You could not tell that anything had been damaged in the first place.

"Who could have done this?" Regan asked.

I braced myself on the sill, feeling the sturdy wood underneath my fingertips. "Given that, besides us, only the fairy and the wolf knew it was even broken, I think it narrows our list of suspects."

"The fairy wouldn't fix it, would she?"

"Maybe to set a trap?" I stepped away from the window as I imagined that scenario. "Or to lull us into a false sense of security?"

Regan's brow scrunched in thought. "It makes more sense that the wolf is involved. He's the one protecting us."

I pulled my phone out my pocket. "I guess there's one way to find out."

"What are you doing?"

"Checking the doorbell camera feed. It may show us if the wolf's been around. It has shown up in our camera feed in the past."

"You caught the wolf on video?" Regan exclaimed. "And you didn't tell me?"

"I didn't want to alarm you."

"We really need to discuss your trust issues at some point."

"Maybe after we fight off a bunch of fairies." I clicked open the app to find the doorbell had recorded a video an hour ago. I hit playback on the file.

The black wolf immediately took up the screen.

To my relief, it appeared perfectly healthy, no signs of wounds from the night before. I relaxed as it pawed around the front yard, sniffing and taking stock of our property. It even came up to the doorbell to sniff around. Then it bounded off, heading toward the back yard.

After the video ended, Regan threw open her bedroom curtains. We found the wolf resting not far from the swing set. It lifted its head to acknowledge us, then hunkered back down for the night.

"It came back," I said.

Regan frowned at me. "It's rude to call him an 'it' when he's clearly looking out for us."

"Okay fine. 'He' came back. But maybe we should go to the hotel anyway."

"Why? We've got a guard dog. That's gotta be better security than what they have at a cheap hotel."

"I suppose." I yawned, lack of sleep finally catching up to me. I should have taken a nap at the office since I had nothing else better to do, but the idea had seemed so sacrilegious to me.

"You should go to bed," Regan said. "I'll feed our friend."

"More turkey slices?"

"I gave him the last bit yesterday, but I think we still have some hamburger patties in the freezer."

"Sounds like I need to make a grocery run, but somehow that seems so low on my list of priorities."

"You slacker," Regan teased. "Attacked by fairies and

you can't even keep the pantry stocked."

"I am literally the worst."

I stayed awake long enough to help Regan deliver dinner to the wolf. I honestly doubted he would attack her at this point, but I wasn't taking any chances. She scratched him behind the ears as he scarfed them down.

"Such a good boy," she said.

He made a low growling sound in his throat. I couldn't tell if he was pleased or irritated, but either way, it wasn't enough for him to quit scarfing up hamburger.

I hung back when Regan grabbed the empty plate and headed for the house. Then, leaning over the wolf, I asked quietly, "Who are you?"

The wolf cocked his head at me, then laid his head on his paws.

My phone rang as I entered the house. Regan looked up from drinking a cup of water.

"Who is it?"

"Jessie." I answered the phone. "Hello?"

"When were you going to tell me?" she demanded in a near yell.

I flinched, looking at Regan, who suspiciously wouldn't meet my gaze. "What are you talking about?"

"The attack at your house the other night. You didn't think I would find out, did you? Well, teenagers have loose lips. Regan told Leah everything."

"Everything?" I gave Regan my best you're-gonna-get-it glare. She retreated to her bedroom in a hurry, the coward.

I had to deal with Jessie first anyway. She kept right on ranting. "I know all about how that crazy lady from school showed up at your house."

"Regan explained how it all went down?" I held a breath, waiting to hear about the black wolf.

"You scared her off with a baseball bat."

Ah, so Regan had told Leah a modified version of the story that didn't involve strange sentiment animals or magical fireballs. That was something at least. I wasn't thrilled about getting committed to a mental institution.

I groaned as I sat down at the counter. "I'm not sure what you want me to do about it, Jessie."

"File a police report."

"Believe me, if I thought the cops would do anything, I would drive down to the station right now. Look, you don't know the full details of what happened."

"Because you won't tell me, which isn't like you. Melissa, what's gotten into you?"

I almost spilled the beans right there about the entire messed up situation. I desperately wanted my best friend's advice on how to move forward. Then maybe I wouldn't feel like I was slowly losing my mind.

Jessie's next words ruined it all. "You told me a long time ago if you ever started acting like your mom, I would tell you. Well, you are. Right now."

My body temperature rose at the accusation. "I'm nothing like Barbara."

"Oh really? Because it seems to me like a normal mom would do everything in her power to protect her child."

"You think I don't care about Regan?" The words came out in a rush of anger. After everything I'd been through, accusing me of not trying to protect Regan was too much.

"You're not acting like it. Instead, you've lost your damned mind."

"Well, maybe I have lost it," I snapped back. "Along with who I thought was a good friend."

And then I did the unthinkable. I hung up.

I stared at the black screen for a long time, half expecting it to light up again with Jessie's smiling selfie or at least a text.

It stayed blank.

I ignored the lump in my throat, convincing myself I was protecting my friend and her family, even though that was only cold comfort.

CHAPTER 19

THE WOLF WAS still sound asleep in the back yard early the next morning, splooting with legs out in both directions and a goofy canine grin on his face. Regan didn't want to wake him, so she didn't refill his water bowl before I dropped her off for debate practice.

"Remember," I said to her firmly before she exited Dirt Dash. "You can't talk about our situation to anyone. Not even partial details."

Regan shrank into the seat. "I know. I'm sorry. I'll be better today, Mom, I promise." Then she left the car with her head held low.

I hated making my child feel so helpless. I needed something productive to occupy myself, so I stopped at the grocery store on the way home.

Generally, I hit the supermarket during the post-work evening rush when suburban moms block the aisles with their overflowing carts, but this early in the day, only a handful of senior citizens dotted the long, empty aisles. Many even scooted over even though they weren't in my way. I made a mental note to switch my shopping hours.

As I loaded my cart, I tried to focus on the day ahead. Despite my big magical problem, I also needed to do my job, or Ida's prediction about me being canned would come true. I had to provide Stronghold Incorporated real value.

But how?

I passed the bakery and paused by a table stacked with delicious, calorie-heavy pastries. A small grandma with a pink hairnet struggled to place a box of donuts at the bottom of her deep cart. I helped her out.

"Thank you," she said.

"You gonna eat all these in one sitting?" I teased.

"It's for my grandkids. I have six of them and they're all coming over tomorrow. I babysit them, you know."

I smiled. "That sounds nice."

She pointed at the donuts. "They always discount the baked goods from the day before, but you have to get here early because they sell out quick."

"Sounds like you snagged yourself a bargain."

She nodded. "Now I'm off to the orange juice. Gotta feed the horde or they'll get cranky. You take care, dear."

Her observation jumpstarted my office manager brain. Everybody loved free food and this was in my price range. On a whim, I snagged up my own box of discounted lemon pound cake. Then I waved at the grandma as I got a container of juice.

When I arrived back at the house fifteen minutes later, Gabriel stood on my sidewalk next to his SUV, arms folded across his chest.

"Where have you been?"

I opened the trunk and showed him. "Grocery shopping. And why are you here again?"

"I told you I would pick you up. You should check the pager."

I bit my lip as I pulled the pager out of my purse. Sure enough, it showed a message.

"I don't know why I need an escort," I grumbled.

"It will make things easier if you just expect me to take you to work from now on. Here." He grabbed two grocery bags from Dirt Dash and made it halfway to the house before I stopped him.

"Those two are for the office."

"Why? We've already got food there."

"I'm just adding to the pile."

He threw them in the SUV as requested. Then he helped me transfer the rest into the kitchen.

As I finished up shoving food into my overstuffed freezer, he asked, "Where's your daughter?"

"She's already at school."

He scowled. "I thought I would drop her off with you."

"I didn't know you were coming, remember? Plus, she had an extra early debate practice."

The cords of his neck tightened. "I see. Well, don't forget in the future. Let's get going."

His foul mood permeated our ride to work. He clenched the wheel so tightly, I worried it would snap off.

I finally cleared my throat. "Sorry I didn't see the pager. Again. I'll get used to it, I promise."

"It's not you." He forced himself to relax. "I'm just mulling over a problem."

"Anything I can help you with?"

"No." The word came out forcibly.

I held up my hands up in surrender. "Yeesh. Okay."

He fidgeted in his seat. "I'm sorry, Melissa. It's just something I need to address once I get back to the office."

I removed all the sarcasm from my tone. "I get it. I really do. You're super busy."

"You have no idea."

That made me pinpoint something that had been nagging at me. "If you're so slammed, why are you chauffeuring me around?"

He turned to give me his full attention. "And miss our amusing conversations that I look forward to so much?"

I wasn't buying it. "Surely one of your other employees can take over driving duty."

He lifted an eyebrow. "You've driven with Vanessa. How often does she laugh with you in the car?"

"I'll loosen her up, like a river over a stone. It just might take a few hundred years."

Gabriel chuckled, returning his focus to the road. "In all seriousness, the 'chauffeuring' gives me a much-needed break. Plus, I enjoy driving. It's one of the few ways I feel relaxed in a city."

"You grew up in the sticks or something?"

"Something," Gabriel said, clearly not welcoming more questions.

I could've ignored him and asked about his employees anyway, but with bait in the trunk, I figured I'd try my way first. Maybe, I wouldn't need to badger my boss in order to impress him.

Once safely inside the Stronghold fortress of doom, Gabriel locked himself away in his office. I went straight to the kitchen and stuffed my goodies away. I wouldn't need them until later in the day.

Instead, I had more Internet research to do. I realized that instead of trying to piecemeal information from random sketchy sites, I needed to find an expert who understood what I was going through. I couldn't be the only person who had ever run across rampaging fairies before. Maybe someone on social media had an experience close to ours? Someone with a shred of credibility and not just a creepypasta story.

Unfortunately, Internet information is iffy at best on well-known topics. Mystic topics brought out the real loonies. I finally gave up after getting stuck on a website that kept popping up badly altered images of gaunt creatures with their eyes gouged out. The site locked up my computer so bad, I had to hold down the power button to turn it off.

"Sorry, Patrick," I muttered. "Hope I didn't just release the mother of all viruses into your network."

By then it was close to midafternoon and time to focus

on my second project. I dragged furniture around the kitchen for my scheme, starting with a cardboard table for food near the door. I cut the lemon pound cake and placed slices on several paper plates, arranging them in a neat circle. I poured several cups of juice and placed them near the door, hoping it would encourage people to enter the room and stay.

Then I waited in my office for my chance.

Nothing happened for an hour. I nervously watched the minutes tick by on my computer clock. I'd have to go home soon.

When I finally heard the lobby doors open and shut, I jumped into the hallway with relief. The trio had arrived. Noah and Naomi rounded the corner first, shell jackets bunched in their hands to expose matching light blue tank tops. They halted when they saw me.

"Hello!" I greeted loudly.

"Hi?" Noah answered, wary.

The twins had to step forward as Henry bumped into them from behind. "What's the holdup?"

I motioned toward the kitchen. "You guys always look so tired. I bought refreshments for you."

Henry pushed past the twins. "We're not interested." I had to step aside so he wouldn't knock me over.

Naomi, however, poked her head in the kitchen. "Whatcha bring?"

"Lemon pound cake and orange juice."

Henry flipped around. "What do you think you're doing?"

While Noah shrunk a little at the grumpy old man's tone, Naomi merely shrugged. "I'm hungry. It's been a long day, and I love lemon cake." Then she slid inside, grabbing a plate.

I couldn't stop a huge grin from spreading across my face as Noah also ducked into the kitchen, careful to avoid Henry's angry stance.

"It's not poison," I promised him. "Just food."

Henry's face mottled red between his sideburns. He marched toward me, and I swallowed a yelp, worried at the violence written all over him, but he kept going back down the hall, toward the lobby.

Well, two out of three wasn't bad. Naomi and Noah had taken the bait and sunk into the plush chairs I'd set up in a ring. Neither talked as they dug into their cake, both savoring each bite.

Step one success. Now onto step two. I grabbed my own plate and sat down with them.

"Busy day, huh?" I asked.

Naomi nodded between gulps. "The crowd was really riled up today. It's getting close to a vote."

I knew they'd been at the Capitol Building and probably had encountered the protesters. "You working for the legislators?"

She shook her head. "No. We're hired security. Crowd control."

"Naomi," Noah said in a whisper. "I don't think we're supposed to talk about our jobs."

"It's not a classified mission," she waved him off with the fork in her hand. "We're even wearing logos on our jackets."

I glanced over at the jacket hung over Naomi's chair. Sure enough, a Stronghold letter logo had been printed over one breast.

"You're making sure the protesters aren't getting violent?" I asked.

Naomi nodded. "Pretty standard stuff."

I could understand why Henry, with his bulk and gruff demeanor, was assigned to keeping an angry mob under control, but these two? They looked barely older than Regan and had that slender college-age look. They didn't look like they could stop anybody.

Naomi noticed my skeptical expression. "You don't think we can do crowd control?"

I raised my cake in front of myself as a shield. "I didn't

say that."

"But you thought it. Typical." She tossed her now crumb-filled plate onto a side table. "I'll have you know that together, my twin and I can handle ourselves in a fight."

"Twins, huh?" I couldn't help but crack a joke. "You two got some sort of psychic powers?"

Noah nearly spat out his juice.

Naomi turned red. "I'll have you know—"

"Nothing," a deep voice said behind us. "This conversation is over."

A chill went up my spine. We all whipped around to find Gabriel standing in the doorway. I hadn't even heard him come up the hall.

"Where'd you come from?" I demanded.

Gabriel shifted to expose Henry glowering behind him. "Henry told me the three of you were lounging in here."

Henry gave me a condescending smirk between his sideburns.

Gabriel turned to the twins. "I think it's about time you guys go home."

"Yes, sir," Noah said, his spine straightening to an unhealthy angle. Naomi followed his lead toward the door, her pale face completely flushed with embarrassment.

I stood up in anger. "Now hold on here. We were just talking."

"About things you don't need to know about," Gabriel clarified.

"Why not? I'm the office manager. Shouldn't I know what everyone in the office is up to?"

"Only under certain conditions," Gabriel said.

The twins shuffled out of sight into the hall. Henry followed behind them.

"Snitch!" I hissed after his hairy butt. He didn't react as he rounded the corner and out of sight.

Gabriel blocked their exit with his massive frame. "Don't blame him for following orders." I guessed

Gabriel's posturing was supposed to intimidate me.

It failed. "What orders were that? Ensuring that I can't do my job?"

Gabriel sighed. "I know you think you understand how to be an office manager, but everything is different in the security world," he began.

I threw my hands up in the air, cutting him off. "And you're doing a bang-up job of trying to help me understand the differences. It's not like you're giving me a lot of tasks to do. You already had someone else organize everything inside the building. I've gone through my computer several times, and I don't have access to payroll. That leaves me with HR issues, and I don't even know exactly who works in the building because no one will talk to me."

"Look, I realize you're under a lot of strain—"

"That's just it. I'm not! I'm literally doing nothing. What exactly did you hire me for?"

To my surprise, Gabriel looked a little sheepish. He shuffled from side to side. I had him cornered.

Unfortunately, Vanessa chose that exact moment to appear behind him in the hallway.

"Sir, I need to talk to you." She motioned Gabriel toward his office.

He glanced at me. "I'm in the middle of something."

Vanessa's eyes narrowed. "We have a situation."

Her insistence snapped Gabriel into attention. "We'll continue this discussion when I return," he promised.

"Sure thing, boss," I replied sarcastically.

As if on cue, the lights began to flicker on and off. I heard the restricted doors open and shut.

"You might want to get that fixed!" I called after Gabriel and Vanessa, but they were long gone.

I stormed back into my office and gathered up my things. It was near quitting time, and I wanted out. I suddenly didn't care if I followed proper protocol either. I was going home with or without my stupid afternoon escort, even if that meant losing my meaningless job.

I almost lost my nerve as I rounded the corner at Gabriel's office, but he'd shut the door behind him. I could hear both Vanessa and Gabriel talking to someone on the phone, but the sound was too muffled to make out anything.

Besides, I didn't have time to eavesdrop. My phone started to buzz in my purse. It startled me since I hadn't ever received a text or call on my personal cell inside the Stronghold building. I wondered how the call made it through until I realized Vanessa had left the metal door to the lobby ajar in her haste to talk to Gabriel.

Regan's name flashed on the screen. My skin went clammy. I answered it.

"Yes?"

"Mom?" Regan sounded breathless. "Can you pick me up now?" Behind her, I could hear a string of bells going off.

My stomach dropped, but I kept my voice low so as not to tip off anyone in Gabriel's office. "Isn't it early? What's going on?"

"I'm fine," she assured quickly. "Someone pulled the fire alarm. Ms. Hopner says we all have to go home."

Ah, she was irritated, not scared. "You're sure there's not a real fire at the building?"

"I'm sure. I saw Lucas skitter down the hallway right after the alarm went off."

"What? Lucas isn't even on the debate team."

"I know. That's why I'm sure he pulled the alarm. It's gotta be some sort of attention-seeking stunt. The guy's an Internet troll come to life, I swear."

I relaxed a little. She seemed safe.

I couldn't leave without a warning, though. "You be careful, okay? Stick with your friends outside. Don't let them leave you alone."

"I will. Just get here quick, okay?"

"Okay."

I hung up, then waltzed straight through the exit door. Still, I hesitated for a moment. Leaving without an escort would infuriate Gabriel. It would probably get me fired.

It wasn't even a choice. Regan needed me now, and I was half expecting to quit anyway. So I walked right out of the Stronghold lobby.

A rush of cold air hit my face as I opened up a rideshare app on the sidewalk. I found a driver looking for passengers nearby. Within minutes, a beat-up sedan pulled over on the street in front of me.

I dove into the car and told the bored-looking millennial to drive to the high school. I refused to look at the Stronghold building as we pulled away, I assumed for the last time. It had to be some sort of record, getting fired twice in as many weeks.

CHAPTER 20

WE WERE DRIVING over Center Street Bridge when my pager went off. I ignored it.

Gabriel was persistent, though. He called my personal phone a few blocks away from the school. I didn't answer.

He finally even texted, *Come back*.

I thought he didn't like to use phones. Still, I ignored it as we turned into the high school. I'd grab Regan first and deal with my termination second.

The good news was that there were no fire trucks or police officers flashing their lights. That meant the whole thing had been a prank and nothing serious, but the bad news was that the campus appeared almost completely closed. The main office windows were dark and even the teacher's parking lot stood bare.

As we approached the drop-off lane, I spotted a group of three students huddled near the sidewalk. The rideshare driver pulled alongside them to let me out.

"Can you wait here for a few minutes?" I asked the driver.

"Sorry." He pointed to the teenage trio as they shuffled toward his vehicle. "They're my next pickup."

I thanked him anyway and paid him through the app.

Getting out of the car, I thought I recognized at least one of the students from the debate team.

"Have you seen Regan?" I asked them.

They all looked around the empty sidewalk. "Not since debate practice ended," a girl with a pink backpack said.

"Okay," I said, trying not to let dread creep into my voice. I moved aside and let them climb into the vehicle. The sedan rolled off toward the street, leaving me alone underneath a cloudy sky threatening an evening storm. It was dark enough that it set off the automatic lamp posts. They cast insufficient light in random intervals around me.

Wonderful. I felt like a horror movie victim who'd just veered off from the crowd to die alone.

I called Regan's number, listening to it ring while watching the eerily quiet campus. The phone rang for a while before clicking over to voicemail.

"Not good," I whispered, power walking toward the building. It couldn't have been more than fifteen minutes since Regan called. Surely someone was still around, dealing with the aftermath of the fire alarm.

Unfortunately, the doors to the main building were locked. I'd have to try the annex where the debate team usually practiced. I walked under an outdoor breezeway that led in that direction, the lights even dimmer here. I jumped at a shadow that suddenly moved, but it turned out just to be a scraggly sapling in a large ceramic planter.

"Keep it together, Melissa," I scolded. I didn't care that I was talking to myself. Better than the oppressive silence of an abandoned high school.

The annex looked as deserted as the rest of campus. The only literal glimmer of hope I found was a light inside one of the classrooms, but when I tried to open the doors to the building, they wouldn't budge.

Desperation mounting in my chest, I tried Regan's number again. The phone rang multiple times. I forced myself to breathe deeply to keep myself calm.

I heard something besides my labored breathing. A

faint melody chimed from somewhere outside. The words "chica cherry cola" reached my ears.

It was the ringtone Regan had set for my number.

The source of the music cut off as the phone went to voicemail. I had to call her number several times to pinpoint the noise across the blacktop, inside a thick grove of trees on the edge of the student parking lot. Not far away, a trail led into a wooded area adjacent to the school's property. I opened my mouth to yell Regan's name, but then clamped my mouth shut. She probably didn't wander this far back on purpose.

Someone must have taken her.

I sprinted forward, dropping my purse so it wouldn't weight me down. I scrambled off the main path under overhanging boughs so no one could see me coming up the path. My ears strained for any audible clue as to who else might be lurking up ahead.

A cry cut through the stillness.

I could see a break in the trees, where the path wound back toward one of the school's less used sports fields. Under the dying sunset, Lucas held Regan by the forearm in one hand, his maroon and gray duffel bag clenched in the other. Lucas pulled in one direction farther away from the school, while Regan dug in her heels, trying to break free.

"You can't go back there!" Lucas growled.

"Let me go!" Regan said at the same time.

Every ounce of my mama bear brain wanted to throw myself at Lucas, but I pressed myself up against rough bark, trying to think things through. Regan didn't look injured yet. I would only have one shot at the element of surprise. I couldn't waste it and put us both in danger.

Regan suddenly broke free from Lucas's hold, dashing in my direction. As quietly as possible, I edged toward the path while staying in the shadows. The pair would eventually pass my position. I could jump out at the last minute and knock Lucas over. It would give Regan time to run.

Lucas skidded to a halt before he reached me. His eyes swiveled in my direction. I crouched behind a tree, wincing as dry leaves crackled around me.

"Show yourself!" Lucas bellowed.

I hesitated. He hadn't seen me. Maybe I still had some surprise going for me.

As sustained howls split the air, all rational thought fled my body. Two pairs of yellow eyes emerged from the darkness, across the path on the other side. Two silver wolves stalked onto the path, teeth bared.

Regan screamed. Lucas pushed her behind him.

A figure appeared behind the wolves. The trim of their robe matched the animals' eyes. With fabric completely covering them from head to ankles, I could only guess the person's gender until a male voice issued from inside the hood.

"I wouldn't do that if I were you."

Lucas reached inside his duffel. "Don't come any closer," he warned.

In response, the wolves took a few menacing steps toward Lucas and Regan.

Lucas looked so primed for a fight, that he startled me when he shoved Regan away from him.

"Run!" he yelled.

Regan skipped backward off balance but found her footing. Instead of fleeing, she stared dumbfounded at Lucas. "What?"

"I said, 'Run!' Get out of here!"

His cries set off the wolves. They leaped across the distance toward them. To my horror, Regan jerked forward to help Lucas rather than flee.

"No!" I dashed out of my hiding spot to grab her. "Regan!"

My shout made Regan turn around. "Mom?"

Lucas ran toward the incoming fangs. We were too far away to help him. As I pulled Regan away, I waited for the agonizing screams to indicate Lucas's final moments.

Instead, I heard only the sickening sound of flesh pounding into flesh. Lucas actually held his ground. He dodged shredding claws in a whirling dance, faster than humanly possible. He even landed a kick to one angry snout, sending yipping cries of pain echoing in the air.

Regan gaped. "How—?"

Lucas's advantage remained short-lived. The robed figure's hands flew into motion, and he emitted a strange series of whines and cries. A tree stirred beside him, and a raccoon scampered down the bark.

With a swish of hands, the raccoon joined the wolves against Lucas.

Raccoons may not seem vicious in comparison, but they know how to defend themselves. Lucas couldn't adjust quickly enough for an additional cannonball of angry fur. The raccoon crashed into his legs, giving the wolves an opening to jump him.

Regan shrieked so loudly that my ears rang.

I quickly changed course toward the fight. I couldn't let a kid who'd tried to save Regan get mauled to death.

I also couldn't fend off wild animals. My only chance of helping Lucas was to take out the Wildlife Whisperer.

The robed guy was so focused on directing his little minions, he didn't see me coming. I dove on top of him, knocking us both to the ground.

His hood fell off as we landed. His face seemed normal enough at first glance—slender nose, thin cheeks, and ruffled hair. A guy in his mid-twenties, although his ears stuck out a bit too far.

Then he turned his enraged eyes to me. They were slitted and green, like a cat.

He waved a hand, and one of the wolves bounded toward me.

I heard Regan scream as I threw a forearm over my face. The wolf would probably snap the bone right in half, but I had no other defense against a charging wolf.

The wolf never got a chance to bite me, though. A monstrous giant with bat-shaped wings fell directly out of the sky between me and the incoming wolf.

The ground shook at the impact of the monster's landing. With massive hands, the monster plucked the wolf off the ground as if it weighed nothing and flung it into the trees. The wolf smacked squarely into the trunk, whimpering as it fell into a heap.

The monster whirled around to help Lucas. I couldn't quite see the monster's entire face, but from this angle, it looked like a statue come to life carved out of stone. Towering above me at almost seven feet tall, it issued a roar that made the wolf's howl sound like a kitten's squeak.

Creepy Cat Eyes had more tricks up his sleeve. He let out a sharp whistle. Every branch above him shook. At first, I thought he'd conjured a wind, but instead the boughs rained down birds. Birds of every size, color, and species. Ravens and owls and woodpeckers and swallows. They swooped down on the angry stone monster.

Creepy Cat Eyes took that opportunity to flee down the path.

The stone monster could have fought back against the nightmare flock. Even the owls couldn't do much to its stone skin. Instead of crushing them to death, the monster roared and spread its massive wings. Despite looking like an oversized boulder, it took to the air in a whoosh that sent my hair flying into my face.

All the birds followed him. They converged as a dotted crowd in the sky, disappearing into a dark cloud.

Awestruck by the entire scene, Regan's voice snapped me back to Earth. "Wait!"

Regan had shouted to Lucas, who ran past me bloodied and battered but still agile. He fled in the direction that Creepy Cat Eyes had gone. The remaining wolf and raccoon careened after him, faster than we could ever catch up.

That left just Regan and I gaping at each other.

CHAPTER 21

I RECOVERED BEFORE my daughter. "C'mon!" I yelled, heading back for the school. "Let's get out of here."

Regan hesitated. "What about Lucas?"

"He's one of them." I only wished I knew who "they" were.

"He may need our help."

I shook my head. "You saw him tangle with the wolves back there. There's nothing we could do but get in the way."

Regan dug in her heels, both literally and figuratively. "That's not true. You tackled the guy in robes."

"I would have gotten killed if that stone giant hadn't shown up." I couldn't help it. A hysterical laugh escaped my lips. "I can't believe this is happening . . . fairies and enchanted animals and now monsters."

A series of sharp staccato beeps filled the air, making us jump. Someone back at the school was frantically slamming their car horn.

Regan took a step toward the sound. "Let's see who it is."

"Wait! We don't know if it's a trap."

"I doubt mythical beings drive cars."

She dashed down the path, forcing me to follow in her wake.

The woodchips led us back to the student parking lot, where we found a familiar black SUV. Relief flooded over me. Gabriel must have followed me to the school after our text message exchange. I'd never been so happy to see someone in my entire life.

But when the driver door opened, it was Vanessa who stepped out. Her eyes bored accusingly into me. "You left Stronghold without permission."

"I had to get to the school quickly," I said without a shred of remorse. "You and Gabriel were busy."

Vanessa took a menacing step forward. "That's a major security risk. Never do that again."

Regan squinted at her. "Who are you again?"

Vanessa turned her hostile gaze to my daughter. "Vanessa Sinclair. I work for Stronghold, your mother's employer. I'm here to take you to a secure location."

"What?" My voice rose a decibel level.

Vanessa folded her arms. "If you hadn't run off, you would have known that Stronghold received a severe security alarm. Because of that, we're placing both of you under lockdown."

My head spun a little as a strange thought occurred to me. "Is what happened here related to Stronghold?"

"You don't have the clearance for me to divulge those details." Vanessa opened the back seat of the SUV. "Get inside."

Her non-answer confirmed it. Somehow the attack with Creepy Cat Eyes was related to their discussion back at the office.

Regan threw her hands up in the air. "Why should we listen to you?"

I placed a hand on her back. "Do you have a better idea?"

My daughter opened and shut her mouth.

"That's what I thought. This is someone I know. It's

about as safe as we're going to get. Let's do what she says."

I scooted into the SUV's back seat, allowing Regan to climb in after me. I found my previously discarded purse tucked away neatly underneath the passenger seat at my foot.

"Thanks," I said riffling through the contents. It still had all my personal effects. "I would have forgotten about this."

Vanessa, who had settled into the driver's seat, narrowed her eyes through the rearview mirror. "That purse has your Stronghold pager, which is supposed to be with you at all times."

Of course, that's what Vanessa would worry about. I rolled my eyes but didn't say anything, happy to be safe, if only for the moment.

Regan slumped in the seat next to me. "I left my bag in the classroom," she said, a hint of accusation in her voice.

"The annex doors are locked," I told her. "You'll have to get it later."

"Easy for you to say," Regan said. "You have your phone."

"So do you." I pulled her phone out of my pocket.

Regan brightened considerably as she grabbed it. "You found it!"

Vanessa blinked a few times. She shook her head as if to clear her thoughts, and then the scowl returned on her face.

"You guys should quit worrying about your stuff and start focusing on what's important."

When Vanessa said a 'secure location,' I assumed we'd go to some downtown hotel or another nearby location. Instead, Vanessa took Highway 22 straight out of Salem's city limits toward the Oregon coast. When we hit hilly forests and turned onto a narrow two-lane road, I finally broke the tense silence.

"Where are we going exactly?"

"The private residence where Gabriel is staying,"

Vanessa answered.

Regan regarded the dense foliage. "Is it in the woods or something?"

"Gabriel likes his privacy."

And his secrets, I thought. I couldn't wait to figure out what he might know about our situation.

We bounced our way through a half mile with thick tree branches scraping against the SUV until we came upon a fancy iron gate surrounded by a solid brick wall. Vanessa clicked a button attached to the sun visor above her head, and the gate swung open.

The bumpy dirt path became cemented over. A sprawling lawn emerged, winding to a two-story mansion with cream-colored cedar siding. A wraparound balcony covered the entire second floor. The ground floor windows provided glimpses of a roaring fireplace beside expensive furniture and a grand piano. Bright lampposts brightened the entire front façade.

Vanessa drove up the circular loop to the ten-foot-tall doors. I exited the car and gaped at the building.

Regan whistled as she stepped beside me. "Why don't we ever stay at places like this?"

"Because I'm trying to send you to college eventually."

"It's just a private rental," Vanessa scoffed.

"Only a billionaire would call this place a 'rental.' This is a freaking villa."

Vanessa's shoulders hunched, clearly unamused. "Come along inside."

She led us into, I kid you not, a foyer with a double-curved staircase leading to the next floor. The interior walls had been painted in natural browns and greens, just enough to remind you of the foliage outside. We followed Vanessa up the stairs into what looked like an upscale hotel hallway with many closed doors. Intermittent alcoves offered chairs with views of the garden and pool house in the back yard.

We walked all the way to the end of the hall to a

mahogany set of double doors with crescent-shaped frosted glass windows. Vanessa deposited us into a sitting room that would have swallowed most of the square footage of our entire house. It had three couches arranged in a U shape with a massive low table between them. A fully stocked bar with gleaming glasses took up an entire wall. The opposite side boasted an entertainment center with a TV that looked more like a private theater screen. There was another set of doors leading farther into the suite, but they were shut.

Regan pointed at them. "Where do you think that leads? A library?"

"My bet's on a basketball court."

"Have a seat," Vanessa said loudly, cutting through our nervous chatter. "Gabriel will be with you shortly." She disappeared back into the hallway.

The weight of what we'd been through finally penetrated my tired body. I plopped down on a couch, throwing my head back over the edge and letting my legs sprawl out in front of me.

Regan paced in front of the entertainment center, eyeballing the many electronic devices attached to it. "This must have cost thousands of dollars to rent."

"Try tens of thousands."

A silence settled between us, broken only by Regan's shuffling feet.

"How long do you think he'll keep us waiting?" she finally asked.

I shrugged, a difficult feat buried in so many fluffy cushions. "He was in Salem when I picked you up. Could take a while."

"How can you be so calm?"

"I'm not calm. I'm drained. Facing death does that to someone in my age bracket."

Regan halted in her tracks. "You're not still mad at me, are you?"

Her voice held so much pain that I pushed myself back

up into an upright position. "No. Why would you ask?"

Her voice broke. "This is all my fault."

"What?" I got to my feet. "No, none of this is your fault."

Tears spilled over her cheeks. "Lucas tried to help me. He wanted me to run, but I wouldn't. I wanted to wait for you. Then the wolves attacked him. I know he's got powers or something, but what if they . . . they kill him, I . . ."

"Oh, honey." I threw my arms around her. My baby girl clung to me the way she used to after having a nightmare. "It's not your fault."

"No," a familiar deep voice replied. "It is not."

Gabriel had entered through the inner doors. Even though he wore his signature business suit, something about him seemed different. His hair was slightly wet as if he'd walked through a drizzle to get to us.

He also had a predatory gleam in his steel eyes that made me catch my breath.

He took a few quick steps toward us before abruptly stopping himself. "Are the two of you uninjured?" he asked, unable to keep the gruffness from his voice.

"Yes, we're fine." I moved to Regan's side so we could have a civil conversation, although I kept my arm around her shoulders for comfort. "It's been a very messed up evening."

"Indeed." He took a few moments to assess us both from head to foot, as if to ensure we were actually intact. Then he motioned toward the bar. "Can I get you two anything to drink? There's juice and soda in there as well."

"I could sure use some coffee," I said out of habit, then immediately felt chagrined. "But water would be fine."

Gabriel smiled, making my insides melt. "I'd be more than happy to make you a cup. Regan?"

"Pop for me. Whatever you've got, as long as it's not diet."

Gabriel went to work on the other side of the counter,

fiddling with the coffee machine as Regan and I took seats next to each other on a couch. Regan discretely wiped her tears away and tried to slap on a bored expression, as if hanging at a mansion after a magical assault was just something we did most weekday evenings.

Her forced bravery kicked my protective instincts into overdrive. "While I appreciate the coffee, what we really need is an explanation."

"You are referring to the second attempted kidnapping tonight?" Gabriel asked.

My head jerked up. "You know about the first?"

He nodded while retrieving a can of pop from a fridge underneath the bar. "It's my job to know."

Regan leaned forward, her hair falling like curtains on either side of her face. "Do you know who's after me?"

Gabriel nodded slowly. "I do, but I can't tell you specifics."

"Why not?" I demanded.

"Because it's classified."

I gripped the edge of the couch, wishing it were his throat. "That's not an acceptable answer."

"It's not," he agreed, catching me off guard. "So, I will tell you what I can."

Gabriel let the coffee pot gurgle while he crossed over to Regan with the aluminum can.

"Thank you," she whispered, sipping on it politely.

Gabriel nodded, choosing to remain standing at a distance so we wouldn't have to crane our heads to look up at him. "We're in a very delicate situation. I work for a higher authority under strict orders not to reveal any of our secrets to civilians. Unfortunately, the two of you have found yourselves entangled in one of my company's primary objectives."

"And what's that exactly?" I asked, unable to keep the sarcasm from my voice. "Are you some sort of magical Men in Black?"

He tilted his head to one side. "Yes, that's a good way

to put it."

Our eyes went wide.

A corner of his mouth twitched into a smirk. "Don't tell me you haven't noticed many unexplainable things going on lately."

"You mean like the creepy cat-eyed guy?" I asked.

"Who summons wolves and rabid raccoons," Regan added in a deadpan voice.

"Perfectly normal," I concluded.

Gabriel raised an eyebrow, not used to our banter. "Yes, that. The people who have attacked you are part of a renegade fae group called the Circle of Elphame. Stronghold monitors them as part of our contract with the US military."

"'Fae?'" I repeated. "As in fairy tales?"

"As in a class of magical people who have been living secretly among humans for centuries. They can be quite powerful, but humans outnumber them exponentially. There used to be a lot of bloodshed between the fae and humans, but the two finally signed a treaty to cohabitate Earth peacefully. Humans would continue to live in a world where magic doesn't exist as long as they left the fae largely to themselves."

It shouldn't have been a shock for him to come out and say this. I'd been dealing with this stuff for a week now, but it still made my head throb a little.

"What does the Circle of Elphame want?"

"What else?" Gabriel almost sounded apologetic. "To rule over humans with magic, like every other rebellion before them."

"There have been more than one?" Regan looked a little ill.

"Of course. Just like in the human world, there will always be people who want more power."

"But why me?" Regan asked, her voice taking on a desperate quality. I took her hand in mine and squeezed as she continued. "I have nothing to do with fairies and magic."

Gabriel went back to the coffee pot as it finished dribbling. "You've caught their attention for some reason. Maybe you fit the profile for some ritualistic purpose. Maybe someone in their organization fancies you as a slave. Whatever the reason, the pixie and the druid are after you."

"Serena's a pixie?" I asked.

He nodded. "Fae come in all flavors of races. A pixie has dragonfly-shaped wings that can generate magic dust, which in turn can be infused with other magic to generate various effects."

I finally made the connection. "You mean glitter?"

Gabriel nodded solemnly. "That was pixie dust."

I stifled the urge to run my fingers through my hair. "What did it do to me?"

Gabriel's jaw stiffened. "Nothing that we can tell, which is peculiar in and of itself."

"How long have you known about our pixie friend?"

"We've been monitoring your situation for weeks."

Weeks? My head's throbbing increased to a steady drumbeat. "That means you knew what was going on with Regan when you hired me."

Gabriel at least had the manners to look sheepish. "I apologize for any deception on my part. The only reason I came to Cascade Vista was to interview you as someone close to Regan. We knew someone was following your daughter but didn't know why. After the attacks became more frequent, I thought it best to keep a closer eye on you. I did not intend to get you fired."

No, he hadn't. I'd done that on my own. "That's why you hired me? To keep tabs on us?"

"Yes."

"So you didn't care at all about my professional qualities?" I accused.

"I find you very capable, Melissa," he said, softly, "but no, I did not need an office manager, as you have probably guessed by now."

"What about me?" Regan butted in. "Why go to all the trouble to protect Mom but do nothing about me?"

Gabriel poured coffee from the pot into a mug. "We did, but protecting you was more difficult. We didn't want to arouse any suspicions, so we couldn't pull you from school. That's why I sent an agent undercover to keep an eye on you."

"Lucas," Regan breathed.

Gabriel nodded. "You may have noticed that he's been at your side for a while now. That was by design."

Regan leaned forward, gripping her can so tightly it bent out of shape. "How is he? Is he okay?"

"He's fine," Gabriel reassured as he handed me my coffee. "He suffered some minor injuries from the attack but is recovering now."

"You got the druid?"

"Sadly no. He escaped."

I took a deep gulp from my mug, letting it send comforting warmth into my core. "Lucas is clearly not human. For someone who hunts fairies, it sounds like you employ a few."

Gabriel regarded me cautiously. "I can't disclose how my agency operates."

"Yeah, I got that from hours of sitting inside that sterile box you call an office." When he opened his voice to protest, I cut him off. "Don't get me wrong. I'm grateful that you've kept us safe until now, but you're making it very difficult for me to trust you given all the secrecy."

"Unfortunately, I am not at liberty to discuss much more. It will have to be enough to know that I'm keeping you safe until the danger passes."

"And when will that be?" Regan asked.

"Hopefully not long, but it's hard to say."

I wasn't liking this whole half-answer BS Gabriel was trying to sell. "What if we refuse your help?"

"That's not an option."

"Oh really?" I stood. "You're going to stop us from leaving?"

He folded his arms across his chest. "You can try, but the grounds will keep you here."

I gaped at him. "Are you threatening to keep us as prisoners?"

"Keep you safe," he qualified. "We've put security measures in place that won't hurt you but also won't allow you to simply walk away."

After everything I'd seen in the past few days, I didn't doubt it. As much as I wanted to play with whatever booby traps he'd set out there, I suddenly felt very drained. I was just a single mom with her kid in the middle of some kind of magical struggle. The term "in over my head" didn't even come close to describing our situation.

But that didn't mean I would just roll over to a virtual stranger's demands, no matter how much he seemed to care about us.

I walked over to poke him in the chest. "I swear, if anything happens to my daughter because of this, I'll kill you."

Regan gasped.

Gabriel simply nodded. "Agreed. That will be on me personally."

"Okay, Mr. Security. Where are our cells?"

He looked pained. "You have private accommodations down the hall. You won't be treated like criminals."

"Great because I'm done with this conversation."

He nodded, reaching into his pocket and fiddling with his pager. Vanessa appeared within seconds.

"Yes?" she asked.

"Can you escort these two to their rooms down the hall?"

"Certainly." She waved at us to come forward.

I let Regan waltz past me first, not wanting to take my eyes off her. As I passed Gabriel, he stopped me with a sigh. "I know this is difficult, but you're welcome to explore the grounds. If you have any needs, message me on your pager. Either Vanessa or I will answer."

"Sure, you'll answer," I said. "Anything that isn't classified, which is just about everything."

He said nothing as I left the room, a conflicted look on his face.

Vanessa led us down several doors to a posh suite with two queen beds. The room had been done in tasteful blues with thick white carpet that would show coffee stains in my house within minutes. There was a partitioned dining area with a mini-kitchen off to one side. The bathroom had a full jacuzzi tub and marble walk-in shower.

"You'll find everything you need in the drawers," Vanessa said. "The closets and dressers have spare clothes too if you need it."

"Even underwear?" I asked sarcastically.

"In all sizes," Vanessa said without humor. "The pantry and refrigerator are stocked with staples for meals. You can also ask me to buy you anything else you need."

"How long are we staying here anyway?" Regan asked.

"As long as it takes," Vanessa said as the door shut behind her.

"Good thing that wasn't ominous," I called after her.

Regan opened up a nearby dresser. She grimaced as she pulled out a sealed package. "She wasn't kidding about the underwear. Says it's been pre-washed and everything."

"Lovely," I said, throwing myself onto the nearest bed. I kicked off my shoes, then climbed under the covers.

Regan nervously shifted from side to side. "What's going to happen now? We can't stay here forever."

"But we can stay here tonight." I twisted around and managed to unclasp my bra without taking off my shirt. With a few delicate yanks, I flung it across the room.

Regan watched it land near the bathroom. "You're avoiding the issue."

"No, I'm just punting it to tomorrow. I can't think

straight anymore, can you?"

"No," she admitted, plopping down on the opposite bed. "I'm scared.

I wanted to say I was too, but I couldn't. One of us had to keep it together. "We'll be fine. I promise."

"How can you say that?"

"Because I'll fix it somehow." And I meant it. I would move heaven and Earth to keep her safe.

I just didn't know how.

CHAPTER 22

ALL MY LIFE, I'd tackled my problems head on. Even when things looked absolutely bleak—like after being told I was pregnant by a doctor—I figured out how to deal with my new reality. It was just part of my DNA.

Which is why, long after Regan fell asleep, I lay awake pondering my next move. I couldn't leave everything up to Gabriel and his super-secret corporation to get us out of this. I had to do something proactive.

Even if that meant looking for my mom.

Like Regan had said, Barbara was the only resource we knew that believed in magic. Deep down, I knew she was crazy, but I was running out of sane options.

Unfortunately, my last known address for her had been over a decade ago. The apartment that we used to rent had been torn down for a nicer set of upscale townhouses. I used my phone's roaming Internet connection to search for where she might have gone, but Barbara Hartley despised the Internet. As far as Google knew, she didn't exist.

I finally gave up around dawn and took a long, hot shower. I found an oversized shirt in the dressers to use as a nightshirt, threw on some of those pre-packaged undies because my own were disgusting, and then finally fell into a dreamless sleep.

I woke up to the smell of coffee and the sound of rushing water. Regan had gotten up before me to take a shower. She came out of the bathroom in a cream-colored robe.

"Good morning," I yawned.

"More like afternoon." Regan pointed to the clock on the nightstand, which had just flipped over to the noon hour.

"Wow. I haven't slept in like this since before you were born."

"Or, you know, most Sundays."

As Regan picked her own wardrobe from the dresser, I poured myself a pitifully small cup of coffee. I missed my ginormous mugs at home.

"Thanks for the caffeine boost," I said.

Regan wore loose sweatpants she tied around her thin waist and a snug V-neck shirt. "I figured you'd need it today of all days. So, what's the plan? Are we going to call the Dunlaps?"

I gave her my severest parental stare. "Tell me you've kept Leah out of this."

She raised her hands in self-defense. "I haven't texted anyone about last night yet, but don't you think we should tell them what's going on?"

I shook my head. "I'd rather keep them out of this if possible." When Regan looked unconvinced, I added, "Do you want to be responsible for the death of your best friend?"

Her eyes widened. "No, of course not."

"Well, neither do I." I took a swig of coffee and grimaced at the bitter taste of the cheap brew.

"We're just going with the flow and doing whatever Gabriel says?" Regan asked incredulously.

"Absolutely not." I added extra sugar packets to my cup. "I tried finding your grandmother last night."

"Really? I thought you said to forget about her."

"That's before I got railroaded by a defense contractor. If there's anyone who has absolutely nothing to do with the US government, it's my mom."

"Did you check all the popular social media sites?"

"Sure. I sent my feelers out to all six of my friends." I gave her a raspberry. "You know I rarely touch that stuff."

"Got it. I'll do the digging there."

"Even though Barbara probably thinks Twitter is the sound that birds make?"

"Well, she's not exactly wrong. And she doesn't have to be active online for someone to mention her."

"Fine, you handle it then, but I need food before we start."

"I'm in for that plan too."

I rummaged around the cupboards and found some sugary cereal. The refrigerator had milk. It wasn't the lunch of champions, but it got us through our initial hunger as we hunkered down for an afternoon of research.

We spent the better part of Saturday following a bunch of ideas: where Barbara Hartley had gotten off to, who our attackers could be, even trying to suss out more information about Stronghold and Gabriel Alston himself. I dove hard into traditional web searches, praying I wouldn't contract a nasty virus on my phone, while Regan hit the social media outlets hard. We worked straight through until the sunlight faded from outside our balcony window.

Regan finally got out of the bed and leaned against a wall to do some of her running stretches. "I've been sitting in one position too long."

I rubbed my aching shoulders. "I'm surprised no one has bothered us."

"Maybe they're taking a cue from us. Gabriel said we could wander around the property."

I made a face. "You want to go exploring?"

"The pool could be relaxing."

"You plan on swimming in our borrowed clothes?"

"Hold on." She pulled out a bikini bottom from the magic drawers. "They really have everything."

I grimaced. "Ugh. There is no way I'm wearing that."

"They have one-piece swimsuits too." Regan pulled out a simple black one and threw it at me.

I caught it one-handed. "I don't know. I try not to show this much skin in public as a rule. No one deserves seeing that many moles on one body."

"This isn't a public place, and strategically placed moles are attractive."

"Says the person with flawless skin." Yet, I knew we needed the exercise. I pulled the swimsuit on. The straps dug into my shoulders, but I supposed better too tight than too loose with these things. Regan's bikini fit her perfectly, of course. At least it was high-waisted with a thick halter top, so she didn't look like she was heading to Florida for Spring Break.

We wrapped bathroom towels around ourselves and walked on bare feet to the ground floor. As we stepped outside toward the pool house, goosebumps formed all over my limbs.

"I know this is rich people problems," I said, "but you'd think with a place this fancy, they could afford a heated walkway."

"We should complain to management." Regan skipped ahead to hold the pool house door open for me.

A wall of humid chlorinated air wrinkled my nose. "Love the aroma."

Regan had become distracted by something other than the smell. "Looks like we're not alone."

Rough cement rubbed against the soles of my feet as I approached the lip of the pool. It stretched out, large enough to accommodate several lap swimmers. Someone had taken to the water, arms forming perfect strides across the far side of the pool.

Gabriel.

My stomach fluttered as he flipped back toward us, his powerful legs propelling him forward. Holy hamstrings, I had not been wrong about him lifting weights. His corded muscles glistened in the water.

I backed up a step to escape. "Maybe this wasn't such a good idea."

Regan dipped her toes in the lane beside Gabriel's. "C'mon, the pool's large enough for all of us. What's your issue?"

She scrutinized me, then an approaching Gabriel, then back to me. "Oh."

"What does 'Oh' mean?"

"You 'like' Gabriel, don't you?"

Her air quotes made my face grow hot. "That would be inappropriate. He's my boss."

"You're acting just like Leah when she's crushing hard. Blushing, weird side eyes, quick denial—all the classic signs." Regan smiled knowingly. "Don't fight it."

"Did you fight it when it was Lucas?" I retorted back.

This time, it was Regan who flustered. "What? No. I mean, it's just—"

While we argued, Gabriel reached the shallow end of the pool near us. He stood, flinging his head and sending droplets flying on either side of him. His eyes widened slightly in surprise when he spotted my legs not far away. They lingered there before traveling up past my towel, lingering on my chest.

Wonderful. He'd seen the raised mole almost in the direct center of my cleavage. I knew I should have had my dermatologist remove it last year.

His eyes roved up to mine. "Melissa?" he said with a rasp, the result of the pool water. "Are you enjoying your stay?"

I hammered down my nerves with trusty sarcasm. "Your ostentatious villa is pretty decked out."

Gabriel looked put upon. "It's just a modest rental house."

"A rental house with a pool," Regan interjected. "Time to dive in."

She smirked at me before plunging into the water. The little punk left me deliberately alone with my ridiculously handsome boss.

"Traitor," I muttered.

"Excuse me?" Gabriel asked.

I lifted my chin, gathering what little dignity I could muster wrapped in a towel. "Regan and I needed a break. We've been holed up in our rooms too long."

"I noticed."

My stomach tightened. "You did?"

He ran his fingers through his wet hair. "I know our conversation didn't end well last night. I was trying to give you some space today."

"Sure, thanks." I waved, trying to sound like it was no big deal, even though I was still mad at him. At least, that's what I reminded myself.

"I know one night's not going to ease your mind." He waded up to the pool's edge and lifted himself out. Water cascaded down his sleek body as he emerged in a Speedo. "I'm hoping you'll eventually come to trust me."

"Yeah," I said dumbly, staring at his face and refusing to look down again. I needed to get out of here and fast. "Boy, that hot tub is calling my name."

"Do you mind if I join you?"

My mind froze. "In the hot tub?"

"I usually take a dip after a swim."

I'd have to be an absolute Puritan to refuse. The hot tub could house more than a few dozen people. "Sure," I said, hoping I sounded like the kind of woman who lounged semi-naked with ripped bodybuilders all the time.

He let me ease into the bubbling water first. I winced as I sank up to my core, a different kind of heat roaring through my body. Although uncomfortable at first, my sore muscles eventually relaxed as I sank into a seat at the far end. The stress of spending the day hunched over my phone eased from my entire body.

"Ahh," I sighed as I settled into my spot.

Gabriel took up space on the opposite side of the tub. He was so tall, his broad shoulders remained above the water line even after he sat down on the underwater bench. His legs spread out in front of him as he relaxed.

I pushed my own knees together. Trying to get a handle on my errant thoughts, I studied his face. He appeared as tired as I felt.

"Long week for you too, huh?"

"You don't know the half of it."

"I thought chasing bad magical dudes was your typical routine."

"I'm working on multiple issues. Your family's safety is just one of many balls I'm juggling."

"Guess I never thought about your balls." It took me several full seconds to realize what I'd just said. "I mean your workload." I'm surprised I didn't spontaneously combust right there.

"Of course." He leaned his head back so I couldn't quite tell if he was laughing or not. "But enough about me. I want to know more about you."

"Me? There is absolutely nothing interesting about me."

"That's annoyingly humble and completely untrue. How did you become the office manager for a software company?"

I grimaced. "You'll laugh."

"With an intro like that, you have to tell me now."

I considered how much to say and decided to throw caution to the wind. "I was initially hired on as a temporary office assistant. One of the hot shot new engineers with a glowing resume ordered me to take notes for some big software planning meeting. He had aspirations of becoming the project lead, but it was beneath him to write anything down himself."

"Sounds about right for Cascade Vista, given what I'd

seen."

"Under new management, yes, but not when Joshua ran the company. This engineer didn't know that yet. I showed up at the meeting, and Joshua ended up being there too. I found out later he'd heard grumblings from the other developers about this new hire's arrogance, and he'd decided to sit in to evaluate the guy himself."

Gabriel grinned. "Sounds like the seeds for office drama."

"Oh yeah. The dude rambled on like a drone using a bunch of computer jargon to emphasize his vague points. I don't know much about coding, but it was clear no one was listening. I started asking questions. He indulged me at first, but when I kept pestering him, he tried to brush me off as being stupid."

"What a jackass."

"Without the 'jack.' Some of the other developers took offense on my behalf. They started asking him questions then. The guy fumbled. It became clear pretty quickly that he didn't really comprehend his own technobabble. One of the developers pointed that out, and he became furious. He melted into a tirade of his credentials at more prestigious companies and how he'd been put in charge of the project. I left the room."

Gabriel frowned. "Because you were upset?"

"Because something seemed off about this guy! I marched right back to my desk and called the HR department of one of the firms he claimed to have worked for. Turns out they had no employment record of anyone with that name."

"So, you swooped back into the meeting and exposed his fraud?"

I shook my head. "I didn't want to fan the flames. Everyone was riled up as it was. Instead, I grabbed a bunch of leftover snacks from a previous client meeting and declared a break. The engineers all simmered down, giving me a chance to pull Joshua aside and tell him what

I'd found."

"How did Joshua react?"

"He pulled the engineer into his office and before we regrouped, he'd been quietly fired. Joshua then stepped back in and put a senior developer in charge, who went on to nail the project. That client became one of our regulars after that. Joshua told me later that one contract alone netted the company millions of dollars in future revenue."

Gabriel's eyes sparkled. "The temp who was just there to take notes saved the day, huh?"

I couldn't help but grin. "Joshua started giving me more HR-related tasks, which snowballed into me taking over other duties. Within a year, I'd become the official office manager for the entire company." I teared up thinking about it. "I loved that job."

"Sounds like you were the best person for the job."

I wiped my eyes. "Don't think flattery will let you off the hook. Now it's your turn. Tell me more about yourself."

His expression became guarded. "I already told you, I can't discuss most of my professional career with you."

Being too close to a hot guy under casual circumstances went straight to my head. That's the only excuse I had for blurting out, "Then how about telling me something personal, like why you don't have a girlfriend?"

Gabriel did a double take.

Before I could explain it away, Gabriel said quietly, "Maybe for the same reason why you're not married."

Now it was my turn to feel taken aback. "Dating and marriage are two different beasts."

"But you have a kid. That changes the game for you."

I flushed, this time with anger. "Are you implying I'm undatable because I have a kid?"

He held out wrinkled hands. "Not at all. Just that Regan's father complicates things."

"I told you before, he's not in the picture." I stood. It was time I got out of the mess I'd created. "Excuse me."

Gabriel stayed silent until I had to pass close by him to reach the stairs. "I'm sorry. I didn't mean to offend you."

It wasn't professional to leave in a snit. I'd been the one to ask about girlfriends, after all.

"You weren't the one to overstep boundaries," I said. "I did. I promise it won't happen again."

He regarded me with those intense steel gray eyes. Was he upset about my declaration? Relieved?

I broke off eye contact first. "Good night, Mr. Alston."

He tilted his head toward me. "Good night, Ms. Hartley."

We were back to last names. I tried to tell myself it was a good thing, but it sure didn't feel like it.

CHAPTER 23

I LEFT REGAN doing laps in the pool and went back to our room. The sooner we figured out a strategy that didn't involve relying on Stronghold, the better. I wrapped myself in a robe and threw myself back into web searches.

Regan poked her head into our room soon after. "Hey, I'm starving, and Gabriel said the kitchen downstairs has better food. You want some?"

"Nah." I'd lost my appetite.

"Mind if I go down and scrounge?"

"Don't let me stunt your growth."

Regan was gone for a half hour. She returned with a cup of coffee for me, mixed with just the right amount of cream and sugar.

"You are my favorite child," I told her as I took a sip.

"Phew. For a minute there, I was worried."

I settled back into the many tabs I had opened in my browser about bizarre otherworldly encounters. A surprising number of people believed in fairies, including some who lived in the Salem area. One local farmer's blog post, dated eight years ago, talked about a fairy ruining his crops. He even posted blurry nighttime pictures of the supposed pests. They all just looked like normal shadows in the woods behind his field to me.

The post ended with glowing praise for a group called the Blessed Order. They'd helped eliminate his fairy problem.

This kicked off a whole flurry of searches as I tried to learn more about this organization. I finally found an obscure website for a group with the same name.

Regan came up behind me and read over my shoulder. "Whatcha got?"

I angled my phone so Regan could read it better, no easy feat since I had to keep it plugged into the wall for a recharge. "This group claims to deal with supernatural exterminations."

She skimmed over the sparse information on their site. "Think this 'Blessed Order' is some sort of religious cult?"

"Kinda sounds like it."

My stomach growled just then, loud enough to break up the conversation.

Regan cowered in mock terror. "Oh no! A demon."

"Don't worry," I said reflexively. "Mommy will banish it."

We both giggled at our little inside joke. Once, when Regan had been eleven years old, we'd watched some demonic horror movie together. I'd thought it was a little too violent for her, but she'd begged me to rent it. My stomach rumbled so loudly during a tense, quiet scene that she'd screamed and spilled our entire shared bowl of popcorn.

Once we stopped laughing, Regan said, "The downstairs kitchen has really tasty clam chowder. They even have oyster cracker packets."

"You had me at 'tasty.'"

I left Regan scrolling on her own device and went downstairs. After strolling through the ground floor ballroom with its ridiculous grand piano, I entered the industrial-sized kitchen. With granite countertops for miles, more appliances than I knew what to do with, and an actual walk-in pantry, the place could accommodate a full-course meal for the entire Cascade Vista crew. I heated up the soup and ate at the breakfast bar, contemplating the fuzzy modern painting hung above me. I tried crossing my eyes to see if any hidden picture emerged from its depths, but nope, it was meant to look like static.

Unable to help myself, I washed my own dishes in the bathtub-length sink and put them back where I'd found them. I almost retreated back up the double-curved stairs when I spotted a lit archway on the other side of the foyer. A short hallway ended in a room with floor-to-ceiling tempered glass. A placard I couldn't read at this distance stated the strange room's purpose.

Curiosity got the better of me, and I approached the glass wall. Vague blobs started to come into shape. I recognized one as a treadmill, so it was no surprise when I finally read the gym placard. Opening the door, I found more exercise equipment, including an elliptical machine, a stair stepper, and a standard set of weights next to a padded floor. The mirror made the space look twice as big as it really was.

Just the thought of using the room made my muscles hurt. I turned to leave when I recognized the muted sound of rushing water coming from somewhere nearby. Perplexed, I followed it to a door with a unisex bathroom symbol.

Gabriel or Vanessa must have just finished a workout and was taking a shower. Not wanting to face either of them, I turned to leave.

That's when I spotted a familiar maroon and gray duffel bag tossed casually to one side of the room.

I stiffened. Lucas's bag.

Gabriel had said Lucas worked for him. I wrinkled my nose in irritation. Gabriel should have told me Lucas would be around, if only so I could warn Regan. Of course, he hadn't said anything, including what kind of superhuman Lucas was.

Maybe Lucas's duffel could give me a clue. I poked it with my foot. It felt full of clothes. I glanced over at the bathroom door, the sound of water assuring me the owner was showering. The thought crossed my mind that maybe I shouldn't snoop around in other people's belongings.

Except these people literally held my family's life in their hands.

Squatting down, I unzipped the duffel bag. Black fur spilled out in a furious cascade.

I jumped back as if I'd just opened a can full of spiders. The fur swished to the floor, and I could see what looked like a limp, deflated paw. Shaking now, I inched forward and grabbed a corner so I could examine it at arm's length. An entire meatless fur pelt unraveled right before my eyes: complete with tail, paws, and eyeball-less sockets.

It was the black wolf's pelt. Someone had skinned it clean off the animal.

My mind reeled. Regan and I knew very little about magic, but we knew for sure that both the black wolf and Lucas had been protecting us. Why would Lucas have the wolf's disembodied fur in his duffel bag if they had the same objective?

Then it dawned on me. We only had Gabriel's word that Stronghold employed Lucas. A person who had stolen Lucas's bag could be in the shower.

Vanessa had shown up awfully quick after our skirmish with the druid. She'd taken us straight here to Gabriel's villa in the middle of nowhere. What did we really know about Stronghold, other than it had used false pretenses to keep me employed?

What did I really know about Gabriel for that matter? Had I let my hormones convince me he was a good person?

The sound of rushing water suddenly stopped. I nearly wet myself as I realized whoever was taking the shower had finished.

I shoved the pelt back into the bag and zipped it up. I

fled the room as fast as I could, down the hallway and back up the stairs. Thankfully, I didn't run into anyone because I couldn't have hidden my fear.

Because despite all my questions, one thing was painfully clear: someone at Stronghold had killed the black wolf and possibly harmed Lucas.

CHAPTER 24

I CRASHED INTO our suite, the door slamming behind me.

Regan jumped, nearly dropping her phone. "Mom, what's wrong?"

"We have to leave. It's not safe here."

"What happened?"

"I wandered into an exercise room downstairs. Someone who just finished up their Pilates workout has Lucas's duffel bag, and it's stuffed with the pelt of the black wolf."

Regan blinked a few times, clearly not processing all this information. I had to relay it to her several times before she understood the implications of what I'd seen.

Her voice shook when she next spoke. "Does that mean Lucas is dead?"

I paced the room. "I don't know, but the wolf sure is. There's no reason why Lucas would hurt the wolf."

Regan looked about ready to cry. "We're in big trouble, aren't we?"

"Yeah."

Her iron resolve took over. She rose to her feet. "We won't let the wolf's sacrifice be in vain."

Pride mixed in with my grief. My little baby wasn't so little anymore.

My pride melted into dismay as she marched toward the door.

"Where do you think you're going?" I asked.

"To confront the wolf's murderer."

I zipped across the room before she could turn the handle. "No."

"He's downstairs right now, taking a shower! He might know what happened to Lucas."

"What if we're wrong, and it *is* Lucas."

She paused, stumped. "We should at least get a look at the killer."

"And what? Ask him or her politely what happened? The person downstairs probably has magic up the wazoo. We can't possibly take him on."

Her eyes searched the room as if it could give her answers. "So, we can't trust Gabriel either?"

My gut twisted painfully as I replied with the stark truth. "No. There's a very real possibility that Stronghold ordered the wolf's death."

"Oh, Mom." Regan laid a hand on my shoulder. "You like Gabriel. I am so, so sorry."

I gave her my best fake smile. "Don't worry about my stupid feelings. Our safety is the most important thing. We have to figure out how to get out of here." I pulled out my phone.

"Who are you calling?"

"Jessie."

"I thought you said not to call her."

"I did, but we have nowhere else to go, and Jessie will help us out no matter what." At least, I prayed she would. We'd ended our last call on a real sour note. Jessie and I rarely fought.

The phone rang, once, twice. As it reached the fourth ring, my heart sank.

Jessie finally picked up. "Oh, so we're talking now?"

"Jessie!" I exclaimed, unable to keep the half-cry of joy from my voice.

She must have recognized my panic because she lost her indignation. "What's going on?"

"Regan and I are stranded way outside of town with no way back. Can you send Paul to pick us up?"

"Paul? Why not me?" Her voice rose a notch.

"Look, we don't have a lot of time, and I'm not gonna lie. It could be dangerous. Could you please have Paul give us a lift?"

To my extreme relief, she relented. "Fine, but I swear you're going to explain what's going on when I see you. Down to the last detail."

"I will." And I meant it. This call got the Dunlaps involved in our mess. I could no longer protect them through ignorance, even if I wanted to.

"Text me the address. See you soon."

Once disconnected, I pulled up the phone's map app and sent Jessie the rough address at the end of the residence's long driveway.

"Now what?" Regan asked as I gathered all my personal belongings.

"Now we sneak out of here and meet Paul by the main road."

"Gabriel said 'the grounds wouldn't let us leave.' What if they have traps out there that could kill us?"

"I doubt any traps will kill us. We're just going to have to chance it."

Regan grew pale but nodded. "Okay. Let's go."

We didn't take anything but the clothes we came in with, our phones, and my purse. I left the Stronghold pager on the bed. Then we snuck out of the room.

Just like before, no one appeared in any of the halls, but I held my breath until we'd made it out of the tall entrance doors without incident. Luck granted us a full moon to light our path. As we jogged away, I worried someone would notice, but before long we'd made it up the paved cement and out of sight.

"Round one goes to us," I said, "but in round two, the difficulty level goes up." I pointed ahead to the metal gate that connected two sides of the brick perimeter.

"You think it's monitored by video?"

"Probably. Which is why we're not going through the gate itself. We'll dive into the trees and find a more subtle place to climb over."

Regan followed me into the woods. The trees drew us into more shadow than I liked, but enough light filtered down to see the way. I scrutinized the fence as we ran parallel to it from a distance. The bricks were rough with large grooves in between. We could probably grip them with fingers and toes.

I stopped when we were surrounded by forest and we could no longer see the well-kept house grounds. "Let's try here."

"No problem," Regan said with teenage cockiness. "I bet I can hoist myself up to the top lip."

I stopped her with my arm outstretched. "No, I'll go first. That way if anything goes wrong, you'll be safe."

Regan's eyes widened. "I don't want anything to happen to you."

"Me neither. Which is why I'm going first."

"Fine," she said, but she didn't sound happy about it.

I crept cautiously up to the brick wall, searching for anything that could indicate a trap. Who was I kidding? I had no idea what to look for. Nothing looked out of place. I tentatively put my hand onto the brick, wincing, half expecting an alarm to sound. Still nothing.

"So far, so good." I clenched my jaw as I wedged my fingers in between two layers of brick. It was now or never. I pushed myself upward, my torso straining as my feet scrambled to find the next foothold. I barely wedged a shoe tip in before edging upward.

"Go, Mom!" Regan cheered behind me.

"My poor noodle arms," I complained. "I should start

lifting weights."

"Put that on your list of things to do when we're out of here."

"Sure thing." I got a forearm over the top of the wall. There was a good six-inch shelf up there. I made one last heave and forced a leg over, grunting as I straddled into a full sitting position.

Regan flashed a victory 'V' with her fingers. "No sweat."

"No, I'm definitely sweating." I scanned the other side of the brick wall. "I don't see anything out there. Looks normal enough." I smiled down at Regan. "So much for Gabriel's fabled security."

"Okay, I'm coming over." Regan took a few bold steps in my direction, then suddenly froze.

My breath caught in my throat. "What is it?"

"I . . . I . . ." She couldn't finish her sentence.

Terrified that we'd walked into an ambush, I glanced around for a possible threat but still saw nothing. "What's wrong?"

Her eyes bored into mine, and that seemed to pull her out of her stupor. "I-I'm scared."

"Of course, you're scared. This is an awful situation."

"No, I mean all of the sudden I'm overwhelmed with fear." She swallowed. "I don't want to go over that wall."

To my astonishment, she began creeping back in the opposite direction, toward the house.

"Wait!" I shouted, but it didn't change her course.

Frustrated, I swung my legs back over and landed on her side. I ran after her and grabbed her by the shoulders to face me.

"What's gotten into you?"

Her eyes had gone wild. "I don't know."

"Get over it. We've got to go. Now."

She shook her head.

I squeezed. "We can do this together. I promise."

She continued to shake but kept hold on my hand as

we marched back toward the brick wall together. She closed her eyes as if she were walking down a pirate plank, so I had to tug her forward to keep moving. By the time she reached the wall, she actively pulled back against me.

"I can't do this!" she shrieked.

"You can," I insisted, not understanding this sudden reluctance. "You go up first this time. It's safe, I promise."

She whimpered as I led her up to the wall.

I grit my teeth in frustration. "You're not going to let your middle-aged mom out-ninja you, are you?"

"N-no." That stubborn streak she'd had since her toddler years gleamed in her eye.

"Then curb stomp your fear and climb this puppy."

She closed her eyes, breathing deeply in and out. For a moment, I wondered if she was just stalling again.

She finally took a flying leap at the wall, springing upward in one fluid motion. Grabbing onto the edge, she swung her legs over the top. Then she fell out of view to the other side.

"Attagirl!" I yelled, then clumsily went over the wall again. I looked like a bumbling idiot next to her graceful leap, but I made it up and over. I followed the sound of her panting and found her leaning against a cedar tree several yards into the woods.

"Sorry about that," she said between sharp breaths. "I'm not sure what came over me."

"As long as it's over now. We've got to get to the road before Paul does."

We jogged down the dirt driveway, deep ruts marking where vehicles had passed over the years. The change in elevation made it hard for us to keep up a conversation, but at least the moonlight fully illuminated our path.

We made it to the road in minutes, its cracked surface indicating the highway department rarely maintained this stretch of road. I sent Jessie a text telling her we were waiting for Paul, then settled on the graveled shoulder to pass the time.

We didn't have to wait long.

The Dunlaps' familiar blue Honda Civic soon zipped toward us. The car screeched to a halt, and the doors clicked unlocked. Regan dove into the back while I took the passenger seat.

"Thanks, Paul . . ." I began.

Jessie shoved her face into mine. Her frizzy black hair indicated she hadn't bothered to comb it before coming to meet us. "What is going on with you?"

". . . or not," I finished lamely. "Why are you here?"

"Paul's having drinks with buddies tonight, and I couldn't reach him. I wasn't about to let my lack of testosterone keep me from helping you out. You're in trouble, aren't you?"

"Big trouble. Let's go."

"What about that explanation you owe me? You've been acting so—"

"Just go," I cut her off, "before we get caught."

She scowled but threw the car back into drive. We sped down the road, leaving Gabriel's villa far behind.

CHAPTER 25

"LET ME GET this straight." Jessie's grip tightened on the steering wheel so hard, I marveled that she didn't twist it straight off the dashboard. "That lady who tried to take Regan out of school was some sort of fairy?"

"A pixie but basically yes."

"And you also got attacked by some guy with kitty eyes who can control animals?"

"Correct."

"Then you spent the better part of a weekend hiding out in your boss's woodland mansion, where you found a wolf skin that you believe belonged to your former savior?"

"I'd call it a 'villa,' but close enough."

Jessie bit her bottom lip. "This is all a bit hard to take, but you are two of the most levelheaded people I know. I believe you."

My muscles unclenched. "Thank you."

"Are you sure you don't want to call the cops?"

"You honestly think they'll believe me when you barely do?"

Jessie grumbled. "There's gotta be someone else you can talk to."

I couldn't help but make a movie reference. "'Who you gonna call?'"

"I think the quote you're looking for is 'I'm too old for this sh—'" She glanced at Regan in the rearview mirror and corrected herself abruptly. "—stuff.'"

"Oh please," Regan said. "I'm sixteen. I know all the damn cuss words."

"Sorry," Jessie said. "Force of habit with a young kid at home."

"Speaking of which, you can't bring us to your place," I said. "Drop us off at a hotel or something." My stomach lurched at the thought of staying at yet another unfamiliar place, but I couldn't ask Jessie to stick her neck out for us any more than necessary.

Jessie was having none of it. "No way, ma'am. The two of you are staying with us tonight. Paul should be home soon. The adults can take turns staying up and keeping an eye on things."

I let out a shaky sigh of relief knowing I would not have to figure this all out on my own. "Thanks, Jessie. You're the best."

"I really am, especially after all the secrecy." Her lower lip protruded in a pout. "I thought you trusted me with everything."

"I do!" When she raised an eyebrow at me dubiously, I tried to defend my position. "Can you blame me for not shouting any of this out to the world? I could barely believe my own sanity for a while. Why would I expect you to act any different?"

"Well, now that you know I'm cool with your delusions, you'd better not leave me in the dark again, or else I'll whoop your butt."

"Does this mean I can tell Leah everything?" Regan asked from the back seat.

"No," we both answered simultaneously.

Regan slapped my headrest. "Why not?"

"Because we're already putting the Dunlaps at enough

risk."

"You just told Jessie!"

"I'll keep my mouth shut with everyone except Paul," Jessie replied, eyes narrowed at the rearview mirror.

"So will Leah," Regan said, but she lost a bit of conviction, falling back into her seat.

I turned around to fix Regan with my best mothers-know-best gaze. "You already told Leah your abridged story earlier, and remember what happened?" I gestured at Jessie.

"It's just not fair," Regan whispered, thrusting her chin toward the window, but I still saw her eyes fill with tears.

"Oh, honey." I reached out to pat her knee. "I know this is a lot to take in."

"Do you?" She jerked her leg out of reach. "Because you don't seem all that upset about Lucas."

I tried to approach the issue reasonably. "I'm worried about Lucas, but I'm focusing all my energy on what I can control."

She glared at me. "What about your boyfriend? Still pining after Gabriel even though he could have killed Lucas?"

Jessie perked up. "Boyfriend?"

I flushed. "Gabriel's not my boyfriend. He's my boss."

"You sure don't look at him like a boss," Regan accused.

"I've handled him like one." I didn't feel like having this argument right now, not when I hadn't had time to examine my own complex feelings about Gabriel.

"Could have fooled me with that whole dip in the hot tub."

"What hot tub?" Jessie exclaimed. "I need all the details!"

What little control I had left evaporated. "I realize I may have let Gabriel get too close to me, but now that he might be a threat to my family, I'm going to do everything in my power to keep us safe. That's what I've always done.

I'm a responsible parent, and I don't have the luxury of nursing my emotions like a spoiled brat."

Regan gaped at me in shock. I never took that kind of condescending tone with her.

My first instinct was to apologize. She'd been through so much in the last few days, but I needed her to understand that we couldn't mess around. I would do anything to protect my daughter.

Even if she hated me for it.

So instead, I left Regan in a daze and twisted back to face the windshield. Beside me, Jessie's lips formed a thin, grim line. I thought maybe she found my tactics overbearing but instead she gave me a curt nod.

She was a mother too. She understood.

She also muttered her breath, "I can't believe there's a hot tub involved."

* * *

The Dunlap children were all asleep in their beds by the time we reached their house. Jessie set us up on the living room couches for the night. Still angry and not talking to me, Regan nonetheless fell asleep right away, further proving my hypothesis that she could nap on a steeple roof if she needed to.

I filled Jessie and later Paul in on everything that had happened. (Except the hot tub bits. Only Jessie heard about that.) Paul acted a bit more skeptically than Jessie about my encounters with magical beings, but he did agree that calling the police would send me straight to a psych ward. The three of us each took two-hour shifts awake during the night.

Penny came out of her room at the crack of dawn. She spotted us guests and squealed so loudly it woke the whole household. Leah demanded to know why no one had told her that her bestie was sleeping over. Jessie made up some excuse about a gas leak at our house and us needing to stay here until we could get it fixed. Regan glowered during the lie but thankfully did not contradict it as the first batch of pancakes was laid out on the table. The children settled down eagerly for breakfast.

With the kids distracted, I did more digging on the Dunlaps' family computer, situated in an alcove off to the side of the kitchen. I wanted to find out more about the Blessed Order, our only real lead. Their barebones website claimed they investigated "supernatural phenomenon" but didn't offer much else besides a web contact form and physical address inside Salem city limits. Apparently, they didn't do phone calls.

I thought of sending them a message but nixed that idea. I didn't have time to wait for a reply. I doubted their office would be open on a Sunday anyway, but I also couldn't just sit on my hands all day.

I waved Jessie over to me. "You got a jacket I could borrow?"

"Why? You going somewhere?"

I showed her the Blessed Order website while the kids ate, blissfully unaware, behind us. "I was going to take a rideshare over there to check this place out."

Jessie did a quick scan of the page. "Not without me. I'll drive you."

"I don't know. I have no idea who these people are."

"Even more reason not to go alone."

"It's too dangerous for you."

Paul walked by just then, my words just loud enough for him to eavesdrop. He stopped in his tracks. "What's dangerous?"

"Sh!" Jessie hissed. Penny cocked her head at us, but Leah was still gabbing so loudly about some viral video that the kids hadn't noticed our pow-wow.

Glaring at me, Jessie pulled her husband back down the hallway. They had a heated argument just out of sight that involved a lot of whispers and handwaving. Penny came out of her seat to go check it out, but I lured her back to the table with promises of syrupy seconds. By the time I'd placed the second round of pancakes out for the teenage sharks, Jessie returned to the kitchen with a lime green rain jacket on. Paul trailed behind her, clearly upset.

"Melissa and I are going out," she called cheerily to the kids. Only Regan glanced up in alarm, but I gave her a nonchalant shrug. Leah thankfully pulled her back into the kids' conversation.

All the adults stepped outside so the kids wouldn't see us. I glanced from Paul, a murderous gleam in his eye, to a triumphant Jessie. "Are you sure this is okay?"

"No," Paul bit out.

"Of course, it is," Jessie said at the same time. "I just had to remind Paul that he doesn't get to dictate where I go."

"This isn't funny, Jess," he glowered. "It could be dangerous. I should go."

"And leave the kids unprotected? What kind of parent are you?"

My right hand involuntarily clenched into a fist. "I'm so sorry about all this, Paul. I didn't mean to drag you into it."

His eyebrows unfurrowed as he let out a big sigh. "It's not your fault. I just wish I could call one of my buddies to go with you."

"You think they'd believe Melissa's story?" Jessie snorted.

"I'll text you the address of where we're going," I promised.

"You'll do me one better." He turned to Jessie. "Give me your phone?"

"Why?" she asked warily.

"So I can enable tracking on it, like we have on the kids' phones."

She dug into her purse. "Fine, but it's coming off the minute I get home."

It took him a few minutes to get it set up. "I love you," he said, handing back Jessie her phone. "And be careful.

Remember, running away is better than engaging in a fight. Call if you need absolutely anything. And don't take any chances."

Paul kept spouting warnings as they lingered near the car, finally drawing Jessie in for a deep kiss. I buckled myself in as they nuzzled each other. As embarrassing as it was, the PDA lifted my spirits. I was happy that love like that existed in the world. Maybe I could find that one day.

And maybe I'd win the lottery too and lose twenty pounds eating cheesecake. A girl could dream.

Jessie drove us toward the northeast corner of Salem, past the major shopping areas to the other side of I-5. Everything seemed safe enough until we found ourselves in junk yard territory. Dilapidated houses with rusting cars made up entire streets. It got worse when we pulled off onto an actual gravel road.

"I thought we were going to some church," Jessie said. "I feel like we're on our way to buy drugs."

"That's the place." I pointed to the end of the road, where massive trees grew so thick it was impossible to see anything beyond the pristine white mailbox sitting on a brick post at the mouth of the driveway. The gold numbers on the box matched the Blessed Order website's address.

A sturdy metal gate barred Jessie from driving in. It had a combination lockbox attached to it, the kind realtors use to store a key to a house so anyone who enters the correct four-digit code can open it.

Jessie pulled up on the road's shoulder. We both exited the car and approached the gate.

I noticed the gate wasn't actually attached to any sort of fence. "We can walk around."

She halted in her tracks. "They don't seem friendly to visitors."

"Let's just find the building and see if they have office hours."

I might as well have been talking to my foot. Jessie had

inexplicably retreated back toward the car.

I gave her my best WTF expression. "What are you doing?"

"I don't think we should go in," she said, her voice shaking.

I turned back to scrutinize the property. Sure, the lawn had some weeds growing on the edges, but other than that, it didn't seem dangerous. There was no barking dog, no signs indicating someone might shoot first. Someone had even planted a row of tulips near the gate. It was by far and away the nicest property on the block.

"It'll only be a quick peek," I said.

"I think we should come back later." Jessie dove into the driver's seat.

"I'm sure it's fine."

She responded by barricading herself in the car. The automatic doors locked with a heavy click.

"Okay, then!" I called. "I'll be right back. Wait here for me."

She responded by starting the car's engine, then backing the Honda down the road.

"Jessie?" I called in disbelief.

She refused to look at me as she sped off back down the gravel road.

"Are you kidding me?" I yelled after her.

The fading hum of her engine answered me until it disappeared out of sight.

"Wonderful." I tried to shake her odd behavior off as a joke, but her quick exit spooked me. I considered leaving myself.

But I'd come all this way, and I had nowhere else to go. What if talking to these Blessed Order people could help?

I summoned up every last ounce of courage I still possessed and strode past the gate. A cool breeze tickled the back of my neck. I pulled the hood over my head to keep warm as I strolled down the dirt path.

Several hundred yards into the trees, I found a well-kept two-story house with a wide porch, complete with swinging bench affixed to the ceiling. It looked like a former pioneer home, complete with skinny, tall windows and a turret on one corner. A matching detached garage stood off to one side. Behind it, I saw an extensive garden with many laminated paper signs indicating what had been planted.

"Nice," I whispered. What had Jessie been freaked out about? This seemed like some sort of historical society, not spooky at all.

I saw a metal plaque by the door with raised letters. Perfect. Maybe it had a phone number I could call.

I didn't make it two steps out of the trees before someone grabbed me from behind. I lost my balance as something slammed into the backs of my knees, causing them to fold. My back crashed into the ground as a shadow passed over me.

"Who are you? Why are you here?"

I knew that barking voice. No matter how long it had been since we'd seen each other, I'd never forget the undercurrent of disapproval that defined my childhood.

"Barbara?" I gasped.

CHAPTER 26

I EXPERIENCED A weird sense of déjà vu, pinned to the ground by my own mother. We'd done this dance many times before, especially after I failed her ritual and she amped up her physical training. We'd go to some remote park and practice throws and blocks. Inevitably, she'd come at me and whip me into the grass. Her natural short chestnut curls would bounce down at me, piercing green eyes that matched my own.

Only now those curls had turned ash gray and wrinkles pinched the edges of her face. I wished I could call them laugh lines, but I think I could count on one hand the number of times that mouth lit up with joy.

Her grimace melted into surprise as she recognized me. "Melissa?"

"Yeah, it's me, your wayward daughter." I pushed against her arm across my throat. "Can I get up now?"

Instead, she tightened her hold, the pale pink gemstone coiled in wire on her necklace tapping me on the chin. "How do I know it's you?"

"Are you serious?"

Her eyes narrowed into slits. Yep, dead serious.

I couldn't go for her actual jugular, so I settled for the

metaphorical one. "You have a scar on your right butt cheek that I can only presume you got when someone tried to stab you in the heart."

Her scowl deepened, but she did ease up on my throat. "It's definitely you. How can you be so inappropriate?"

"Because life's inappropriately hilarious. Double hilarious since I found you here." This time when I strained against her grip, she moved away.

We stood at arm's length from each other. She wore her standard attire: jeans, comfortable sneakers, and a black leather jacket. She looked so familiar, I half wondered if I was in a waking dream.

"What are you doing here?" I asked.

"Isn't that what I should be asking you? You're trespassing."

I rubbed my temples, feeling the beginning of a headache coming on. "Please don't say you're part of the Blessed Order."

She pursed her lips in a thin line. I'd forgotten she did that when she was considering how much to tell me.

I should have pressed for more answers, but her presence evoked old habits. "Fine. Don't say it. I knew this was a long shot, and now I know it's not worth my time. Not if you're involved." I skirted around her to leave.

She stopped me with that death grip, this time attached to my shoulder. "How exactly did you get here?"

I jerked my arm out of her hold and shuffled to the side before she could snag me again. "I have this newfangled device called a cellular phone. It has a program full of up-to-date digital maps so you don't need to buy a paper version. You should try it sometime."

"Not here to this physical location," she snapped. "How did you get past the gate?"

"It's not exactly Fort Knox. I'm perfectly capable of walking around a freestanding gate."

Her eyes widened ever so slightly. "Not that gate. It's special."

"I don't have time for your statements shrouded in mystery. I've got real problems."

"Wait!" she yelled as I stalked away. "Why were you looking for the Blessed Order?"

"Definitely not for a family reunion," I called over my shoulder. I expected a snarky reply, and when I didn't get one, I turned around.

My mother had vanished.

I gaped at the spot where she'd been standing a second ago. "Barbara?"

"You're in trouble," she said right behind me.

I squealed, whipping back around to find my mom suddenly between the road and me.

"How'd you get there so fast?" I demanded.

She answered by grabbing me by the wrist. "C'mon. You're not leaving until I get some answers."

Ah, yes, the good ol' lecture tone. That worked when I was eighteen, but as a middle-aged woman, it'd lost authority.

Still, I hated that I sounded like my teenage self as I whined, "I can go wherever I want."

I tried to get out of her hold, but she put a second hand on me this time. I might have learned a bunch of tricks from her, but she'd always been able to overpower me.

I flushed, hating that a senior citizen, even one as athletically obsessed as Barbara, was gaining the upper hand. "Get off me!"

"Not until we talk."

We struggled against each other, my panic rising. I had serious mommy issues, but besides our training sessions, she had never physically tried to hurt me. I yanked back against her hold, and when that didn't help, I kicked at her calves. Not hard, but enough that she flinched in surprise.

She tried to maneuver her legs to provide leverage, but I got the jump on her before she could stabilize herself. We fell into soggy pine needles, all limbs and shouts and family angst.

Of course, Barbara wound up on top of me again. She held me face down in the dirt.

"We need to talk," she grunted in my ear. "I promise to let you go after our chat, but you can't just walk away from this conversation like a petulant child. Show me that you understand."

I slapped my hand furiously on the ground.

"Do it again if you agree not to run away."

Anything was better than suffocating to death. I continued to pound the dirt.

She released me, and I pushed away from her, breathing in lungfuls of sweet, oxygen-rich air.

Barbara marched us back to the gate. When I could finally speak again, I panted. "Did I flunk . . . your little test . . . again, Barbara?"

She entered a code on the lockbox. "I guess that depends."

"On what?"

The lockbox swiveled open. Instead of a key, a flat rock fell into her palm, the kind you might use to skip on a riverbed. She held it out to me, displaying a smooth hole in the stone's center.

"Do you feel anything?" she asked.

"Does the urge to call an elder care agency count?"

She glowered at me. "Be serious."

"I'm serious about those emotions. You're asking me if your rock donut gives me the tingles."

I expected her to retort at my flippant response, but instead she stared at the rock, confused.

After the silence got too unbearable, I asked, "Hello? Did I just break you?"

"If you could have done that, I would've died years ago." Her green eyes focused on me with an intensity I hadn't seen in years. "After all this time, you're finally showing your true potential."

I made an exaggerated show of wiping my hands

together, washing them of this situation. "I'm out. I ain't doing that whole Rite of Passage BS again."

"You don't have to do it again. I finally know what you can do."

"I've known what I can do for a long time. I can walk away."

"You're not even curious what I've discovered about you?"

"Nope," I said, popping the "p" for emphasis as I stalked away.

She waited until my shoes hit the road's asphalt before declaring, "You came here because of magic, didn't you?"

I halted in my tracks. This was my last shot at finding someone for help, but then again, this was my crazy mother.

I probably still would have walked away, but Barbara said the one thing that gave me pause. "It must be about your daughter."

I whipped around. My mother's shoulders slumped. I knew her as this rock-solid woman with a will to match, but her expression betrayed just the opposite.

Barbara was scared.

"How do you know this is about Regan?"

"Because parents often pass magic down their hereditary line."

I snorted. "Like you down to me?"

"Exactly."

A mirthless laugh escaped my lips. "Sure. You're magical. I totally believe that."

It was an argument almost as old as our relationship. Barbara always refused to show off her "abilities." Sure, she'd drop hints that she could do something mind-blowing, but she insisted she couldn't tell me anything until the time was right. When that time never came, I'd finally concluded real magic didn't exist.

Except things had changed in the last week. I should have adjusted my expectations about my mom accordingly.

It still took my breath away when she disappeared right before my eyes.

I blinked, but she didn't appear.

"Barbara?" I looked to the left and then the right.

She whistled behind me, yards down the road. She couldn't have gotten there without passing directly by me, which she hadn't.

She grinned at me, adding a digit to the number of times I'd seen her smile.

"Believe me now?"

CHAPTER 27

THE INTERIOR OF the pioneer home included many of its original features. Wall paneling continued up twelve feet to chipped crown molding. The front rooms were small and cramped with scratched hardwood floors throughout, the living room leading to the dining room, then to the kitchen. A massive black stove that looked more like a fireplace than an oven dominated the space. At least someone had taken the liberty of renovating the place with plumbing and electricity, so Barbara didn't have to light a fire to make tea.

I sat down at a worn round table cramped in the corner as she fiddled with the ancient sink. She didn't ask questions as she scuttled around, which I appreciated because I needed the time to collect my thoughts. Not only did I need to determine what I should tell her about my situation, I had to absorb the fact that she had superhero abilities.

"Must be convenient," I said out of the blue.

Barbara lifted the dented tea kettle to stop the flow of liquid. "What's convenient?"

"Being able to teleport. You never have to drive anywhere. Need more eggs? Just teleport to a grocery store, and you're good to go."

"It's not like that." She placed a mug in front of me, straight black tea. She hated sugar the way snails loathe salt. "I can only go short distances, usually to a spot where I can see or at least very close by."

"Still useful. You can escape boring conversations at cocktail parties."

She took a hearty swig of her own drink, probably to avoid swearing at me.

I grimaced. "I finally realized why you cook such bland food. If you can down this tea without flinching, you must have burned off your taste buds years ago."

"Is everything a joke to you?"

"It's a coping mechanism. It helps me get through stressful situations."

She raised an eyebrow. "Is that so?"

"Hey, I'm still coherent, aren't I? I just found out my estranged mom has powers straight out of a comic book. I think it's doing the job."

"Melissa." She dragged out my name. "Are you going to tell me what's going on with your daughter or not?"

I took a sip, letting the bitter heat seep into my worn body. "Maybe after you tell me what the Blessed Order actually is."

She pursed her lips. I thought she would refuse.

I was wrong.

"We're warriors who make sure the fae don't take over the human race."

"So, you're fae hunters."

"Only when they cross the line."

"How often do they do that?"

"Often enough."

I wanted to scream at this piecemeal information. "If my vice is joking at inappropriate times, then yours is the inability to lay everything on the table."

"I've taken a vow not to talk freely about the fae except when necessary."

That sounded a lot like Stronghold's policy. "It's necessary now. A pixie's trying to kidnap Regan."

"Tell me everything."

"After I hear more about what the fae are and why you're scared of them." I wanted someone else to give me their take on what was going on.

"They're scary magical creatures, Melissa. Surely inside all that garbage you watch on TV you ran across a fairy tale or two. Those old stories are based on historical fact, made palatable by time and morality. Fae have been on Earth for centuries, perhaps millennia."

"So why don't they rule everything?"

"Because we outnumber them."

That jived with Gabriel's story.

"And they're foreigners," Barbara continued. "They come from another realm, one apart from ours."

That's an interesting tidbit Gabriel hadn't mentioned. "They're interdimensional aliens?"

"I've never fought a little green man, if that's what you're asking," Barbara said dryly. "Not even a leprechaun."

"Oh good. Those aren't real."

"They are real. They're even short. They're just not green."

"How come only you seem to know about the fae?"

"Because they made a deal with humans a long time ago. In exchange for peaceful coexistence, we provide them anonymity. Only a select few government leaders and the Blessed Order even know they exist."

"And that works?"

Barbara folded her hands in front of her. "It works exactly because the Blessed Order keeps them in check."

"Why not just tell them to go home? Get off our lawn and all that?"

"They claim they are refugees. They won't tell us much but spout nonsense about some kind of war in their world. Personally, I don't think they want to go back."

At least Gabriel's story meshed with Barbara's, even if my mom provided more colorful commentary. Still, that left one obvious problem. "So how do you, presumably human, have magical powers?"

She straightened. "There's fae in our heritage."

I would have fallen down if I wasn't already sitting. "What?"

"Every paladin in the Blessed Order has some fae relative buried deep in their ancestry. Like I said, magic often passes down hereditary lines. That's how some humans like myself have abilities." She paused to point a knobby finger at me. "And now you too."

"Me? What can I do?"

"You walked right past the adder stone's defenses."

"You mean that donut rock you had in the lockbox?"

Barbara glared at me. "That adder stone emits a powerful aura around the front gates, causing extreme stress and fear to anyone who comes within its radius. Didn't you feel anything?"

"No." My pulse quickened, thinking of Jessie's terrified retreat. "If that's the case, why aren't you freaking out?"

"Everyone in our unit of the Blessed Order has imbued our blood into the stone. It doesn't affect us."

"You smeared that rock with a bunch of people's blood?" I wrinkled my nose. "Ew."

She ignored my disgust, leaning forward for emphasis. "You waltzed right past the adder stone. That's unheard of, even for the most powerful fae."

"Maybe it's because of your little blood oath. Your DNA is similar to mine, right?"

"It doesn't work like that. I can feel the stone's presence when I am near it, like a distant annoying buzz."

"Fine, so I can't feel a rock's aura. Who cares?"

"It means you're immune to its effects, which is called void magic and very rare." Her eyes lit up. "I always knew you were special."

I wanted to shake her. "Are we back to that stupid Rite

of Passage thing already?"

"It's not stupid! You are gifted, and if I had figured this out years ago, you would have been inducted into the Blessed Order as a paladin like me."

The regret in her voice jolted my memories. Suddenly, a childhood full of lonely nights, excessive training, and a host of other bizarre behavior made sense. My mom had been out hunting freaking fae while I made myself sandwiches for dinner.

Suddenly, tea wasn't the only bitter taste in my mouth. "I must have been such a disappointment to you."

She missed the sarcasm oozing off my words. "It was a blow believing you didn't possess any magic. I couldn't make any sense of it. The Blessed Order has no use for ordinary people. I kept waiting for your ability to manifest."

"And when it didn't, you pushed me away." *Like you always do*, I silently added.

"Even now, I don't understand exactly what you can do," she said. "You clearly are immune to some magic, like the adder stone. How far your ability extends needs more testing."

"Sorry to burst your bubble, but I'm long past the days where I ask myself what I want to be when I grow up. I have no interest in joining your little club."

She waved a hand dismissively. "Of course not. You're way too old to begin induction now, and you've obviously grown accustomed to a modern lifestyle."

"I'll have you know I have a healthy BMI for my height." Okay, mostly healthy.

"It's not about your physical form, although I can clearly see that needs work." I opened my mouth to protest that I run faster than a lot of other middle-aged women, but she continued. "Magic takes time to hone. You're like a pen someone bought two decades ago and never used. Who knows how much ink will actually come out now?"

I'd had about enough of being compared to useless objects. I stood. "Thanks for that stunning analogy. Maybe it's best I get going."

She let me stomp all the way to the doorway before asking, "What about your fae problem?"

I paused.

"You need the Blessed Order or you wouldn't be here," she said quietly. "I've told you my secrets. Now, it's time to spill yours if you want help from us."

Much as I hated to admit it, she was right. I sulked back to my chair.

She half-smirked. "It's just like old times, isn't it?"

"You acting high-and-mighty and me with no other option than to deal with you? Yep. Nostalgia overload."

Barbara nursed her tea and waited.

I started with short sentences. "Someone's been trying to kidnap Regan. Someone with dragonfly wings."

The sentences got longer as my story became more complicated. I didn't trust her enough to tell her everything, so I went with outlining the attacks, from the first glitter bombing to Creepy Cat Eyes. I stuck to the basic threats I knew plagued us, leaving Gabriel and Stronghold out of it, not quite trusting her enough for that part of my problem yet.

I wanted to see first how much new information she would tell me. "The people who attacked us called themselves the Circle of Elphame. Have you heard of them?"

"No, but that's not surprising. Fae rebels come and go like the seasons. It's hard to keep up."

Wonderful. "Why would they be interested in Regan?"

Barbara paused to consider it. "They might have discovered that Regan comes from a magical bloodline. They probably want to test her to see what kind of abilities she has."

My blood ran cold. "What would they do if they caught her?"

"Exploit her, of course. You've read stories where fairies steal babies from their mothers? Those aren't just disciplinary tales by spineless parents. The fae can use a gifted child in all sorts of ways. Their favorite tactic is to force them into magical slavery, since our human magic is diluted but still useful."

Great. Another point for the kidnapping column as motive. "They won't take her," I vowed.

"Of course not. Not if the Blessed Order's on your side." Barbara bowed her head in thought. "Does Regan display any magical talent?"

"She's smart, hardworking, kind . . . but no, I've never known her to control the weather or shoot lasers out of her bellybutton or anything like that."

Barbara straightened her shoulders. "I want to meet her and see for myself."

Somehow, this angered me more than all my childhood trauma combined. "Oh, so now you're finally interested in your granddaughter?"

"How else am I supposed to protect her?"

"Protect her or recruit her for your little cult?"

Barbara frowned. "What caused your sudden mood swing?"

"I asked you to come see Regan when she was a baby, and you couldn't be bothered!"

She narrowed her eyes. "When you ran away from home, you made it quite clear you didn't want anything to do with me."

"I wanted you to be excited about your granddaughter."

"Don't you think I was?" She slapped her fist on the table, her face twisted into a terrible mixture of grief and rage. "You wanted a normal life, one apart from my world. I gave it to you! No fae, no magic . . . isn't that what you wanted?"

I jerked backward in surprise. It was. She had. I'd never thought of it that way.

Her shoulders continued to heave. "I've dedicated my entire life to ensuring that the fae leave normal people alone. It's a stark existence." I thought I saw a freaking tear at the corner of her eyes, but she blinked it away before I could be sure. "I couldn't be part of your lives, even if I wanted to."

I sucked in a breath. "So, you *are* human."

She looked like she wanted to strangle me. "Melissa—"

"Sorry, I didn't mean to sound dismissive. It's just . . . wow. I never knew."

"You couldn't know. It wasn't your problem."

"Until now," I corrected. "You had to have made enemies in your line of work. Do you think they're after Regan because of you?"

"I doubt it. I've gone to great lengths to hide my identity and your relationship to me by proxy."

"This is the modern age. Information is everywhere. It wouldn't be hard to look up public records and find our connection."

"I suppose," Barbara said, although she sounded doubtful. "The fae are terrible with technology though. They're only now dabbling in it, and they're not good at using it effectively."

I blew out a long breath. "What now? How can you and your buddies help us?"

"We can hunt down this pixie and her druid accomplice. Take them into custody for interfering in human affairs, as per our agreement with the fae."

"Great!" I said, feeling a weight lift off my shoulders.

It all came crashing back down with Barbara's next words. "It may take some time, though. Our diocese is stretched thin at the moment. And in the meantime, you need to disappear."

"What do you mean?"

"I mean go into hiding. It would be best if we put you in a safehouse for a while."

A sharp ringing broke between us before I could argue.

Barbara pulled a phone out from her jacket pocket. After viewing the caller's name, she swore.

"I've got to take this," she said. "Don't go anywhere."

She slipped out to the front rooms, her voice becoming an inaudible murmur.

I took a swallow of tea, which was now cold as well as bitter. I knew what Barbara said was probably the smart thing to do. We couldn't keep putting Jessie and her family in danger. Regan and I should go off the grid for a while, at least until we knew exactly what we were up against.

That meant uprooting our lives completely. Regan would miss a ton of school. It would devastate her.

Barbara stuck her head inside the door and gave me one of her signature phrases. "I've gotta go. You stay here."

"Hey!" I called, scrambling after her. I caught up with her outside on the porch steps. "You can't just leave me here like I'm a little kid."

"I can. The adder stone will protect you here. You're safe." She didn't so much as break her stride as she marched toward the detached garage, a set of keys jangling in her hands.

"But not Regan. She's still at my friend's house."

This made Barbara pause as the garage door lifted, revealing a beat-up hatchback that looked like it had more dents than bolts.

I couldn't believe she still that had hunk of junk. "Your old beater still runs?"

"Japanese engines last forever." Barbara unlocked the driver's side door. I tried to pull open the passenger side, but it wouldn't budge.

She settled down behind the windshield, rolling down the window so we could still talk. "What's your friend's address? I'll pick Regan up."

"I can give you directions on the way."

"You can stay where I told you."

I backed away from the car as the engine roared to life.

"I could just wander off, and you'll never see me again."

She tried to melt me with her fiery gaze. "You wouldn't dare."

"Wouldn't I?"

The engine sputtered between us.

Grumbling, she leaned over and unlocked the passenger door. "Fine. Get in."

Barbara barely allowed me time to shut the door before she sped away, nearly giving me whiplash.

CHAPTER 28

BARBARA DROVE LIKE the controlled maniac she was, weaving in and around other cars as I gave her directions. Only one person gave us the finger as she cut them off. Not a bad ratio, all things considered.

"Isn't there any other way to get to your friend's house?" she grumbled.

"I'm afraid it's unavoidable, Speedy McWreckage. We need to cross the river."

I tried to duck out of the gaze of a startled jogger who gaped as we whizzed past her at fifty miles an hour. "Wouldn't it be faster if we took Center Street?"

"We can't." She took a sharp corner, narrowly missing the curb. "The protests are blocking traffic."

I groaned. "On a Sunday? I mean, don't get me wrong, I'm all about preserving our remaining forests, but can't they at least wait for business hours to bother the legislators who'll vote on the bill?"

"They're desperate," Barbara said grimly. "And desperate people do desperate things."

We whizzed past an intersection. "Like running stop signs?"

Barbara rounded on me. "I swear, if you keep up your

inane mumbling, I'll boot you from this car."

"Okay! Okay!" I waved at the windshield. "My lips are sealed. Just keep your eyes on the road."

She cut back onto a main thoroughfare, whizzing south toward the bridge. We passed through another commercial hub of town, a mixture of old homes, warehouses, and sporadic retail chain stores. We must have gone a half mile with light traffic, Barbara even easing up on her vehicular daredevilry, before we hit a dead stop. We got stuck in the right lane with parked cars on one side and a growing line of bumper-to-bumper vehicles on the other. Barbara cursed as the cars ahead of us didn't move after a full green light.

"We're a decent way from the Capitol." I craned my neck, unable to see around a pickup truck. "I wonder what the holdup is?"

Barbara answered by unbuckling herself and exiting the vehicle. She slammed the door shut before I could ask if she'd lost her mind. Weaving between cars in a spy-like slouch, she disappeared in a sea of metal.

The middle-aged blond in the car next to us gave a reproachful shake of her head. I returned it with a shrug of whatcha-gonna-do, but internally I agreed with her.

At least Barbara had left the keys in the ignition. As I considered scooting into the driver's seat, I heard a distant hum gathering in front of me. It grew louder through the next green light, and we still didn't move. A group of pedestrians powerwalked past us on the sidewalk, not quite running, but reminding me of animals fleeing a forest fire.

I quickly figured out why.

Protesters were suddenly everywhere: on both sides of the sidewalk, the oncoming lane, even beginning to trickle between the two lanes of stalled cars. They shouted some sort of chant about forests, but it was too garbled to make out their slogan. The blond shrank in her seat with fear.

Barbara suddenly reappeared at the passenger door, giving me a jump scare. She opened the door, and the decibel level rose.

"It's the protesters!" she yelled over the din.

I didn't have time to make a Captain Obvious jab as she reached around to unbuckle me. "What are you doing?"

"We've gotta go."

My jaw fell. "And abandon the car?"

"Yes." When I blocked her, she hissed in frustration.

"You're crazy! Just wait for it to pass and then—"

"It's the Circle of Elphame, Melissa. They're here."

I stopped fighting her. She used that opportunity to release the strap and pull me from the vehicle.

"Where?" I asked, barely audible over the shouts of angry environmentalists.

"I spotted a woman wearing that Celtic knot you described up ahead." Barbara opened the trunk and retrieved a ragged backpack. She flung it over her shoulder, jogging into the flow of people. "C'mon!"

I followed her in between the lanes of traffic, where the crowd was thinnest. I avoided looking at the frustrated people inside the vehicles, wishing I were one of them. A pair of dudes carrying signs tried to cut my mother off and slow us down, but she elbowed past them. When they turned around to complain, she bored her eyes into them as if stripping away their souls. They cowered, recognizing a superior menace.

I came up close behind Barbara so we could talk loudly at each other. "Why didn't we just stay with the car?"

"We'd be too vulnerable. Best to hide."

I looked at the salmon-like sea of protesters swirling around us, doubtful.

She continued. "If she gets too close to you, rip the Celtic knot off her. It's probably her focus object that she uses to channel her pixie dust."

"I'll get right on that if she doesn't fry me first."

The cars thinned out, forcing us to swell together into a mosh pit. Barbara grabbed my forearm to keep us together. Unfortunately, I reflexively pulled away, a habit born out of too many recent surprise attacks.

Once separated, people pushed in between us. I lost sight of her in the crush of sweaty bodies. Someone accidentally shoved me, and I stumbled. By the time I regained my balance, I'd lost even the direction where I'd last seen my mother.

"Barbara!" I cried, but no one could hear me over a chant that rose within the ranks. I scanned faces, catching glimpses of a mustached man, a girl with a round face and glasses, and a bald senior citizen. Everyone carried signs and chanted about trees.

Then I recognized a flash of auburn hair over gaunt cheeks. It could be Serena Fawcett. She began to turn her head in my direction.

The mob shifted and I lost sight of her.

Frantic now, I pushed in the opposite direction. Maybe she hadn't seen me, or maybe I'd been mistaken. There were so many people in the crowd.

A strange fog formed around me out of nowhere. Some of it went up my nose, tickling the hairs within. I sneezed. I wiped something brushing against my cheek and studied my fingertips.

Pixie dust.

The person next to me suddenly collapsed. Then another. A muffled cry rose around me as more people fell, accompanied by the sickening thud of flesh slumping to the concrete.

Out of the glittery haze, a gap opened up between Serena and me, a swath of unconscious bodies between us. She targeted me with those crazy eyes, her wings stuffed back into a hump underneath a heavy sweatshirt pinned with the Celtic knot. The knot shimmered with a crazy iridescent glow. I had nowhere to go, not with people at my feet and more protesters trying not to trample over the fallen.

Serena lunged for me, stomping over the backs of the

people she'd knocked out.

Before she could reach me, Henry from Stronghold dove out of the crowd. He slammed into Serena with a punch to the gut, but not before she could fling pixie dust in his face. He inhaled some of it and fell to the ground, choking.

As I tried to escape from both of them, the rest of the crowd realized something was terribly wrong. Chants morphed into the clamor of alarm. People screamed as they backed away. I nearly lost my balance but steadied myself. When I looked back, someone suddenly appeared to grab me, keeping me upright.

It was Barbara. I wouldn't have recognized her with the goofy gas mask if she hadn't also worn her signature black jacket.

"Didn't you hear the voice tell the crowd not to breathe that pixie dust?" she demanded.

"No," I replied, confused.

Then she shook her head. "Of course you didn't hear the warning. You're magically immune to sprite magic."

Before I could answer, a hysterical man knocked us apart, a surge of people filling his wake. I tried to squeeze back to where I'd last seen Barbara, but the crush forced me in the opposite direction. I couldn't see where I was going, taller people blocking my view. Before long, I didn't even know which direction I'd come from.

I eventually found myself plastered against a brick wall. A storefront. I crawled along the perimeter until I found an alley with a handful of other people seeking shelter.

Since I couldn't locate Barbara, I decided to put as much distance between Serena and me as possible. I ran down the alley onto another side street, then two more blocks, the protest crowd evaporating. I eventually reached one of the narrow side streets next to the river, an old railroad track embedded in the road. An empty field of weeds and trees lay sandwiched between two concrete warehouses. I hunched over my knees, taking huge gulping breaths. I was finally alone.

Or so I thought.

"There's nowhere else to hide."

A dark robe with yellow trim emerged from the street I'd just come from. Creepy Cat Eyes the druid must have followed me from the mob. He hadn't bothered to keep his hood up, letting his pointed ears jut out like miniature sails around his head.

I dashed toward the nearest warehouse, the only cover available, but before I could get close, the grass in the field next to it rustled. A low growl preceded two silver wolves emerging from the brush, trapping me between them and their druid master.

"We've been looking for you, Ms. Hartley."

I summoned false bravado. "My calendar is booked for the foreseeable future. You'll have to find another family to freak out."

He smiled at me, exposing crooked teeth. "Oh no. We definitely want your daughter. Where is she?"

"You think I'm gonna tell?" I would have sounded much more snarky if my voice hadn't cracked on the last word.

"Maybe," the druid said, "or maybe you'll just feed my wolves. Either option will suffice."

He whistled, and the wolves snapped forward.

A dark shadow passed over me, a whooshing sound filling my ears. My muddled brain associated it with the impending wolf attack, their mouths frothing.

A roar exploded in the sky, vibrating the marrow in my bones. The dogs whimpered and skidded to a stop as the stone giant, the same one that had swooped in during the high school attack, slammed into the ground in front of me.

My jaw went slack as the monster turned around, its rocky hide somehow flexible. For the first time, I got a good look at its face, framed by familiar dark brown hair with graying temples and inlaid with steel eyes.

The world spun.

The stone giant was Gabriel Alston.

Creepy Cat Eyes executed a series of whistles, sending the wolves scattering back into the field. Then he also took off in the opposite direction, retreating.

Gabriel's gray bat wings spread out as he roared a second time. He meant to pursue the druid.

I don't know what possessed me, maybe the compulsion to make sure I wasn't hallucinating, but I grabbed Gabriel by the rock-hard bicep. His skin felt like rough pavement.

He glanced down at me, his eyes filled with murderous rage. For a second, I thought it was aimed at me.

His expression softened. He placed a heavy hand over my own. "Are you okay?"

I nodded. I still couldn't speak. My voice had melted somewhere into the puddle of acid that now compromised my stomach.

Satisfied with my answer, Gabriel turned back to Creepy Cat Eyes, but he'd disappeared. A low rumble came from his throat, the sound of a jungle cat defending his territory.

I tried to make sense of the fact that my boss stood before me in inhuman form. The more I examined him, the more details I took in. His hands had grown large black claws like obsidian fingernails. He wasn't wearing anything, so I tried hard not to stare at his anatomically-correct crotch. A pointed devil's tail swished back and forth behind him.

"You're a demon," I breathed. The only thing missing were horns.

He jerked as if I'd slapped him. "No, I'm not."

"But you're not human."

He still grimaced, but he didn't deny it. "Why did you run away? I've been looking everywhere for you."

I blurted out the truth. "I found the black wolf's pelt."

He cocked his head in confusion. "What?"

I poked him in the chest and nearly bent a fingernail. "You killed the black wolf. I found his fur in your gym in a duffel bag. He's dead!"

Gabriel shifted, causing his wings to billow behind him. "He's very much alive."

"I just told you, I saw the pelt. Did you skin him alive?"

Dawning lit Gabriel's eyes. "It's not what you think."

"Nothing is what I think! I've got a pixie chasing my daughter, an animal whisperer with terror eyes who almost fed me to his wolves, my mom's a freaking fae hunter, and now this!" I waved my hands in his general direction.

"You found out your mom's part of the Blessed Order?" he asked.

"Really? Out of everything I just said, *that* is the detail that shocks you?"

He shuffled after me. "Melissa—"

Right above our heads, an intense light flashed brighter than a firework. I peered through the glow, everything an unnatural white, stunned by its sudden appearance.

Gabriel cried out, shielding his face from the light, as if completely blind. With the stone monster incapacitated, a new figure ran toward us, holding a blazing welding torch. I recognized the stocky man with the buzzcut as the crazy jaywalker I'd seen during a previous protest.

Buzzcut intended to cut through Gabriel with fire.

I acted without thought, putting myself between this new threat and Gabriel. "No!" I screamed.

The welding torch bore down on me.

Buzzcut noticed me midleap. He lowered his free hand, and the weird glow around us dimmed significantly. Unfortunately, he was committed to his attack. Momentum would not stop his welding torch from sizzling through me.

In the split second where Gabriel regained his sight, he smacked me aside with his tail. It knocked the wind out of me as I slammed into the ground, but it saved me a visit to the burn ward.

Gabriel intercepted the welding torch instead of me with a raised forearm. Gabriel roared as the weapon scorched his stone flesh. In one fluid movement, he swung his free arm and struck Buzzcut across the chest.

Buzzcut let out a rasp of air and flew backwards, landing in a heap several feet away.

Gabriel shook his head and blinked several times, still dealing with Buzzcut's too bright light. He saw me stir and helped me wobble to my feet.

"Are you hurt?" he asked, his voice strained.

"Only my pride." Then I winced as I touched my leg. "And maybe a bruise or two."

Gabriel emitted a low growl, refocusing his attention on a moaning Buzzcut. He let go of me to face his new opponent.

"Alston!" my mom's voice snapped down the street. "I should have known you were involved."

We all turned to find my mom with hair plastered to her sweaty face, her gas mask gone. She had glitter all over her pants but somehow not on her sacred black jacket.

She also wielded two pearl-handled switchblades. She never left home without some sort of pocketknife. I'd never actually seen her use them other than to open packages. Now she bent forward like some sort of ninja with the blades clenched in her hands.

"What are you doing?" I called to her.

Barbara never took her eyes off Gabriel. "Everything will be fine, Melissa. Just walk away from the gargoyle."

"G-gargoyle?" I repeated.

Gabriel's growl deepened. "Keep the Blessed Order out of this, Hartley."

"The Blessed Order got involved when your pixie went rogue."

"The pixie is not acting under the Court's orders. Neither is the druid."

Barbara's eyes narrowed. "So you say."

I could barely keep up with this surreal conversation.

"You two know each other?"

"The way an exterminator knows a rat." My mother pointed a switchblade at Gabriel. "You got my daughter involved in fae business, didn't you, stone lapdog?"

"My intelligence team says the two of you are estranged. You have no right to be here."

Barbara raised a superior eyebrow. "Melissa came to the Blessed Order for help."

Gabriel sucked in a breath, glancing at me. "Is that true?"

"Y-yes," I stammered.

Barbara beamed with victory. "The rules are clear here, Alston. She's under my protection."

Gabriel glowered. "It doesn't matter that she asked the Blessed Order for help. She's under my employment."

Her arrogance wavered. "She works for a software company."

"Not anymore. I hired her last week. She's under Stronghold protection."

"But not Regan!" Barbara announced. "You can't employ a teenager. The Blessed Order officially extends our protection to her."

Gabriel's face darkened.

I finally found my voice. "Will someone tell me why the two of you are posturing as if we're at an auction?"

"She's a fanatic . . . " Gabriel said.

"He's manipulating you . . . " my mother said at the same time.

That's when Buzzcut decided to regain consciousness. He stumbled to his feet and immediately bathed us all in a bright light, his hand clearly the source of this particular magic.

Apparently only I could see him because Gabriel and Barbara both concealed their faces from the light.

I'd had about as much as I could take of gargoyles, secret societies, and people with superpowers. I flew across the short distance and tackled Buzzcut back to the ground.

CHAPTER 29

I STRUGGLED AGAINST Buzzcut in a heap of limbs, fabric, and raw emotion. He tried not to hurt me, but I was done being passive. It was the world's most awkward wrestling match.

It took both Barbara and Gabriel to pry me off Buzzcut. Barbara explained he was another Blessed Order paladin named Chuck. He'd been monitoring the protests for a while. That set off Gabriel, who claimed that Stronghold had sole authority to protect the state capitol from fae mischief.

The two might have continued arguing all day if I hadn't reminded them that the pixie and druid were still nearby. While they agreed we shouldn't just stand around in public, neither of them could decide where to seek shelter. Both Barbara and Gabriel wanted to take us back to their own secure headquarters and refused to step foot in enemy territory. I finally pointed out that my neutral house was located not far away. Gabriel hopped me across the Willamette River with a few flaps of his wings while Barbara teleported the Blessed Order pair.

No one was on the trails or at the park, so we walked to the house unnoticed. Even Nancy's curtains were thankfully drawn up and closed, probably for her afternoon nap that she swore she never took. Once inside my living room, I marched into my bedroom to use the master bathroom. I could have used the hallway bathroom, but I needed the additional distance. Besides, the extra time might give Gabriel and Barbara just enough time to kill each other, which would save me the effort.

I took my time relieving myself of the day's coffee, then washing my face with refreshingly chill water. Muted sunlight trickled in through the window, highlighting my frizzy hair. On impulse, I brushed my grimy teeth. For a brief moment, everything felt ridiculously normal, like I'd slept in during a weekend. I couldn't even hear anyone yelling down the hall.

"Maybe it was all a dream," I told my reflection.

Barbara's voice cut through, loud and clear. "Quit dallying and get out here, Melissa!"

Nope, not a dream. "I'm almost done!" I said, sounding just like Regan when we were running late. Perfect. We were really coming full circle on this mother-daughter relationship.

I walked into the living room to find Gabriel dressed as a human in a T-shirt and jeans by the fireplace. He stood still as a statue, which now that I thought about it, was completely appropriate for a gargoyle.

"Where'd you get the clothes?" I asked him.

"Lucas brought them." He pointed out the front window to show Lucas rummaging around the backseat of one of Stronghold's black SUVs, parallel-parked on the street. He wore only a pair of athletic shorts and was barefoot for some reason. Chuck, who stood guard on our front porch, watched him with palpable animosity.

"Lucas is alive!" I exclaimed.

Gabriel's eyebrows scrunched in confusion. "Of course, he is."

"I thought he might have been killed." My eyes wandered over to the couch, where Barbara sat. Thrown haphazardly over the seat next to her was a familiar black fur pelt. "Where'd that come from?"

"It's Lucas's," Gabriel said slowly, as if the pace of his words would make me understand.

"She doesn't get it, gargoyle," Barbara said as Lucas came back inside, shutting the door on Chuck's watchful face. "She's never met a shifter before."

"What's a shifter?" I asked.

Lucas retrieved the pelt and flung it over his hair as if it were a hooded towel, the back legs dangling behind him. "Let me demonstrate," he said.

I averted my eyes as Lucas kicked off his shorts. "Why is he stripping in front of us?" I screeched.

Gabriel answered, "Lucas is showing you what kind of fae he is."

Soft rustles followed, then a bark. When I turned back around, Lucas had disappeared, the black wolf wagging his tail where the boy had stood.

"How?" I breathed.

Gabriel straightened from his sentry at the fireplace. "Lucas is a wolf shifter. He can change between his human and wolf form at will. As a human, he always leaves his pelt behind."

I stared at the wolf. "Lucas was protecting us as a wolf this whole time?"

Lucas nodded, trotting over to me. He smacked his forehead against my hand, asking for affection.

"I'm grateful, I really am," I told him, "but I feel weird petting a teenager."

"It takes some getting used to," Gabriel said.

I looked at Gabriel. "Are you a shifter too?"

"Not exactly. Gargoyles can transform directly between human and stone forms without a pelt."

"What happens to your wings?"

"Wings and claws extend or contract depending on which form I take."

"Does it hurt?"

"Does it matter?" Barbara interrupted. "He's a fae under Mab's control."

Gabriel bristled. "Queen Mab has faithfully maintained the treaty between human and fae for centuries. She is not responsible for the Circle of Elphame."

"What a wonderful excuse for her."

"Who's Mab?" I asked.

"Queen of the fae, the one who is supposed to keep them in line," Barbara said before Gabriel could answer. "There are the normal fae subjects who live off the grid or coexist with normal people, but then there is her inner circle. Alston here runs one of the country's biggest military defense contractors. That's not a merit-based position. Part of the treaty states the two sides must engage in mutual cooperation. It's a check and balance system between the fae and world governments. Stronghold's integration with our military is one of many concessions the humans have made to keep peace with the fae."

Gabriel's steel gray eyes turned cold. "Every society has a difficult history, but given how humans have been able to mostly live in peace, I'd say the fae have upheld their end of the treaty well."

"Then tell me why there's always so many 'rogue' fae to clean up after?"

"Because not all fae want to honor the agreement. Your pristine human world isn't full of saints either, the last time I checked."

"Of course not, but most of us don't have magical abilities to lord over weaker prey."

"No, money and power do that just fine."

I rubbed my temples against my swelling headache. "Can you guys spare me the simmering animosity? I don't care about politics."

"Well, you should," my mother scolded. "Politics is what brought one of Mab's most loyal servants to Salem, Oregon." She pointed at Gabriel.

"Stronghold is monitoring the protests," Gabriel said. "The Circle of Elphame has been causing Queen Mab problems for years. Killing innocent people, recruiting fanatics to their ranks, basically disregarding the treaty."

"Imagine that," Barbara said dryly.

Gabriel ignored her, continuing. "We tracked the Circle of Elphame to the Capitol protests."

"Why would they care about human legislation?" I asked.

"Because many fae live secretly in forested areas," Gabriel said. "Some are upset about the Oregon state government selling off more public lands. The Circle of Elphame is trying to fan hatred among those fae who may lose their homes if the bill passes."

I thought of the trio of workers I saw every afternoon. "So, you sent Henry, Naomi, and Noah to monitor the protests as Stronghold employees? Are they fae like you?"

Gabriel hesitated for a brief moment but nodded. "Henry is a sasquatch. He can turn invisible at will."

That explains his excessive body hair, I thought wryly. "And the twins?"

"Sprites. They can telepathically communicate."

"So that's what you meant during the riot," I told Barbara. "I wouldn't be able to hear the twins because of my void magic, right?"

Barbara made a swift cutting motion across her neck to get me to be quiet, but it was too late. Gabriel straightened with interest.

"You possess void magic?" he asked.

I nodded. "We just figured it out at the Blessed Order house. I walked past a stone that should have made me hysterical or something. It definitely worked on my friend Jessie."

"An adder stone," Gabriel said. "Like the one we had installed on the rental perimeter. No wonder you and Regan got past it."

Come to think of it, Regan had been acting weird when

we jumped the wall at Gabriel's villa. I hadn't made the connection until now.

Gabriel looked thoughtful. "This explains many strange things, such as why pixie dust doesn't affect you. Your void magic makes the dust useless."

Barbara scowled at me. "I wish you hadn't told him. The last thing he needs is more ammunition to hold over your head."

"It's better if I know as much information about Melissa as possible," Gabriel argued. "How else can Stronghold protect her?"

"Given your current track record, you can't."

Gabriel narrowed his eyes at her. "And I suppose that you and one other measly knight can stave off the entire Circle of Elphame when even Queen Mab can't pin them down?"

"We're paladins, not knights," Barbara corrected. "And unlike your precious queen, the Blessed Order can handle unruly fae."

This would get way out of hand if I didn't keep steering the conversation in a useful direction. "Okay, now I understand what's going on at the State Capitol. Do the protesters have anything to do with the people after Regan?"

"No," Gabriel said.

"Probably," Barbara answered simultaneously.

Gabriel rounded on her. "Do you have some sort of insight that I don't?"

"I just don't like coincidences," Barbara said. "I've done my best to distance myself from my daughter and granddaughter to hide their magical heritage, and yet suddenly, Stronghold is in town and my family is under siege. How else did these fae freaks learn about Regan's ancestry?"

My heart lurched as I connected the dots. "Regan took a DNA test recently."

"That shouldn't matter," Barbara said. "The fae should

not have access to her medical records." I could tell my mom was just getting warmed up for a fight with Gabriel.

I had to set her straight. "No, not a test at her doctor's office. She did it through a private company, the kind that share results with people who 'match' familial DNA."

Barbara paled. "She what?"

Gabriel nodded. "That information is often made public by such companies. Easy to obtain, even by the fae."

Barbara rounded on me. "Why would you let your daughter do something so reckless?"

"I didn't let her do it. She did it behind my back."

"But why?"

I wrung my hands in my lap. "Because she wants to find out who her father is."

"Why didn't you tell her yourself?"

Oh, that was rich, coming from her. "For the same reason I assume you never told me about my dad. It's none of her business."

Gabriel cleared his throat. "Regan's father is not nearly as important as determining what kind of magical powers Regan possesses. If they are minor, the attackers will likely stop trying to abduct her."

"She has no powers," I said.

"That you know of," Barbara said.

Gabriel actually agreed with my mom on this one. "Teleportation and void magic are pretty strong abilities. I'd be surprised if magic had skipped over Regan completely."

"It could take years to find out what Regan can do," Barbara said. "Most abilities manifest anytime between puberty and early adulthood. She has some time yet to go."

"Unless we can diagnose them now," Gabriel said. "The fae have a special way of determining one's potential magic."

Barbara pursed her lips. "What is that exactly?"

"It would be better to show you back at the Stronghold

office."

"Ah-ha, there's the catch," Barbara said. "You want to lure Melissa and Regan under your supervision and lock them away where the Blessed Order can't reach them."

"The rules are clear on this. We are under no obligation to allow you onto our property," Gabriel said. "Besides, we both know Regan and Melissa will be better served under Stronghold protection."

"And I know they'd be safer under the watchful eyes of the Blessed Order."

Lucas growled, his hackles rising.

I cleared my throat to get everyone's attention. "Not to rain on either of your parades, but I believe I'm the person with all the decision-making power here."

"You're my employee," Gabriel said.

"And you're my child," Barbara added.

"I can quit, and you haven't been an active parent in my life for decades." I straightened my spine to let them know I wouldn't back down on this. "Either my mom can escort us anywhere, including into Stronghold's office, or Regan and I won't come."

Gabriel's steel eyes tried to melt me on the spot. "Barbara is a member of an organization that looks for any reason to kill fae, and you want me to let her into a building full of them?"

"Not my problem," I said.

Barbara crossed the room to lay a hand on my shoulder. "You can't bully a Hartley."

I scooted out of her grasp. "Don't think this means I trust you either. You've got to swear to be on your best behavior and not hurt anyone, or I'll personally boot you from the building myself."

Barbara glowered at me. "Whose side are you on?"

"Neither, which is why I'm dragging both of you along. I'm tired of the half-truths and lies both sides have decided to dish out so far."

Gabriel didn't look happy, but he said begrudgingly, "I

can agree to this bargain. Barbara Hartley can accompany you inside Stronghold under her sworn word that she will harm no fae inside, but no other Blessed Order member may accompany you. Vanessa will conduct a thorough search of Barbara before she enters the building."

"So you can kill me once we're inside?" Barbara asked.

"I swear no harm will come to you unless you start it first," Gabriel vowed.

"This sounds like a good deal," I told Barbara. "Take it."

"Fine," she said, "but be warned, gargoyle. One false move, and I can teleport my granddaughter out of there before you can say 'stonewall.'"

"You'd leave me in there to die, wouldn't you?" I asked her dryly.

"I doubt I could carry you with void magic. And besides, you should have thought of that before you made me agree to such a stupid idea."

"Nothing is going to happen to Melissa," Gabriel said, his voice a low growl.

The two continued posturing with each other, but I let it slide. Despite the tenuous situation, I finally felt I had things tentatively under control.

CHAPTER 30

OF COURSE, MOST plans fail when met with the reality of a prickly teenager.

"What do you mean I might have magical powers?" Regan shrieked. The two of us were holed up inside Jessie and Paul's bedroom while everyone else waited for us to finish out in the front room.

It had been an awkward reunion to say the least. I had met Jessie and Paul on their front lawn. First, Jessie apologized profusely about her previous behavior, so I had to reassure her she'd been manipulated to ditch me at the Blessed Order house. Then she noticed my mom, and I had to fight her not to rip Barbara a new orifice for not being involved in Regan's life. When Gabriel stepped out of the dark SUV, Paul threatened to shoot him if he so much as dipped a toe off the public sidewalk. All this while the poor kids watched from the upstairs bedroom windows with wide eyes.

Gabriel and Barbara had not wanted me to tell Jessie and Paul anything, but that boat had sailed, so I filled them in. Paul looked sick while Jessie's expression turned murderous as I gave them the entire rundown. They were then sworn to secrecy upon pain of death, although given her expression, I gave Jessie good odds at the first kill. They both promised to keep this all from their children.

That just left breaking the news to my stressed-out child. I filled her in on every painful detail.

"I don't want powers," Regan whined loudly.

"Will you keep it down?" I hissed. "We don't want Leah and the others to know what's going on."

"Why?" she asked, though she did bring it down to a conversational volume. "Are you afraid they'll hate me because I'm a freak?"

"I'm trying to keep them safe from the same people who want to hurt you."

This made her calm down a notch. "You think they're in danger?"

"We're all in danger. That's why we're going to Stronghold to try to figure out what kind of magical abilities you might have. The more information we have, the better we can defend ourselves."

Regan plopped on her back over the Dunlaps' sunflower bedspread. "I can't believe this is happening. Who wants to have superpowers anyway?"

"I thought it was every kid's dream to be special."

"That's what they say they want, but they're also desperately trying to act like everyone else."

I chuckled. "Good thing we're not like everyone else. I've got magic too."

She drew her knees up to her chin. "You do?"

"Barbara called it void magic, meaning magic doesn't affect me. You remember when we climbed the wall at Gabriel's resort, and it freaked you out?"

She nodded.

"That wall had a series of magical stones to prevent anyone from scaling it. Normal people would run away from it in terror."

Her eyes widened. "So that explains why I felt so scared around it."

"Yes, but I didn't feel a thing. Gabriel thinks you might

have a dash of void magic too, given that you were able to get up and over the wall at all. Jessie and I encountered the same thing this morning at the Blessed Order house. Jessie ran away as if she'd seen a ghost."

"She was acting really strange when she came back home without you," Regan conceded. "Paul forced her to take a long bath to relax while he tried to figure out what had happened to you."

I rubbed her knee gently. "I don't know what the future will bring, but we'll face it together. One step at a time."

"Baby steps. Starting with figuring out what I can do." Regan flashed me a shaky grin. "What will you do if I can walk through walls?"

"Walk around naked in my bedroom so you'll never want to do it around me."

"That would do the trick."

With the mood somewhat lightened, I ushered her back to the living room. The Dunlaps quickly gathered around the front door to say goodbye. Regan gave Leah a lingering hug.

"Something's going on here," Leah declared after they untangled themselves. "I'm going to find out."

"Regan's just going to hang out with her grandmother for a while," Jessie said cheerfully, although she couldn't hide the strain in her voice. "Isn't that nice?"

"I thought you all hated her," Leah said. "This is super weird."

"Family relationships are complicated," I said wearily. "C'mon, Regan. Let's go."

As we marched to the SUV, Leah called out to us. "You'll be at the debate tournament, right, Regan? I'm volunteering for you. You can't miss it."

I nodded absentmindedly as I opened the back door for Regan. The debate tournament didn't really matter now, of course, but I didn't want to cause a scene.

Barbara scooted over to make room for Regan. My

normally aggressive mother couldn't quite meet Regan's eyes, although she examined her granddaughter as if she were precious gemstones.

"Hello," she said softly.

"Hey," Regan snapped back. She refused to even look at Barbara.

I caught Barbara's crestfallen expression before she slapped on her characteristic frown. Well, what did she expect after ignoring the kid during her entire formative years?

I could have forced Regan to let me in beside her, but she clearly needed some space from her absentee grandmother. So, despite my misgivings, I settled into the passenger seat next to Gabriel.

He eased away from the curb, casting glances at me now and again. I kept my focus solely ahead as if my life depended on it.

"I'll keep a security detail on your friends' house," he finally said. "They'll be safe from the fae, I promise."

"Okay." I should have sounded more grateful, but I was too overwhelmed to care.

Gabriel must have picked up on my tone because he asked, "Are you doing okay with all this?"

My sarcasm would not let that one go unanswered. "Absolutely. Just what I always pictured my midlife crisis to be. Thanks for asking."

He sighed as we flowed into midtown traffic. "I'm sorry things turned out this way."

"You mean that I found out anything at all? Sure, that tracks."

"I didn't mean that."

"Could have fooled me."

He stopped trying to talk to me, which was for the best, even if it made the lump in my throat three times larger.

Vanessa met us in Stronghold's underground parking lot, baton in hand.

"Really?" Barbara asked as we all exited the SUV. "A scrying wand?"

"It's the only way to determine whether you're bringing in something magical," Vanessa said in flat tones, motioning Barbara to step aside.

The thing chirped immediately as Vanessa waved it over Barbara's extended arms.

Barbara rolled her eyes. "It's reacting to my teleportation magic."

"I adjusted it for any internal aura." Vanessa continued to wave the wand over both Vanessa's arms and move slowly down her torso. "If you have anything else on you—"

As if on cue, the chirping crescendoed to a loud squawk. Regan flinched beside me.

Vanessa patted the offending area of Barbara's leather jacket. "Hand it over."

Grimacing, Barbara reached into her jacket and removed her pearl switchblades.

"They're imbued," Vanessa said. "What do they do?"

"None of your business."

Vanessa pursed her lips. "Maybe you don't know because you stole them from the fae?"

"Wouldn't you like to know," Barbara sneered.

Gabriel grabbed a bucket near Vanessa's feet. "Put them in here."

Barbara hesitated. "How do I know you won't mess with it?"

"You have my word."

"I'll need that spelled out, please."

Gabriel glowered at her. "We promise not to alter your belongings. You may have them back untouched the minute you leave the premises."

Barbara turned to Regan and me. "Lesson one in dealing with fae. Get them to be as specific with you as possible. While they are masters of deception, they prefer avoiding telling a direct lie." Then she tossed the switchblade into the bucket, followed by the gemstone necklace she wore around her neck.

With nothing else magical on Barbara, Vanessa followed us into the elevator. She faced us as we crammed into the tight space together.

Barbara squinted at her. "What kind of fae are you?"

"The kind that can take you down."

"She's too tall for a lot of types," Barbara told us as if Vanessa were an interesting object in the room and not a person right in front of us. "Not a dwarf, obviously. She's got the look of a court elf, but I doubt Mab would let someone of that stature be commanded by a mere gargoyle, no matter how high ranking."

Vanessa's eyes flashed dangerously. "If you're so curious, why don't you fight me and find out."

The elevator dinged and we spilled out into the lobby. We found Lucas standing watch in human form at Vanessa's podium leading into the inner offices. His eyes lit up when he saw Regan.

"Hey." He extended a hand, relief in his eyes as he viewed my daughter.

Regan marched up to him and punched him in the face.

Mild chaos ensued as Vanessa latched onto Regan while Barbara tried pushing the other woman over. If Gabriel hadn't managed to get between everyone, it would have been an all-out brawl.

"Enough," Gabriel said in a voice that boomed in the high-ceilinged room. When everyone stilled, he turned to Regan. "What was that about?"

She pointed at Lucas. "He tricked me by being a wolf and not telling me."

"I was protecting you." Lucas rubbed his jaw where she'd clocked him.

"You made me care about you."

His jaw fell open, but no sound came out.

Barbara placed a hand on her hip. "Lesson learned, child. Never trust a fae."

I pulled Regan closer to me. "We all just need to calm down."

"Easy for you to say." Regan created distance between us. "You're not the one getting thrust into a secret underbelly of society that's been trying to kidnap you."

"And neither are you," I lobbed back. "Do you really think I'd let any of these people near you if I thought they'd hurt you?"

She fumed but didn't reply.

Gabriel seized the opportunity to motion us into the main office. "We'll need to access the restricted area to test Regan."

We fell into a tense silence, Gabriel leading the way with us Hartleys behind him, Vanessa and Lucas taking up the rear. I had to admit, I was both nervous and excited to see what this restricted area business was all about.

We snaked through the corridors to that last hallway, where those plain metal doors with that out-of-place blue cube frame stood like horror movie twins at the end of the hall. This time, the thin, credit card-sized rock stuck at the frame's apex caught my attention. It had a perfect hole in the middle of it.

An adder stone.

Not surprisingly, my mother halted before she could even see the door. Regan cowered behind me.

"Get that thing out of here!" I heard my mom demand.

Gabriel reached up and gave the adder stone a sharp twist. It fell neatly into his hands.

"At least now we know why this didn't affect you," he said to me.

"Lucky me."

After shoving the adder stone into his pants pocket, he began to pull other stones off the frame. They appeared to be held in place by stakes jammed into the wall. Instead of pocketing those much larger stones, he swapped them with other stones' positions, solving some sort of puzzle in a pattern that only he knew.

"I'm waiting!" Barbara yelled.

Regan began to whimper. I threw my arms around her. "It can't hurt you. It's all in your head."

Gabriel put one final cube back in place, then stepped back. I wondered why until, like someone had flipped a switch, a strange glow surrounded each stone. It lit up carvings I hadn't noticed in each cube for a few seconds before fading back into normal looking rock.

As if on cue, the lights in the hallway went haywire. Now I knew what had been causing the weird power surges over the last few days.

With the light show finished, Gabriel opened the doors. I tensed, imagining what kind of wonderous place all the Stronghold employees always disappeared to. Would it be a golden hall? A breathtaking mountaintop? Some high-tech military complex?

Instead, the door led to a plain cement room with shelves. It was the kind of utility room you might find inside any office building, and not a very big one at that. Gabriel stepped inside just far enough to toss the adder stone on a bare surface, then came back and shut the doors.

Something like fear crossed Barbara's face as she watched Gabriel rearrange the stones again. "That's a fairy ring!"

Regan's eyebrows furrowed in confusion. "What does that mean?"

"It's like an instant doorway," Lucas said. "We use them to travel quickly to predetermined magical locations.

Barbara's entire body had gone stiff. "It's a trap! It will probably lead us right to Queen Mab herself."

"It doesn't," Lucas insisted.

She didn't look like she believed him. "Or maybe this goes straight back to your accursed motherland."

"Hardly," Gabriel said wryly. "Even if it were possible to open a fairy ring to the Old Realm, which it absolutely isn't, your world would be overrun with terrible monsters that would destroy everything you hold dear in less than a week."

I chuckled before I realized no one else thought it was a joke. "Are you serious?"

"Yes," Gabriel said. "There's a reason we don't return to our home. It's not ours anymore."

"What sentimental lies," Barbara said. "You don't want to go home because you like exploiting humans. So much easier prey than your powerful brethren back home."

"Believe whatever fanatic doctrine the Blessed Order has taught you, Hartley." Gabriel slid the last stone into the place, and the doorframe lit up again to expose the stones' many runes. "Not everything is so black and white as your fanatical leaders would have you believe."

My mom opened her mouth, probably with some derisive comment, but it became lost as Gabriel opened the doors to a truly breathtaking landscape. A wide cavern spread before us. Columnar stalactites appeared to hold up a tall ceiling. A wide hole in the roof sent beautiful rays of sunshine down to the shimmering turquoise pool below. The glistening rock surrounding the body of water held patches of yellow and green algae, covered by an artist's worth of refracted light patterns.

Gabriel stepped through the doorway toward the pebbled beach. "It's time for a dip in the Aesir Pool."

CHAPTER 31

WHILE LUCAS AND Vanessa had no problem strolling into what looked like a Hollywood set of a mystic cavern of wonders, the rest of us mere mortals hung back.

Barbara could at least articulate her reluctance. "Aesir Pool? As in the old Norse gods? Is this some kind of fae booby trap?"

"The place was named by regional humans eons ago when they mistook fae for the old gods," Gabriel said. "Those ancient fae created this pool to wash the birth from their newborns born on Earth."

Regan wrinkled her nose. "And you want me to swim in it?"

A smile tugged at Gabriel's lips. "Those days are long gone. The pool is quite clean, but all those washings gave the water here special qualities. Anyone with fae blood who dips into the pool will experience a change to their skin."

"I'm not sure our dermatologist would approve." I said, worried for my daughter.

"It's quite safe," Gabriel said. "Here, let me demonstrate."

He removed his socks and shoes. The T-shirt also came

off in a hurry, exposing his finely chiseled chest. As he shed his jeans and reached for his boxers, I flushed and turned my head.

Barbara elbowed me. "For pity's sake, they're just genitals."

Regan snickered.

Gabriel put one large foot into the water. Us Hartleys stayed on the Stronghold side of the door, able to watch everything due to the slope of the cavern.

Nothing happened at first besides Gabriel sinking lower and lower, the reflected pool highlighting all his muscular curves. As he approached waist deep, though, a dark sheen appeared over his skin. Pitch black at first, it hardened into an obsidian-like glaze until it covered his body, even the parts of him not yet submerged. His wings slowly crept out of his back, made of the same stuff. By the time he stopped at heart level, he looked almost like an ebony version of his gargoyle form.

"Whoa," Regan said.

"As a gargoyle, my skin hardens into rock, which is reflected in these waters" he said, his lips strangely fluid for looking so stiff. "Your transformation may give us a hint to your abilities."

Then he climbed back out of the pool, his wings receding into himself while his body shifted back to normal.

"I don't like this," Barbara said so quietly only I could hear her. "You don't know if that water will do something else to your daughter."

"Then I'll try it first." I stepped into the doorway.

I smacked my face against an invisible barrier. Hard. I yelped and stumbled backward.

Regan steadied me by the shoulder. "What happened?"

Gabriel's steel eyes went grim. "Apparently Melissa's void magic applies even to fairy rings."

"You'b gob to be kibbing me," I said with nasal overtones, hand over my throbbing nose.

"Maybe we should call off the whole thing?" Regan looked hopeful.

I tweaked my nose like a rabbit. It was already starting to feel normal, so I thankfully hadn't broken it. "And wonder what kind of magic you might have? That seems like a losing strategy."

Barbara looked from me to Regan and shrugged off her jacket. "Fine. If someone needs to do this, it might as well be me."

"What are you doing?" Vanessa demanded as my mom kicked off her boots on her way to the water.

"Testing this before my granddaughter." She shimmied out of her pants, her skin wrinkled but still more firm than many people decades younger than her. As she removed the rest of her clothes, she pointed at me. "If I die in here, you tell Chuck everything you saw. He'll take care of Regan."

"You're not going to die," Lucas growled.

"Says the fae mutt." Barbara waded thigh deep into the pool.

I blinked as a wavy shimmer surrounded my mom, almost like watching a highway desert on a hot summer day. It surrounded her body, making her entire figure blurry. Before long, all you could see of her was a weird rippling at the water's surface where she'd been.

"That's freaky," I said.

"Feels fine though," she said in a begrudging tone. The disturbance in the water moved back toward shore, her body slowly shimmering back into view.

Gabriel regarded my naked mother as she scrambled for her clothes. "Are you convinced now it's harmless?"

I turned toward a nervous Regan. "It's up to you. I won't make you do anything you don't want to do."

She watched the pool's lapping surface. "What will happen if I don't have any powers?"

"Nothing," Gabriel said. "You'll just get wet."

"I mean, after that. Will the fae stop chasing me?"

"They'll have little reason to go after you if you don't have any magic," Barbara said, adjusting her tank top back over her chest.

Regan straightened with purpose. "As long as I don't have to take my clothes off, I'll do it."

"Whatever makes you the most comfortable," Gabriel said.

Regan kicked off her shoes and stuffed her socks inside, leaving them on the Stronghold side of the doorway. She took a step forward, but instead of just marching through to the other side, she faltered. She raised one hand above her forehead and lurched, as if facing off against a strong wind.

"Is something wrong?" I asked.

"It feels like it's pushing me back." Regan gritted her teeth as she waded through the doorframe.

Gabriel regarded her struggle. "It must be a side effect of the partial void magic you inherited from your mother."

Unlike me, Regan eventually made it through to the other side. Then she marched down to the water's edge. I pressed my forehead against the invisible barrier, which felt completely solid to me. I wished I could go with her, but this vantage point would have to be enough.

For the first time since she was born, I silently pleaded she was a dud.

Regan waded into the pool, her water-logged jeans slowing her strides. She shrugged out of her jacket and threw it back to shore, leaving her in a T-shirt.

"It's cold," she complained, rubbing her bare arms.

She trembled as the water went past her waist. We all held our breath waiting for something to happen, but as her teeth chattered with the water lapping near her shoulders, nothing happened.

Regan whipped and flashed me one of her brilliant smiles. I raised my hands to give her two thumbs up in return.

That's when the light began to shine around Regan.

It started small beneath the water's surface, as if someone had switched on a light bulb underneath her feet, but it soon spread, enveloping her entire body so that she appeared made of light. The natural dust in the air ignited like fireflies, casting a golden hue on the slick, wet cavern walls.

Even more impressive than the illumination was how it affected everyone in that room. Gabriel and Barbara stared at my daughter as if they had never seen anyone so beautiful in their lives. Unflappable Vanessa opened her lips and began to sing, her gorgeous voice belting out an opera-worthy aria in a foreign language that made my cheeks flush. No wonder she preferred live music if she could sing like that. Lucas even howled in human form.

Stunned by this response, Regan's smile drained away, morphing into terror. The light evaporated. The entire room darkened as if someone had thrown a blanket over it.

It felt like the beginning of a horror movie.

The cavern's occupants similarly shifted moods. Vanessa's glorious song became minor key. Barbara and Gabriel crouched low as if facing a threat in the water. Lucas hunched over and growled, a deep sound that cut through the sudden tenor in Vanessa's voice.

"Get out of the water!" I yelled at Regan.

Regan scrambled for the shoreline, the water now black and shiny like some kind of slippery ooze. It crept over Regan, emanating from somewhere inside her.

I worried it would swallow her whole.

"Hurry!" I yelled.

"I'm going as fast as I can!" she snapped. Lucas howled as if to accentuate her point.

I banged a fist against the invisible wall, wishing I could get in there and praying the others wouldn't attack her.

They didn't. They merely watched as she ascended from the pool, sopping wet and angry like an alley cat.

The moment her soles hit dry pebbles, the atmosphere

of the cavern returned to normal. Regular sunlight filled the room and the water returned to its pristine quality. The occupants shook themselves out of their dreamlike stupors. Vanessa's song died on her lips.

"What was that?" I yelled.

Gabriel shook his head. "I think we can say that, without a doubt, Regan has magical abilities."

CHAPTER 32

"SO NOW WHAT?" I asked, sipping coffee at the conference table. I needed all the comfort juice I could handle.

After the Aesir Pool incident, the Hartleys and Gabriel had hunkered down in the Stronghold conference room. Gabriel had found a towel for Regan to sit on as we tried to outline a plan for what to do next. Lucas had left to guard the front door, while Vanessa had been dispatched to get some dry clothes for Regan.

"Can you even tell us what kind of magic Regan has?" I demanded.

"Some sort of power that affects the mind, but we can't be sure exactly what." Gabriel maintained his infuriatingly patient demeanor, as if it might rub off on my frazzled nerves.

"I've never seen anything like it," Barbara said. She stood by the door, ever the sentinel, but even so, she looked a little spooked. "It's as if something from inside Regan permeated my very soul."

"How can we figure out specifically what she can do?" I asked.

"This isn't like your comic books where a radiation

blast turns a man into an overgrown hunk of muscle," Barbara chided. "Abilities will manifest in their own due time."

"Time that we don't have right now," Gabriel said. "We must continue to keep Regan safe under Stronghold care."

"Don't you mean 'our' care?" Barbara said. "Last I checked, Regan hadn't formed any sort of alliance."

"I vote for dual protection," I said. Better to keep both parties close until I could figure out who was easier to trust: my overbearing fanatical mother or my super-secret fae employer. Ugh, what a choice.

Regan shifted from her balled up position in the swivel chair next to me. "Does anyone care what I think?"

"I'm sorry, honey." I rubbed the crook of her elbow. "Do you want to add anything?"

She yanked her arm away. "Only that I don't want to be under anyone's supervision. I have a life, you know."

"There will be no more school activities," Gabriel said. "Not until we can subdue your attackers."

"I hate to agree with the stone devil," Barbara said, "but there's no way to keep you safe in public."

"Someone from Stronghold can look after me like Lucas did before," Regan protested.

Gabriel steepled his fingers in front of him on the table. "After what the Circle of Elphame did to your mother at the protest, it's clear they are getting more desperate."

This made me pinpoint something that'd been bothering me. "How can they get away with that, actually? Everyone in that crowd had a camera in their phone. That whole incident should have gone viral by now."

"Fae magic and electronics don't mix well," Barbara said. "Cameras often can't record it. The video will either abruptly end or get all blurry."

That explained why Lucas's video of Serena in the high school office had been cut off. "There were tons of witnesses in that mob."

"The key word in that sentence is 'mob.' The authorities tend not to give protesters a second thought."

"Can we get back to what's important?" Regan interrupted. "What happens to us now?"

"We'll take you someplace safe," Gabriel said. "I'll place a rotating group of Stronghold employees on guard—"

"As well as the Blessed Order," Barbara interjected.

"—until we can find the pixie and the druid," Gabriel finished.

"How long will that take?"

"Anywhere from a few days to a few weeks, depending on how far they've gone underground."

"You're going to lock us away like prisoners for a month?" Regan looked like she wanted to throw up.

My shoulders slumped in defeat. "I'm not sure what else we can do at this point."

Regan opened her mouth, but no words came out. She realized we were making the best choice possible. It was just a bitter pill for someone so young to swallow.

"Excuse me," she said. "I need to use the bathroom." Then she slipped away on a hiccup.

I felt my own eyes well up.

Barbara scowled at me. "Stop with the crocodile tears."

Anger raced through me. "Slipping back into stellar parental habits there, eh, Madam Paladin?"

"Regan's not a baby," my mother said. "She's old enough to understand the stakes."

"She's also still a kid."

"I was fighting fae scum when I was her age."

Gabriel cleared his throat, which was just as well because we'd been escalating into a classic Hartley showdown. "We'll do the best we can for Regan, but first of all, we'll need to get her out of the building safely with a decoy. I'll dress one of my employees in bulky clothing and release her out the front door. Then we'll make a big show of escorting the decoy away from the building in case anyone's watching. No one will know the difference if we execute it right."

"You think the Circle of Elphame knows we're here?"

"I think it's better safe than sorry. In the meantime, we can arrange the fairy ring to take Regan directly to my rental house in the woods."

"You mean the villa," I said.

Before he could correct my choice of words, Barbara spoke up. "It should go without saying that I will stick to Regan like glue wherever they take her since you, Melissa, can't accompany us."

"Sounds good."

I waited for Gabriel to disagree, but he merely nodded. "We'll escort Melissa separately when the coast is clear," he said.

I thought of a better idea. "Or you could just use me as the decoy. Regan and I have the same general build and hair color."

Gabriel frowned. "I don't know if I like putting you at that kind of risk."

"You'll be putting me at risk either way the moment I step out the door. Besides," I couldn't help adding a little jab, "you're the top muscle around here, right? Are you worried you can't protect me?"

"You don't need to stoop to insults," Gabriel said coolly, although by the set of his jaw, I could tell my barb had hit its mark. "Let's get Regan to safety first, then be on our way."

* * *

Of course, what's an escape without a little drama?

Not because of any rogue fae or anything like that. Just teenage hormones as we tried to bustle Regan through the fairy ring to Gabriel's villa. She wore some new clothes courtesy of Vanessa, who went through the portal first.

Lucas had turned back to his black wolf form at some point. Before he could follow Vanessa, though, Regan blocked his path so he couldn't reach it.

Regan pointed at him. "He's not coming."

Lucas growled.

"Why not?" Gabriel asked. Barbara and I stood behind him.

Regan lifted her chin. "I don't want Lucas around anymore."

"I thought you liked him," I pointed out.

"Mo-o-om!" Apparently, I'd committed a three-syllable offense. She reddened but made her case to Gabriel anyway. "I don't trust Lucas anymore. He spent too long stalking me. It's creepy. You've got a whole crew. Find a replacement."

"He's not going anywhere," Gabriel said. "We need his skillset."

"Why?" I asked. "He's barely a teenager."

When it was clear Gabriel wouldn't elaborate, Barbara gave out a disgruntled sigh. "Shifters in their animal form have some immunity to mental attacks. If Regan's powers develop further, he'll be less likely to be affected by them."

"I don't care," Regan said. "Find someone else."

I stepped up to my stubborn daughter. "Regan Allison Hartley." Yes, I'd pulled out the dreaded middle name. "It's time to face reality. Lucas stays."

A flash of pure anger, even worse than when we'd fought over the DNA test results, lit her face. "You're just going to let these strangers call all the shots?"

"These strangers can catch the people who want to harm you."

"And then what? It's not like we can pretend I'm not some sort of freak. Do I live in hiding for the rest of my life? Or maybe I'll go join Grammy Barbara's club and learn how to kill fairies or something."

"'Grammy?'" Barbara repeated as if she'd just swallowed gum.

I held open my arms to Regan, pleading. "I don't know what the future holds, honey. I'm just as confused by this as you are. Together, we'll figure it out."

Regan glanced at each of us. Her focus settled on me. "I hate you."

Ouch.

Hurtful remarks aside, she was going through a lot. I motioned her toward the door. "C'mon."

Regan gave us all as wide a berth as possible in the narrow hallway and leaped through the fairy ring.

Barbara opened her mouth to make some scathing remark, but whatever was written on my face made her pause. She quietly followed, Lucas on her heels.

"She doesn't mean it," Gabriel said softly beside me.

"I know. It's the oldest trick in the offspring book." Yet it stung enough that I had to take a deep breath before adding, "Alrighty. Ready for me to play decoy?"

"You shouldn't be so glib about this."

"Sorry. It's what I do."

He laid a strong, heavy hand on my shoulder. The contact sent warmth throughout my body. Then he motioned for me to come to his office.

I thought I would just wear something generic to cosplay as Regan, but someone must have gone to our house because on Gabriel's office chair, I recognized the rainbow heart patch on Regan's favorite hoodie.

"Who gave you permission to rummage through my house?"

Gabriel shrugged. "We've done it before. Who did you think fixed the gaping hole in Regan's bedroom?"

My mind whirled. "You guys did that?"

"Not me personally. Ida did. She's one of our best engineers."

"Whoa." Suddenly, I understood Ida's irritability over the last few days. If I could fix a blasted wall in one day, I wouldn't want to be called a mere "building manager" either. I tugged Regan's hoodie on, wishing it wasn't so tight in the chest.

Gabriel escorted me back through the main lobby and down into the underground parking garage. Naomi met us there, already seated in one of the two company SUVs with Noah sitting in the passenger seat. I waved at them, but they didn't reciprocate the gesture.

Once inside the second car, Gabriel explained his strategy. We would drive slowly around downtown, Gabriel on the lookout for anyone following us. The twins would trail behind at a safe distance. Once we confirmed we didn't have any stalkers, we'd make our way to Gabriel's house in the woods.

Gabriel drove around Salem like a grandpa despite the roads being relatively clear, checking all his mirrors constantly. He caused more than one irritated suburbanite to whip past us like a maniac.

As we watched a harried housewife in a minivan zip around him through traffic, Gabriel asked, "Why do so many mothers drive like that?"

"Insane levels of stress. There's always something to do: groceries, housework, playdates, educational activities . . . and that's just for the married ones. When you're parenting solo, you also have to cram in a full workweek in there somewhere with no outside support."

Gabriel cast me a sympathetic look as we stopped at a red light. "And I thought I had it hard leading a company."

I dismissed that compliment with a wave. "That's not to say you aren't busy. Most working people are whether they have children or not."

"Raising a child isn't just a paycheck, though. You mess up your job, you get fired and move on. Mess up a kid, and you've ruined someone's entire future."

I couldn't prevent my face from flushing. I'd never had any bachelor ever understand my life like that before, and I'd worked with plenty in the software industry.

"You sure you don't have kids stashed away somewhere?"

"Absolutely not. I would raise my own children with my mate."

I couldn't help but tease. "How do you know she'd stay with you?"

Gabriel's steel eyes went dark. "Gargoyles don't do family halfway. It's everything to us."

Something about the intensity of his expression made me believe it. "So, you've never found the right gargoyle?"

"She doesn't have to be a gargoyle. And no. Running Stronghold doesn't leave me a lot of time for dating."

"That, at least, we have in common."

He gave me a long, assessing look. "I suppose we do."

My fingers curled into the leather seats as I thought of him dipping naked into the Aesir Pool. Then I mentally kicked myself. There were way more important things than my libido going on. I needed to get a grip.

The light changed to green, and Gabriel returned to his Sunday driver speed. A long silence spread between us.

I thought maybe he'd gone back into surveillance mode, but he surprised me by suddenly declaring, "I know you don't fully trust me. I have to earn that."

"Where did that thought come from?"

"My line of work won't allow me to be completely honest with you. That doesn't mean I don't care what you think. I do. I'll find a way to prove that you can trust me through my actions."

I wanted to believe him. I was an independent woman, through and through, but that didn't mean I liked adulting solo. I wanted to find someone to live my life with. Someone like Jessie had in Paul, who could share in life's ups and downs. An equal with whom we could face life together.

Then Gabriel had to burst my romantic bubble by adding, "It's my duty not only as your employer, but as Stronghold's leader to maintain peace between fae and humans. We will figure this out."

My poor desperate heart had jumped to the wrong

conclusion. Gabriel didn't see me as a potential partner. That was my hang up. To him, I was just another security risk he had to solve.

And dammit, I was grateful if his duty kept my child safe. I fought back loneliness to remind myself of that.

"Yes," I agreed. "We'll get through this rogue fae thing together, and then Regan and I will be out of your hair. We're not going to burden you forever."

I thought I saw his eyes narrow at my statement, but then he got distracted by pulling onto a quiet industrial street. A construction site loomed at the far end, abandoned for the weekend. Gabriel drove over the dirt-encrusted entrance, past the warning signs to keep out and behind the steel frame of the building.

We exited the vehicle. Gabriel opened the trunk and began rooting around for something, so I surveyed the lot. Construction vehicles rested among piles of rubble and stacks of supplies. Then Naomi's SUV pulled up, ready to take over our car.

I realized I didn't see a third vehicle. "I don't see how we're going to drive to the villa."

Then Gabriel slammed the trunk shut, and I got a good look at him.

Gabriel had turned into gargoyle form, his wings stretching in outspread glory. He towered over me, a monster with fangs and tough stone skin. The sight of him naked in this form should have made him less appealing, but my heart sped up to full-sprint levels.

"We're not driving," he said.

Before I could unpack that statement, he scooped me up in his arms and took off into the air.

CHAPTER 33

MY STOMACH LURCHED as Gabriel soared upward at an alarming rate. I watched a bulldozer shrink to toy size and buried my face in the crook of his neck. I got my nose flattened for my trouble.

"Ouch," I muttered miserably.

Gabriel looked down at me, the wind tousling his hair as his bat wings propelled us still upward. "You okay?"

"Peachy," I said around chattering teeth. I was still wearing Jessie's borrowed jacket, and it didn't mask the change in temperature. The altitude made my ears pop painfully.

"You're cold." Gabriel drew me in closer. Despite Gabriel's hard exterior, he radiated heat like any other living creature. I just had to make sure I didn't bruise myself, physically or emotionally, trying to get closer to it.

"You could have warned me about your flight plan."

"You might have refused."

"You think?"

"It's the safest way to get you to Regan. Even if the pixie tried to follow us via flight, she'd have to expose herself above the treetops to keep up."

We had reached cruising altitude, about as high as

migratory geese. We'd already passed most of the city, the outlying forests taking over residential neighborhoods. Only snaking roads and the occasional farm property hinted at man's breach into the mountainy wilderness below.

I clutched him tighter. "Don't let me fall."

"I won't. I know my wings are made of stone, but they fly just fine."

I hadn't realized that, but upon closer inspection, his bat-like wings did have a textured edge to them. "How does that even work?" I demanded.

"They're lighter than they look."

I couldn't stifle a groan. "I'm going to die."

"You need a distraction." He scanned around us in all directions. "Look behind us, straight to the west."

I craned my head over his shoulder, and the sight took my breath away. Mt. Hood, Oregon's tallest mountain, broke out on the range like a god, its eternal snow cap glistening shades of orange and pink in the declining sun. A haze of clouds surrounded it as if drawn by a master artist, giving the summit a heavenly halo.

"Okay, you win. That's beautiful."

His arms tightened around me. "Very beautiful."

My blood warmed another few degrees. I tried to comprehend this ridiculous moment. I was soaring through the air in the embrace of a very attractive gargoyle. Had you told me a month ago this would be my life, I would have snorted coffee up my nose laughing so hard. Right now, though, it felt like a waking dream.

But all dreams come crashing into reality. Mine did in front of Gabriel's villa, where Regan and my mom waited for us inside the massive front archway. Barbara had the same look on her face the time I snuck out of the house for junior prom and she caught me coming home at midnight.

Gabriel did not seem nearly so concerned. "Is something wrong, Ms. Hartley?"

"Chuck can't get past your adder stone barrier." She pointed to the gate near the brick fence. "You need to let him in."

Gabriel opened the door and motioned us in. "No."

Barbara stormed in after us. "That wasn't the deal. The Blessed Order is supposed to protect Regan on equal footing with Stronghold."

"The Blessed Order is allowed to aid in Regan's defenses, which is the only reason why you're even allowed on the premises. I won't compromise my defenses beyond one fanatic inside."

Barbara turned to me. "Are you going to let him do this?"

"Chuck can stay outside the gates, can't he?" I called to Gabriel's back.

"He can be wherever my security systems allow him to be."

"There," I said with a majestic wave of my hand. "Problem solved."

"Problem not solved," my mother retorted. "What if there is an enemy breach inside the house?"

Gabriel, still in his gargoyle form, swiveled to give her an arrogant smile with lots of fang. "Then I suppose that means the enemy is better at infiltration than the Blessed Order is."

My mother sputtered, unable to conjure an appropriate comeback.

Gabriel led us back to the suite we'd stayed in before, only this time, Henry stood guard outside, slumped against the doorframe in boredom. He straightened when he saw us approach.

"Who's that guy?" Regan asked, glaring at him.

Henry's eyes narrowed at her. "I see manners flow downhill in this family."

"This is Henry," Gabriel said. "He's on rotation to help guard you."

"Why?" Regan demanded.

"Because you're the one everyone's after," I said, my patience wearing thin. I wrinkled my nose at Henry. "But why does it have to be this guy?"

"'This guy,'" Henry gestured to his hairy neckline, "saved you from that pixie, or have you forgotten?"

"Whatever, Bigfoot."

Henry's face reddened.

Barbara tittered behind me. "They hate being called that."

The hairs in Henry's sideburns actually stuck out when he got angry. "They also hate being talked about as if they aren't right in front of you."

"Enough." Gabriel's harsh command broke through our squabble. "Barbara, you can take the suite across the hall. It has a similar setup as the other one. I think we all could use some food and rest for the night."

My rumbling stomach reminded me I hadn't eaten much that day. Letting things mellow until tomorrow sounded just perfect to me. I didn't have much energy left, and by the haggard looks all around, everyone could use some sleep.

Everyone, that is, except Regan. As we shifted to go our separate ways, she flung her hands up in the air. "So, that's it?"

"What now?" my mom asked.

"You just expect me to follow orders? Have Mommy"—she pointed at me—"tuck me in for the night and just go to sleep? Wake up in the morning and start my life as a prisoner?"

"You're not a prisoner," I said, exasperated.

"Oh yeah?" She flipped to Gabriel. "Can I leave your little villa?"

"It's not a villa," he said emphatically. "And of course not. We're protecting you."

"Do you want to get kidnapped by those lunatics?" Barbara asked.

Regan ignored her. "Can I at least go for a walk

outside?"

"If a guard accompanies you," Gabriel said.

"Or me," Barbara added.

"What if I don't want company?"

"It's just a precaution," I ground out. "I'm sure they'll stay a few steps back—"

She interrupted me. "Can I even go swimming in the pool by myself?"

Gabriel's wings, which had remained folded tightly behind him in the relatively narrow hall, threatened to jerk open. "I will do my utmost to give you privacy, Regan, but you must be monitored at all times."

Regan shook like a volcano about to burst. "Constant surveillance sounds like prison to me."

I opened the door to our suite. "C'mon. Let's talk about this."

She breezed past me into the room. "At least give me my own cell to wallow in." Then, before I could respond, she slammed the door in my face.

Henry tucked his chin into his chest hair, obviously trying not to laugh.

"Well," I said, unable to keep the irritation out of my voice. "I guess I'm staying in another room."

Barbara clucked in disapproval. "You're going to let her get away with that stunt?"

"It's not a stunt," I snapped, unable to contain my own raw emotion. "Regan's in over her head, just like me, only she's sixteen. She doesn't know how to handle it. To her, it feels like her whole world is falling apart." *Because it very well may be*, I silently added to myself.

My mom never did employ any type of empathetic parenting. "If you've been indulging her like that all these years, no wonder she acts like a spoiled brat."

"The way you raised me, dear mother, is obviously the kind of performance that deserves an encore." I turned to Gabriel before she could respond. "I don't suppose you have yet another suite? Because if I have to share a room with Barbara, I'll sleep in the pool house."

Gabriel gestured to the next door down the hall. "All the suites on this floor are similar. Help yourself."

"Don't mind if I do." I tipped my imaginary hat off to everyone. "It's been real, but not real fun." Then I skittered off to my room before anyone else could throw a temper tantrum, including myself.

CHAPTER 34

IF I THOUGHT a few days of rest would cool things down, I was wrong. If anything, living in limbo made everyone crankier. Regan kept mostly to her room, unwilling to talk to me. I tried to engage her, and when that didn't work, I channel surfed through the suite's ginormous cable options, not focusing on any one program for more than five minutes. She ended up increasing the volume until I took the hint and left.

Henry and Lucas took shifts guarding Regan's door. While the black wolf seemed content with this duty, Henry looked like he'd rather eat nails. I heard him ask Gabriel if he could be put on the team searching for the Circle of Elphame, but he was denied. I tried to say "Hello" a few times, but that just made him more upset because he had been trying to be invisible, a trick that didn't work on me. I eventually ignored him completely, which he reciprocated.

I wish I could have also pretended Barbara didn't exist. She tried to talk me into ditching Stronghold for exclusive Blessed Order protection roughly fifteen times a day. My constant refusals made her usual sour mood spoil to epic proportions. She claimed she wanted to be out searching for the Circle of Elphame, but we'd "tied her hands" because Gabriel wouldn't share any information on where they might be. She generally spent her time either working out in the gym or calling Chuck on her cell phone to give him updates.

My only sane daily conversation was with Gabriel, who would usually come back to the villa in the evenings. I'd spot him landing as a gargoyle on the master suite balcony, not far from my bedroom window. He would knock on my door a few minutes later in human form, dressed in casual clothes.

"Still no trace of either the pixie or the druid," Gabriel repeated on the third day, standing in my suite doorway. Apparently, our last skirmish had caused them to go underground.

"How could they just disappear? I thought you had ties to fae communities."

"We do, but as you well know, many fae are upset about the proposed forest bill."

"What does that have to do with tracking down the druid and the pixie?"

"Fae protect each other," Henry spoke up behind him. He was doing a shift outside Regan's door. "They're not going to lift a finger to help two pitiful humans when they have to worry whether their brethren will have a home tomorrow. In fact, they might even be inclined to help a rebel fae to make their anger known."

"Which is why it's madness for you to put your trust in Mab's crew," my mom's breathy voice echoed down the hallway. She had a towel wrapped around her neck, having just come back from the gym downstairs.

Gabriel's steel eyes hardened on her. "Are you insinuating that I'm not doing my job?"

I joined Gabriel in glaring at her. "Just suck it up, Barbara, like the rest of us."

The doorknob behind Henry jiggled. A red-eyed Regan stuck her head out the door. Snarls snaked through her hair, her pale complexion only adding to her zombie-like appearance. "What's all the commotion out here? You caught the guys yet?"

Barbara snorted. "Hardly. We were just discussing Gabriel's lack of progress."

"Great. Thanks for waking me up for that update." She turned to hide back in her suite.

"Regan," I called before she could shut the door again. "Are you hungry? I can get you something to eat."

"I'm fine." The door slammed shut.

Barbara tsked, crossing to her door. "Someone needs to look after that girl."

"It won't help," I tried to warn Barbara, but to my surprise, Regan opened the door and smiled at her grandmother. I tried unsuccessfully to squash my jealousy as Barbara disappeared into Regan's suite.

I must have stood there looking absolutely pitiful because Gabriel's gentle hand came to rest on my shoulder.

"We'll catch them. I promise."

"Thanks." I detached myself from his soothing touch to make my own escape to my room.

* * *

I didn't sleep well that night, so I finally just got up early. Dawn had barely made any inroads against the heavy clouds hanging outside. I got dressed in my last set of clean clothes. My suite had run out of coffee, but I knew there were extra supplies in the larger kitchen downstairs.

All thoughts of roasted brew vanished when I found no one guarding Regan's suite. A quick peek confirmed no one was inside. Alarm bells buzzing, I checked Barbara's room across the hall. Also empty.

Worse case scenarios flickered across my brain as I ran downstairs, searching for anyone. No one appeared on the ground floor either, not even in the gym. I was about to go into full panic mode when I saw a familiar black wolf stretched out by the pool house.

Jogging to Lucas, I called out to him, "Is Regan inside?"

He barked in affirmative.

I let out a long, deep breath of relief. I hoped this meant Regan had finally decided to quit sulking.

The hot rush of air that greeted me when I opened the door came as a welcome reprieve to the cool early morning. I held the foggy door open for Lucas to enter the pool with me, but he made a point of hunkering down in the damp grass. I supposed the heat of the pool would be torture with a fur coat on.

I found not only Regan, but Barbara swimming laps in the turquoise water. My mom had clearly made it a competition, pushing Regan to go faster and keep up with her insane pace.

I settled on a mesh metal chair next to a matching table to watch them. My heart twisted seeing them together doing the kind of things Barbara and I used to enjoy. Those sweet memories had been tainted knowing they'd all been to prepare me for a life of fae hunting. On the flip side, Barbara had gotten Regan to snap out of her hermit funk, something I'd failed to do the last few days.

Regan didn't notice me until they'd finished swimming and pulled their dripping bodies out of the pool. Wearing matching Stronghold bathing suits highlighted their genetic similarities, my mom's facial features reflected in my daughter.

"What are you doing here?" Regan asked as she toweled off.

"Couldn't sleep. You?"

"Doing something more useful than moping around," Barbara answered for her. Her disapproval shifted to something like pride when she said, "Regan's quite the athlete."

"She's been on the track team since middle school," I said.

"I'm a pretty mediocre runner," Regan added. "Where I really shine is debate." That declaration caused her eyebrows to droop.

"Oh, honey." It dawned on me the significance of today's date. I walked toward her with open arms. "I'm so sorry."

She ducked past me and ran out of the pool house, Lucas hot on her heels.

"What's got her in such a snit?" my mom asked.

"Regan's been preparing for months for a debate tournament that starts today. She's their star competitor."

"Life's full of disappointments. She better get used to it sooner rather than later."

"Wow, that's insightful. Do you charge for each grizzled tidbit of wisdom you dispense?"

"Make jokes all you want, Melissa." Barbara wrapped her own towel neatly around her waist. "Regan's different now. She needs someone who can help her navigate life with magical abilities. That's not something you learn at a public high school."

I balked. "You think I'm going to let you cart her off to the Blessed Order when all this is done?"

"I don't think you have much choice. It's either that or let her get crushed by the fae."

"Or she could just live a regular life. I stayed integrated in the normal world even though I have some magical juice. It's possible."

Barbara headed toward the pool exit. "Possible because no one knew you had any so-called 'juice.' The cat's out of the bag with Regan. It's only a matter of time before she'll need to figure out where she belongs."

Regan and Lucas had long since disappeared inside the main house. We would have done the same, too, if a furious thwapping sound hadn't caught our attention high above our heads.

Gabriel swooped toward the villa in full gargoyle form. Initially heading for his balcony, he spotted the two of us and changed course to smack down in the grass, uprooting dirt as his claws dug in.

"Where's Lucas?" he demanded.

"He went upstairs with Regan," I said, my adrenaline pumping. "What happened?"

"We have a lead on the Circle of Elphame." Without explaining further, he lumbered into the house, bellowing the shifter's name.

Barbara and I scurried after him. Gabriel zipped up one side of the double staircase in the foyer, both of us following on his wingtips. Lucas came zipping back down the second story hall, Regan sloshing after in her damp swimsuit.

Gabriel ignored the gathering crowd of Hartleys and focused on Lucas. "We found the pixie's former hideout. Documents left at the scene indicate the duo plan on making an appearance at the high school today to intercept Regan. It's the perfect opportunity to ambush them."

The wolf howled.

Regan's face went pale. "They're going to attack the school?"

Gabriel nodded. "They think you're at a debate tournament. With Lucas's nose, we should be able to track them before they get anywhere near the building. The tournament doesn't start until this afternoon."

"And if you don't?" Regan asked, voice rising to hysterical levels. "What about the people inside?"

"They'll be safe," Gabriel said. "I can get a whole team in place by noon. It shouldn't be an issue."

Regan shook her head, looking at me. "Mom, Leah's going to be there. You can't just put her in danger."

To my surprise, my own mother spoke up in favor of this plan. "It should be fine. Chuck and I will accompany the gargoyle to ensure the mission goes smoothly. Noon, you say?"

Gabriel narrowed his eyes at her. "Stronghold can handle it alone."

"Just like you've been 'handling' it the last few days?" Barbara walked over to put her arm over Regan's drooping shoulders. "You are ruining this poor child's life. The least you can do is accept all the help you can get."

Gabriel turned back to Lucas, ignoring my mother completely. "Let Henry know he's on duty here, then immediately come to my room for a debrief. We're going to need your tracking skills."

Lucas dashed off at full tilt, presumably to find Henry. Gabriel also lumbered off toward the master suite.

Regan's hands shook in fists at her side. She pushed my mother's arm off her shoulders and, without a word to either of us, fled back to her suite.

"Looks like she took the news well," Barbara said dryly. "Are you going to go talk to her?"

"I don't think anything I say will help right now," I said quietly.

"Well, somebody should try to comfort the poor girl." Barbara said, pulling her phone out of her pocket. She disappeared into my daughter's suite.

That left me alone and bewildered on the landing. I had no idea what to do. Even during the lowest points of my life, I'd always had a plan.

Now I just stood there, waiting for someone else to solve my problems.

"There's nothing you can do," I told myself, but I couldn't erase the sense of helplessness that had settled in my gut.

CHAPTER 35

AROUND NINE O'CLOCK I got sick of channel surfing. It wasn't distracting me anyway. I turned off the TV in my suite and picked up my unwashed clothes off the floor. I'm sure Regan had a similar batch. Doing something productive wouldn't necessarily snap me out of my funk, but it would make me feel useful. Plus, hooray for clean underwear.

I carried a garbage bag half full of dirty clothes into the hallway. Henry wasn't on guard duty, and Regan's door was ajar. Barbara had probably convinced Regan to do more physical training. I squelched another surge of envy and instead focused on the wrinkled pile at the foot of Regan's bed. I shoved all her clothes into the same garbage bag and slung the pack over my shoulder, Santa Claus style.

I only belatedly realized that I had no idea where the villa's laundry facilities were. I searched the entire second story with no luck. I had to switch my pack to the opposite shoulder as I hauled the clothes downstairs. I finally found the stupid laundry room tucked in an alcove not far from the gym. A man had definitely designed this building. No woman in her right mind would stash the laundry machines as far away from the bedrooms as possible.

The facilities contained an extra-large washer and dryer set. I separated the clothes into two piles, light and dark, then shoved all the lights in the washer. I thought for sure that I'd find detergent in the cabinet above the large stainless-steel sink, but no, the room contained no useful laundry supplies.

Argh! Off on another round of the world's worst scavenger hunt.

I wandered around the first floor in search of a utility closet. My search led me across the foyer, past the ballroom and its ridiculous piano, and into the spacious kitchen. Henry sat at the long breakfast bar staring off into space. Three coffee cups surrounded him, indicating he'd been having a drink with the others at some point.

"Hey," I called. "You know where I could get laundry detergent in this forsaken mansion?"

Not a single muscle on Henry twitched.

"Rude much?" I grumbled, heading for the pantry. It wasn't until I'd made it across the room while he hadn't so much as blinked that I realized something was wrong. I switched course to stand next to him.

"Hey." I snapped my fingers in front of his face.

That at least got him to sway a little. "The coffee's great," he muttered, cupping one hand around the mug. "Thanks."

"Henry?" I grabbed his shoulders and gave him a shake. "Snap out of it."

My touch set off some sort of instinctual response. He jerked out of my grasp, losing his grip on the mug. It smashed into a few slick pieces on the tile floor between us.

"What's going on?" he demanded, his voice a low growl.

I raised my hands and took a step back so he wouldn't attack me. "I don't know! You tell me. Where's Regan?"

Henry put his hands on either side of his head as if

working through a headache. "She told me to enjoy the coffee."

"Did she do something to it? Did Barbara?"

"No." He tilted as if disoriented. I'm glad he didn't step into any mug shards as he sat back down on the stool. "Regan kept telling me to stay and drink some coffee, over and over. It…didn't feel right."

I froze, remembering what had happened in the Aesir Pool. Had Regan somehow used her emerging magical powers on him?

His next words seemed to confirm it. "Barbara had her fingers in her ears, humming a tune." He glanced up at me with wide eyes. "As if she didn't want to hear Regan speak."

"Where'd they go?"

A muffled boom rattled the wall, making the fancy chandelier above us shake. Hanging pots underneath a cabinet crashed to the ground, adding to the disorientation. We both grabbed the breakfast bar counter to steady ourselves as the vibrations settled back down.

"There!" Henry pointed out the window facing the front of the house. A trail of smoke plumed out from behind a grove of trees near the gate.

I ran out the huge front double doors, Henry keeping pace with me. He wobbled unsteadily at first but eventually evened out as we sprinted down the long driveway. I had flashbacks of Regan's and my first escape down this road, only this time I was looking for Regan rather than trying to get her to safety.

What had she done?

We got our answer as we approached the wrought iron gates. Or what was left of it anyway. A six-foot crater of smoking rubble had been blown straight through it.

Henry pointed at chunks of smooth rock off to the side. "They blew up the adder stone!"

The sudden roar of a vehicle's engine sounded from beyond the fence. We leaped over the smoldering debris just in time to see a dented pickup swerve down the dirt path, the back of Regan's hair clearly visible in the driver's seat.

My body went rigid with disbelief. "You don't even have a license!" I screamed.

Regan's blue eyes met mine in the sideview mirror. I read the shame written there even as she sped off, alone, into the foliage toward the road.

She left behind Barbara and Chuck standing side-by-side, waving like two doting idiots after her. Chuck even yelled, "See you later, honey!" with moisture in his eyes.

Henry couldn't move, dumbfounded. I, however, had no room left for shock. I had nothing left but rage, aching for an outlet.

I found it in my mother's face. I marched right up to her oddly serene smile and slapped her as hard as I could.

She wobbled backwards, hands covering where I'd struck her.

"Regan!" she yelled at me, snapping out of her calm demeanor. "What are you doing?"

"Wrong Hartley," I corrected, pointing at the dirt cloud that indicated where Regan had gone.

Horrified realization split across my mother's face. "Regan?" she asked softly. Then she stood back up and waved her fist at the sky. "Come back!"

I grabbed my mother by the leather jacket and pulled her so close I could smell the coffee she'd drank on her breath. "What have you done?"

CHAPTER 36

BARBARA CONFESSED TO helping Regan practice her weird mental magic. Regan could talk people into doing things for her. This really shouldn't have come as a surprise, given Regan's recent success on the debate team.

But it certainly would have been nice if Barbara had told us instead of trying to exploit Regan's power for her own selfish reasons.

It took everything I had not to strangle my mother right there. "Let me get this straight," I said in a low whisper to recap Barbara's story. "You convinced Regan to hypnotize Henry so you two could ditch him? And then you had Chuck blow up the adder stone so you could escape?"

Barbara smoothed her hair, a clear tell of guilt even if she would never admit her fault. "I told you the Blessed Order should be in charge of protecting Regan. Once your gargoyle neutralizes the rogue threat, the fae will do something horrible to her. Since you wouldn't listen to me, I had to get Regan away from the fae before that could happen."

A near hysterical laugh burst from my lips. "Then why are you two zealots still here, while Regan's cruising around in Chuck's pickup?"

"Because she turned traitor by using her hypnotism on us." Barbara scowled at me. "Really, this is all your fault."

My jaw was so rigid, I should have cracked a tooth. "How do you figure that?"

"You clearly groomed her disobedient nature. She's just like you, running off when she's told to stay put."

There wasn't a chainsaw in the world strong enough to cut through the layers of my mother's cognitive dissonance. "She was supposed to stay here under Stronghold care. You're the one who encouraged her to run away!"

Barbara shrugged nonchalantly. "I guess that's one way of looking at it."

I had no choice. I leaped forward to grab her throat.

Henry, of all people, pulled me back before I could get in a squeeze. "You can't kill her."

"Just let me maim her a little!" I managed to twist out of his grasp, but he restrained my arms again. "She'll heal. Mostly."

"We're wasting time," Henry said. "We need to figure out where Regan's gone."

"Why don't you teleport after her, *Mom*?" I yelled her parental title sarcastically. "Fix this mess you made."

"Because I told you, *child*," she scolded in the same tone. "I can only teleport places within sight, and I can't just pull off tens or hundreds of jumps in a row. She's out of my reach in a vehicle."

As much as I wanted to come to blows with my mom, I had bigger problems. Regan was out there, completely vulnerable, with nasty people gunning for her. I stilled enough that Henry cautiously let me go.

"Where do you think she'll go?" Henry asked.

"The high school," I answered with certainty. "She's worried about her best friend getting caught in the crosshairs at the debate tournament this afternoon." I turned to Henry. "You got an extra vehicle stashed somewhere? If we hurry, maybe we can catch up to her."

Henry ran back toward the mansion. "There's a garage out back."

We all followed Henry down a paved road that curved off the main driveway toward a discrete corner of the villa. Four RV-sized doors boasted the garage's capacity. Henry pulled a clicker out of his pocket, and each gleaming white door curled upwards to expose matching black SUVs.

"Gabriel doesn't like variation much, does he?" I asked as we entered the garage.

Henry patted the hood of the left-most vehicle. "I need to go inside to find the keys. Be right back." He jogged up a set of mini stairs with beautiful wood carvings—because even the villa's garage had fancy features—and disappeared inside the house, leaving the door open behind him.

Once he was gone, I faced my mom and Chuck. "You two are not coming with us."

"Of course, we are," my mother said. "You don't know what you're up against."

"Henry will call Gabriel. We're covered."

She flinched as if I'd spat in her face. "You'd trust a fae over your own flesh and blood?"

"I trust the person who didn't plot to run off with my daughter. If it wasn't for you and ol' Chuckles here, we wouldn't even be in this mess."

Chuck grimaced, turning the scar on his chin white. "I don't laugh."

"The name works because it's pure irony."

Out of the corner of my eye, I saw Henry return wearing what appeared to be a gas mask. I half turned to him, but he shook his head fiercely. He must have been invisible because the others didn't notice him.

I realized what he meant to do and faced my mother again. "I mean it," I said. "You're staying here."

"I don't care what you want," Barbara declared. "I'll teleport us into the car if you attempt to leave. It's not like you can drive off without me seeing where you're—"

Henry came up behind her and sprinkled something in his gloves over her head. She cut off mid-sentence, slumping to the floor in an unconscious heap.

Chuck whirled around, searching for an enemy that he couldn't see. Henry walked right up to him, glove diving back into a leather pouch. He threw the same shimmering particles on the other paladin. Chuck, too, crumpled onto the cement.

A few of the twinkling dust particles fell onto my shoulders. I wiped some onto my fingertips.

"Pixie dust?" I asked Henry.

He gingerly tied the leather pouch back together before taking off the gas mask. "It will put them to sleep for a while." He shoved the gloves, mask, and pouch into a corner of the garage. "Just for the record, it still freaks me out that you can see me all the time."

"Still, let's give a shout-out to teamwork." I held my hand up for him for a high five. "Nice job!"

He pulled a key fob from his pocket to click an SUV open.

"C'mon, don't leave me hanging," I scolded.

He slipped inside the car, the engine roaring to life.

I opened the passenger door before he drove off without me. "Yeesh. With that sunny attitude, I'm surprised you're going to let me come."

"I wouldn't except Gabriel told me my number one priority is to keep you safe, no matter what. If I left you here with the Keystone Knights, who knows what would happen to you."

"Score one for bureaucratic orders, I guess?"

He braked while backing the SUV out of the garage to give me a hard stare. "You'll stay out of trouble, do you understand? One false step, and I'll whack you unconscious, boss's orders or not."

"It's not my favorite threat, but I can live with it."

Henry gunned backward out of the garage in a dizzying

twirl. With lips grim between his sideburns, I decided to keep my mouth shut from any other quips for the time being.

* * *

We'd hoped to catch up to Regan on the road, but she had too much of a head start. Plus, drivers on rural mountain roads were literally the worst. We got stuck behind a middle-aged man in a shiny new sports car. He drove at just the suboptimal speed to create a parade of annoyed cars behind him, our car at the forefront. No one could pass him because of the curvy roads, and he sped up whenever there was a passing lane so we couldn't get around him.

Henry edged the SUV toward the center line, wondering if he should try to chance swerving around the sports car illegally.

"Don't you dare," I warned. "If you think Gabriel's going to be mad when he finds out Regan's gone, think how he'll react if I get squashed by an oncoming semi."

Henry grumbled but resigned to riding the guy's bumper.

Out of habit, I pulled out my phone and absentmindedly opened my email app. That's when I noticed an email message sent two days ago from the school which had fallen into my spam folder. It was from the debate coach and labeled, "Urgent."

My heart raced as I clicked it and found that the debate tournament had been moved to start in the morning due to a scheduling issue with the athletic department. All debaters and volunteers were asked to be at the school no later than 9:00 a.m.

It was already 9:15.

"The debate tournament started early today!" I screeched at Henry. "That's why Regan looked so awful this morning. She must have seen the message earlier and knew that setting up a trap by noon would be too late."

"Why didn't she say something?" Henry demanded.

"If you haven't noticed, she's not big on trusting you guys. Can you call Gabriel and let him know about the time change?"

Henry shook his head. "Gabriel and Luke can't carry phones in their nonhuman forms, and Vanessa's magic tends to mess with cell phones. I can leave a message for her, but it's a stab in the dark."

"Well, it's something. Do that."

He did, even though he grumbled about it being a waste of time.

After another fifteen excruciating minutes, the roads finally widened into two permanent full lanes, and we were able to pass the sports car driver. By that time, we'd reached the outskirts of Salem, just a mile from the high school. Henry booked it a good twenty miles over the speed limit. We thankfully didn't encounter any traffic cops as we pulled onto the school's street.

The front parking lot lay mostly empty, except for a cluster of beater cars the students drove. We spotted Chuck's pickup truck right away

"Bingo!" I cried.

Henry parked not far from Chuck's pickup. As I got out of the car, a howl filled the air. My body tensed as I whirled around, expecting the druid to appear with his minions. Henry must have thought the same thing because he dashed around the SUV to stand in front of me, the vehicle's metal body protecting me from the rear.

Instead of the druid's pet wolves, though, a familiar flash of black fur bounded out from the wooded area behind the school. Lucas snarled, ears flattened on either side of his head and teeth bared. His yellow eyes caught mine, but instead of coming toward us, he made a beeline straight to campus, disappearing in the breezeway that led to the annex.

We didn't have time to follow as a massive shadow

suddenly blocked out the sun above us. Gabriel's bat wings sounded like whipping sails as he landed beside us. Vanessa glided down not far behind, radiant feathers creating a light halo around her entire body. As she made contact with the ground, her wings disappeared in a flash of brilliant warm light. I gaped at her.

Henry was less impressed, rolling his eyes. "Freaking angels. So dramatic."

Vanessa waved her hands in his direction, smacking him on the shoulder. "Quit hiding," she admonished. I had no idea that Henry had gone invisible.

Gabriel towered over Henry, apparently now viewable to everyone. "What are you doing here? Melissa's supposed to be at the villa." Gabriel's steel eyes were so furious, I couldn't even enjoy the fact that he'd finally referred to his place as the 'villa.'

Henry stood his ground, even if his shoulders shrank a little. "Hey, things happened out of my control." He gave a quick overview of Barbara's betrayal and Regan's escape.

After the recap, Vanessa looked like she wanted to punch something. She faced me to let me know I might be a good target. "We shouldn't have trusted the Blessed Order."

"You're right," I snapped back, "because trusting a shadowy government contractor full of magical beings would have been so much better."

Gabriel let out a guttural growl. "We don't have time for petty bickering. Lucas tracked the pixie's and the druid's scent here. They're already inside."

"No," I whispered. Images of the druid attacking Regan after debate practice flashed through my mind. I couldn't let them have my baby girl.

I shot toward the breezeway, going faster than I'd ever run in my life.

Gabriel yelled after me, "Stop!"

I couldn't stop, not with my daughter's life on the line. I made it all the way through to the other side, sneakers pounding on the sidewalk leading up to the annex when Gabriel flew to catch me. I heard his uneven breathing hovering just behind me. I twisted my head to tell him to back off.

He smacked headfirst into some sort of transparent shield.

His stone face crunched with sickening force, and he bounced backwards away from me. He crashed onto the ground, creating a mini-impact crater in the concrete.

"Gabriel!" Vanessa landed at his side, her glowing hands waving over his obviously broken nose. The stone shifted to repair itself under her light.

Henry jogged toward me, stopping a few yards away. Holding out his hands, he patted around like a mime, feeling the barrier that had smashed Gabriel's face. "We can't get through here. It's solid."

"Didn't Lucas just come this way?" Vanessa asked as she put the finishing touches on Gabriel's face.

"They must have just erected the barrier." Henry rubbed his palm up and down the barrier's surface. "And it gets worse."

He showed off bits of glitter stuck to his hands.

"Impossible." Vanessa extinguished the light from her hands, giving Gabriel room to hobble back to his feet. She scoured the skies. "How could the pixie use her dust if she isn't here?"

"She must be using a magical amplifier." Gabriel stretched his muscles around his shoulders, testing to make sure everything worked.

"She's insane," Vanessa said. "An amplifier of this magnitude will kill her."

A low grumble issued from Gabriel's throat. "The Circle of Elphame is nothing if not extremely devoted to their cause."

"Let the amplifier do its job then," Henry said. "Once the barrier breaks, we can get in and take care of business."

My face flushed. "How long will that take?"

No one answered. Henry especially couldn't look me in the eyes. Gabriel finally said, "It could be just a few minutes."

"'Could be?'" I repeated. "You don't know?"

"It's hard to tell without exactly knowing the amplifier in question."

"We don't have time to wait," I said, taking a step toward the annex.

"Melissa," Gabriel said, lacing his voice with supreme authority. "Come back here. Now."

"Who will help Regan?" I demanded. "She may need us right now."

"Lucas can handle it," Gabriel said in slow measured tones, as if trying to talk someone off a skyscraper ledge. "He's got natural resistance to pixie dust in his wolf form."

"Lucas can't take on both the druid and the pixie by himself. He already tried once and failed."

Gabriel hesitated to respond, which told me he agreed with my assessment. "I'm sure Lucas will buy us some time before anything happens to your daughter."

"That's not good enough." I turned my back on him and strode with purpose toward the annex.

Gabriel let out a guttural roar that shook me deep to my core. Henry flinched. Even Vanessa's wings reappeared with a hazy glow as Gabriel's frustration rang out across the campus.

When he finished, he looked at me with raw anguish. "You'll be killed."

He wasn't wrong. It was a real possibility.

The alternative was worse. "I might as well die if they do something to Regan!"

His face was unreadable for a few long seconds. I thought for sure he would launch into another tirade, but instead he drew his lips into a thin line. "Fine."

Vanessa let out a loud breath. "You think our office manager can go toe-to-toe with rogue fae?"

"No, but she can help us get inside." Gabriel bunched

his hands into fists at his side, as if willing himself to remain calm. He turned to give me all of his intense focus. "You need to find the pixie and destroy whatever amplifier she's using to create this barrier."

"What will it look like?"

"You'll know it when you see it," Vanessa said. "Given how wide a range she's projecting her dust, the amplifier will be visibly interacting with her magic."

Gabriel nodded. "She'll be solely focused on keeping the barrier erect. One slip, and it comes tumbling down. So, take her down, and stay out of the druid's way."

"Okay," I said, pumping myself up to hide my fear. "Find the pixie and destroy her magic trinket. Got it."

Gabriel then began barking orders to Henry and Vanessa to search for any weakness in the barrier they could exploit to fight their way in.

I jogged up the sidewalk to the annex and gripped the front door's handles. Before slipping inside, I stole one last glance at Gabriel. He'd been staring after me, deep concern in his eyes. He mouthed 'Stay safe' then soared upward into the air, raking his claws against the barrier in a futile attempt to slice it open.

CHAPTER 37

THE ANNEX'S FRONT hallway hit me with a quiet punch. The overhead lights should have been casting an obnoxious fluorescent glow on the lockers lining the walls. Teenagers should have been bustling through the hallways, waiting in between debate rounds. The tables in front should have been manned by either cheerful debate coaches or surly students, asking participants to register as they signed in.

Instead, the hallway lights had been turned off, allowing only muted daylight to slide inside from the occasional overhead window. No one walked the halls. All the classroom doors were closed. Someone had knocked over the two registration tables, sending papers and permanent markers all over the floor. I skirted around the mess.

A giant ball of silver fur huddled past the upturned tables. I jumped at the sight of one of the druid's pets. I thought it might attack me until I noticed a red streak leading to its body like bloody emergency lights on an airplane.

The druid's wolf had been injured.

I tiptoed to within several yards of the beast, hearing a

slight rasp that told me the animal was still breathing but just barely. Although it tried to fully open its eyes, it couldn't even manage that.

This had to be Lucas's handiwork. Hopefully, he'd cleared the entire hallway. I kept the injured beast in my direct line of sight as I scurried to the closest classroom door.

A peek through the window grids showed me that the room had been set up for a debate. Two opposing desks faced each other in front of the chalkboard, a longer desk with a podium in between. A judge's table sat off to the side with scoring sheets.

I was about to turn away when I noticed movement in the far corner of the room. Squinting, I pressed my face into the glass.

A round face with wavy hair popped up in front of me. "You want a piece of me?" Leah screamed, spittle flying from her mouth. "Come on and fight!"

I barely jerked out of the way as she flung the door open and came at me with a chair, the rubber foot caps facing me as if she were taming an unruly circus lion.

Years of training with Barbara kicked in. I let Leah flail past me, then yanked the chair away from her. Using her own momentum against her, I pulled her back into the classroom and shut the door behind us.

That's when Leah finally recognized me. "Melissa?"

I nodded. In the classroom's corner, a boy dressed in a nice dress-up shirt and slacks sat comatose underneath a poster with Hamlet quotes. He was a debater from another school. I recognized a second boy with short dark curls as a freshman on Regan's debate team. He held a sobbing middle-aged woman in a rumpled business suit.

"What's up with her?"

"She's a parent judge," Regan's debate teammate said quietly. "She went nuts when the wolves showed up."

As if to accentuate his point, the woman's sobs grew louder. The freshman boy whispered words of comfort into her ears.

These kids were more level-headed than a grown woman. I wanted to smack her straight, but she'd only slip into more hysterics. Just great.

I took a deep breath. "Tell me what happened."

Leah's body shook as her bravery melted. "Regan showed up at the last minute. I was so happy to see her after not hearing from her for so long, but she acted funny, demanding to talk to her coach. I told her I last saw Mrs. Hopner on the far side of the building, and she took off."

I grew cold. "Did she ever come back?"

Leah's shivers turned more violent. "No. The first round started, and I had to keep track of time in this room. Within minutes, a pack of wolves showed up. They were being controlled by some freak in a hooded robe. He asked us where Regan was. I-I shouldn't have told him where she'd gone, but I was scared. He told us to stay put or else the wolves would eat us."

I put an arm around her. "It's okay, Leah. You did your best."

"We tried to call the police," the freshman added, "but our phones aren't working. They won't even turn on."

They wouldn't either, not with the amount of mojo Serena was pumping into the invisible barrier around this place. Her magic probably explained why the lights were out too.

"Did you see anyone else besides the guy in the robe?"

They both shook their heads, but the freshman said, "I thought I heard the guy order a wolf to guard the auditorium."

"Where's that?"

"Way on the other side of the building."

That was probably where Regan went too. "How do I get there?"

"The main hallway leads right to the auditorium's front entrance," the freshman said, "but there's a stage entrance that's closer than the front doors. Take the first side corridor you see. The unmarked double doors after the bathroom will get you backstage."

Leah steeled her shoulders. "I can show you."

"Absolutely not. I'm going alone. If you both stay put, you should be safe here." At least, I hoped so. They certainly couldn't leave the building until the pixie's barrier came down.

"Be careful, Melissa," Leah pleaded. "And please, don't let anything happen to Regan."

I don't know if they saw me shiver, but my voice was steady when I replied, "Will do."

I didn't stop at any of the other classroom doors after that, making my way down the sole main hallway. All the classrooms were shut up tight. I tried not to think of those rooms full of vulnerable kids.

Just like the freshman said, there was a narrow corridor that took me off the main path. The bathrooms in this hallway were inlaid into the wall with no doors, one leading to the ladies' room and the other for men. Both rooms were pitch dark given the power outage, but I didn't think to check the shadows, too intent on getting to the double doors at the far end.

I should have paid closer attention.

Without warning, a wolf burst out of the women's bathroom, tackling me to the composite tile. I managed to get an arm up in self-defense, which the wolf grazed with its teeth, leaving a hot gash of pain. I couldn't evaluate the damage as it bore down on me, hot breath ratcheting up my panic. I tried to push back but couldn't get leverage against the beast. My upper chest and face were open to attack.

The wolf should have snapped my neck in two.

Instead, a flurry of snarls overwhelmed my ears. More weight crushed my lower legs, dog nails poking into my skin. I let out a short cry, and to my amazement, the weight came off.

The fight had moved off me.

Lucas in black wolf form had driven off my attacker, but he'd become intertwined with his enemy. Black and silver fur flashed as each struggled to find a chokehold on the other. High-pitched yips indicated when one of them struck a vulnerable spot. Lucas already had bloody mats in his fur from the previous fight and was sluggish against his opponent.

Frantic to help, I glanced around and found a fire extinguisher mounted on a wall. I yanked it free and pointed the spray at the dogs before realizing I had no idea how to operate the stupid thing. I discovered it's not easy to read instructions when a life-or-death struggle is happening in front of you.

Dog claws scraping across the floor warned me of the pair's approach. The silver wolf had gotten a biteful of Lucas's withers and shoved him down. Lucas squealed as his enemy's jaws thrust from side to side.

Screw the instructions. I raised the fire extinguisher, and as Lucas went limp from pain, I slammed the fire extinguisher's metal end onto the silver wolf's head.

A sickening wet crunch told me I'd hit my target. The silver wolf collapsed, its front legs draping over Lucas.

I thought I saw brain matter on the fire extinguisher and flung it aside before I puked. I kneeled next to the black wolf.

"Lucas?"

He let out a pathetic whine.

The silver wolf weighed a couple hundred pounds, but I managed to shove its body aside. Lucas took the opportunity to crawl to the men's bathroom entrance, tucked out of sight in the darkness.

"Hey, there." I put a gentle hand between his ears, trying not to lose what little composure I had left. "You gonna make it?"

He managed to open one eye into a mere slit and nodded. Then he slumped back again onto the tile.

Panic threatened to claw its way out of my gut. Lucas may have been fae, but he was also a teenager. He couldn't die this way.

I noticed his chest rise and fall in an even rhythm. No wheezing mingled with his breath. Although covered in blood, most of it seemed like it came from the other dogs. He honestly reminded me of how he'd looked the night Serena attacked our house, and he'd lived through that encounter.

I stood up, praying he'd be okay. Now there was only one of us who could rescue Regan.

CHAPTER 38

I STEELED MYSELF as I stood outside the backstage doors. If another wolf waited on the other side, I'd be puppy chow. A part of me wanted to run away screaming. If a freaking wolf shifter like Lucas couldn't stop these fae without severe injuries, what could I do?

But even if I died opening that door, it was the only way forward. I would willingly get mauled to death for my kid.

I winced as I turned the handle and pulled it open.

The hinges didn't creak. Nothing tore off my face. As I crammed myself inside, all I could see was cement walls and the far edge of the stage curtain. I shut the door behind me so the light wouldn't give me away.

Thrown into darkness, I had to rely on groping around with only a pulsating light leaking from around the curtain. At first, I couldn't hear anything except my own pounding heart, but as I treaded across the wooden floor, muffled voices reached me. I couldn't make out any words, but I recognized one cadence instantly.

Regan was in the auditorium, and she was clearly distressed.

I stubbed my toe on something solid, wincing through

the pain. The throbbing abated as I reached the thin sliver of light coming from one corner of the curtain.

I peeled the fabric back an inch. The rush of voices transformed into words.

" . . . let me go," Regan ended on a sob. I couldn't see her, but I knew from her hiccups she'd spent herself crying.

"You're wasting your time trying to manipulate me in this form." The druid replied.

I gingerly lifted the curtain farther back so I could see into the theater. Stage left came into view first. Like the rest of the building, the auditorium had lost all functional electricity, but that didn't matter given Serena's surreal glow.

It took me a moment to realize it wasn't her body glowing, but her Celtic knot pin. What had once looked like shoelaces and ribbon now shone as bright as any LED light, illuminating glittery dust motes floating around her body. The light vibrated in and out of intensity, giving objects murky form in the otherwise dark room. Serena herself looked gaunt and haunted, each strobe causing her obvious anguish. She also wore noise-canceling headphones as a bizarre accessory.

"Hurry, Ander," she hissed.

Creepy Cat Eyes apparently had a name.

I crawled forward until I could see stage right, which was closer to me. I saw the curious stones first, faint but visible beneath Serena's glow. They'd been arranged inside of a metal framework so that they created a rough archway, like a door, at the edge of the stage. Only a small space at the top was missing rocks so that the two lilting columns weren't yet touching.

A shadowy figure on four legs leaped up onto the stage near this strange construction. I thought it was another wolf at first, but it was clearly much larger and sleeker, a whiskered face coming into view as he called out to Serena.

"I'm almost done building the fairy ring. Just a few more stones." He paused before adding, "Not that you can hear me."

The druid had turned into a cougar, and unlike Lucas, he could still speak in a clear human voice. The apparently shapeshifting druid plunged offstage toward the seats. He came back a minute later with another rock in his mouth to place in the ring. He had to stretch on his back legs and lean against one column to do it, but he managed to nudge it into place.

"Please, don't do this!" I heard Regan plead somewhere in the seats, but I couldn't see her yet.

Ander paused, his eyes softening, but then shook his furry head. "Be quiet or I'll knock you unconscious. Would you like that?"

Regan whimpered.

"You should feel honored. Your existence will change the fate of all fae kind. Finally, the prophecy will be fulfilled, and we can return to our rightful place."

I pieced together the scenario as best as I could. At some point, the pair must have figured out what Regan's magical powers were. In cougar form, Ander wasn't as affected by Regan's magic persuasion. Serena was similarly protected by the headphones. As long as Serena kept Stronghold's team at bay, all the two had to do was use a fairy ring to portal Regan away to someplace I could never reach her.

Ander only had a few more stones left before he had completed the makeshift archway. I could run out on stage to knock some of the rocks out of alignment to buy some time, but the cougar would maul me to death before I could do much else. Same went if I tried to tear the Celtic knot pin off Serena. It would lower the barrier, but I doubted anyone from Stronghold could get here before Ander killed me.

I needed a better plan if I wanted to save Regan and myself.

I inched forward the most I dared, hoping to catch a glimpse of my daughter. She could still talk. Maybe we had a chance if I could take off Serena's headphones, and Regan ordered Serena to defend me. The timing would have to be flawless to keep Ander from tearing me to shreds.

I located Regan on a third-row aisle seat, curled up in a ball. She was a sobbing mess, but otherwise had all her limbs and no obvious wounds.

While I'd pondered my strategy, Ander had retrieved and placed the second-to-last stone in the fairy ring. "All your school friends will come out unscathed if you just come with us." He nudged the stone into proper alignment with his paw. "You don't want to be responsible for their deaths, do you?"

"I-I don't want to go." Regan's voice broke, and her body clenched into an even tighter ball.

Ander jumped back offstage, and this time I could see his tail saunter off toward the back of the auditorium near the triple set of entrance doors. A ray of light coming in through their windows revealed a nearly flat backpack resting against the balcony's support beams. One last rock remained in the pack.

With both his back to me and Serena doubled over in pain, I risked sliding onto the stage, waving my arm to catch Regan's attention. She unfortunately chose that moment to sink her face into her arms and sob.

No. Not now.

I glanced over at Serena. I'd definitely have enough time to take off the headphones, but would Regan catch on fast enough to compel Serena to protect me? Even though the gore-encrusted fire extinguisher had made me want to vomit, I should have brought it with me. At least I'd have a weapon. I was so stupid.

I tried to think of another plan, but time had run out. Ander had reached the backpack, bending his feline head down to retrieve the last stone. This was as far away from me as he would ever get.

It was now or never. I ran for Serena.

"Regan!"

Regan lifted her head as my feet pounded the stage toward the pixie. Her red-rimmed eyes widened in recognition.

"Mom?"

Behind her, Ander let out a horrific snarl. He kept the last stone in his mouth as he scrambled down the aisle.

I made it to the oblivious Serena, reaching for the Celtic knot and the headphones.

"Use your power!" I screamed at Regan.

Serena jerked at the last second as she realized my presence, but it was too late. I pulled the headphones off, then ripped the Celtic knot from her shirt.

Unfortunately, removing it set off an energy blast that sent me skittering halfway across the stage. I landed by the nearly complete fairy ring stones. I should have been grateful that I didn't hit my head on a rock, but my right hip bore the brunt instead, the radiating pain even worse than my wolf-chewed arm.

Dazed from the unexpected blow, I had no time to fend off an oncoming Ander. The emergency lights of the auditorium blazed to life, probably because Serena no longer was projecting her magic with the Celtic knot. They gave me a perfect view as the cat leaped onstage with claws extended, shredding the wooden boards at the stage's edge. Regan shrieked something, but it was lost as his enraged yowl made my ears ring.

I would have died if Serena hadn't come between us.

Her angle of impact threw both her and Ander to the side, allowing me time to scramble away in a crab walk. The two tangled over one another in a mass of bodies, Serena somehow getting her arms locked around Ander's back even as she bled from horrid scratches to her face.

"Get off me!" Ander hissed.

"No!" Regan shouted. She climbed on stage to stand

next to me. "Don't let go!"

Tears streamed down Serena's injured face as she clenched tighter to the cougar. "I can't release you! The girl's controlling me!"

Regan tried helping me to my feet, but my hip wouldn't bear any weight. It hurt too much to move, much less walk out of here.

I shooed her away. "Go. Run while you can."

"I won't leave you."

My breath stammered through a fresh wave of pain. "You have to. Otherwise, we'll both die."

Her death grip tightened on my arm. "It's my fault!"

I wanted to tell her it didn't matter. All I cared about was keeping her alive.

"Step aside!" Ander suddenly raked his claws from Serena's right shoulder all the way down to her left side. Blood splattered across the stage floor.

We all stared at him in horror, Serena the most shocked of all.

"A-an-der . . . " She attempted to speak but a pink bubble cut off his name. She collapsed in a wheezing mess, clutching her torso.

Regan trembled so violently, I worried she would faint. "Y-You killed her."

"She was dead anyway, expending that much energy." Serena's blood dribbled down Ander's foreleg. He picked up the last stone with his mouth from where he'd dropped it in the scuffle. As he stalked toward us, he looked exactly like the lethal predator he was.

We shuffled backward as he placed the last stone in the ring, carefully arranging it with his paw. Just like back at Stronghold, this set off a chain reaction of light that surrounded each stone, igniting the runes carved on top. A new glow formed inside the archway, spreading outward, sending sparks like a Tesla coil as images slowly formed: a vast field of snow with a dark night sky full of hundreds of sparkling stars.

Ander had opened a portal to some wintery location far away from Salem.

He faced Regan, his tail twitching. "You have a choice, Regan. You can come quietly with me right now, and I'll let your mom live. Or you can refuse and I'll kill her."

"No." I struggled to put myself in between them.

Regan easily sidestepped me, walking out of my reach. "Just don't hurt her."

Ander regarded her with cool approval. "You don't know it, but you are chosen for greatness. In time, you will see that." He beckoned her toward the portal so they could cross over together.

"Stop!" I yelled after them. I couldn't reach them in time, but the tips of my fingers brushed against one of the fairy stones. "You can't have her!"

I lurched forward and knocked a single stone out of place. Most of the rocks held within the metal framework, but the small misalignment did the trick. The surreal snowscape vanished inside the archway like the image on an old TV set, growing smaller into a line that slowly stretched out of existence.

Ander screeched at the disruption, hackles rising. "I warned you!" He knocked Regan over to get to me.

I didn't want to die, but I'd made my decision. I straightened as best as I could, prepared to fight off Ander for as long as possible, praying that someone else could still save Regan.

A roar filled the auditorium. I thought it was from Ander until it flew past me from backstage, tearing one set of curtains down completely in its wake. Gabriel's stone form slammed into Ander before he could reach me, a trail of fabric stuck to a barb on one wing. It tore with a snap as the gargoyle pummeled Ander into the ground.

Henry ran up next to me. "You okay?" he asked. I thought I detected concern in his voice, but it was probably just the pain radiating from my hip.

"I'll live. Too bad for you."

"Of course, she jokes," he said, then dashed over to Gabriel, attempting to subdue Ander for capture.

Or so I thought. Feline bones crunched under the gargoyle's devastating blows.

"It's over," Henry said, trying to catch his boss around the arm and restrain him.

Gabriel shrugged him off, a scowl on his face as he went for another punch.

"Gabriel!" Vanessa nimbly danced around the shredded curtains as she also entered from backstage. "We need him alive for questioning."

"It's too late for that," Gabriel said, but he did throw Ander's body back to the carpet. I turned away. One glance told me I didn't want to see more of that mangled corpse.

Gabriel took one flying leap and ended up hovering over me. His pained expression took my breath away.

I gave him a shaky wave. "Thanks for the save. I really owe you one."

His eyes found my side wound, and he snarled. "Vanessa," he rasped. "Heal her."

"I can't, remember?" Vanessa said quietly. "Magic doesn't work on her."

I placed a gentle hand on Gabriel's arm. "It's not fatal, I promise. It does hurt like hell though."

Gabriel's stony Adam's apple bobbed as he swallowed something in his throat. Then he scooped me into his arms and lifted me as if I weighed no more than a small child.

"Honestly, Mom, you can use a better four-letter word than that," Regan said behind him. "You deserve it. You look like death warmed over."

Gabriel squeezed me at the mention of the word 'death.' Then he took off running through the building, getting outside in record time so he could take to the sky.

EPILOGUE

I THOUGHT GABRIEL would drop me off at a hospital, but instead, I spent a few days back at the Stronghold villa in my suite. Unwilling to place me under medical care outside his control, Gabriel struck a bargain with Barbara to have one of their paladins check me out. Dr. Reno looked more like an old farmhand, having the sunburned skin of someone who spent most of his time outdoors, but he apparently knew his medicine. He gave me local anesthesia and stitched me up just fine. He also gave me liberal doses of painkillers, which both let me sleep in relative peaceful chunks and made me a little loopy.

I vaguely remember different people visiting me at my bedside: Regan with guilt written all over her face, Barbara standing guard, and Dr. Reno checking in on me. But the person I remember most was Gabriel, always hovering just on the edge of my periphery, standing silent sentry.

That's why it didn't surprise me when I woke out of my stupor at some point to find him staring quietly out of my suite window. His size blocked out the sunlight trying to stream in. He wore a rumpled T-shirt and jeans, such a stark contrast to the confident businessman who'd hired me back at Cascade Vista.

Gabriel must have heard me stir because he turned to face me. The trouble melted out of his eyes when he realized I was awake and alert.

He cleared his throat and managed a "Hey."

"Hey." I sounded equally hoarse. "How long have I been out?"

"Just a few days. Dr. Reno's just been by, though, and says your wounds are healing well."

My injured side faced away from Gabriel, so I felt comfortable taking a peek under the sheets. I grimaced at the stitches poking from my arm at odd intervals.

"At least my side's only bruised. I'll be back in a bikini in no time." Then I blushed, pursing my lips shut. I didn't even like wearing two-pieces. Why did I say stuff like that in front of Gabriel?

To hide my embarrassment, I asked questions. "Can you tell me what happened after you rescued us from the school? Is Regan really okay? What about the kids at the debate tournament?"

Gabriel answered everything in order. Regan had been recovering fine at the villa. She'd insisted on having company, though, so Gabriel had graciously allowed Leah to visit. She'd been told about Regan's magical background and sworn to secrecy upon pain of death.

As for the school, many students had been able to call the police after I'd taken the Celtic knot off Serena. Vanessa and Henry had cleaned up most of the mess, removing the fairy stones, Lucas, the fae bodies, and one of the dead wolves. Acting in his official business capacity, Gabriel had told the authorities that Stronghold had taken a "fringe terrorist" into military custody that had let loose a single wolf onto school grounds. He refused to make any public statement in the name of national security and told the police no record of the incident would exist on his end. Because no one had good footage of anything that had happened, nothing substantial ever got leaked. Even the social media buzz was just a blip of teenagers making wild claims that no one took seriously.

I leaned back into the soft pillows. "So that's it? Everything's been squared away?"

"Yes, even Lucas is recovering nicely." Gabriel leaned forward, his elbows on his knees. "Everything's settled but what to do with you and Regan."

"Uh oh. I don't like the sound of that."

"The Circle of Elphame will come back. You'll need protection."

"I suppose just pretending none of this ever happened isn't an option?"

"After everything you've been through, do you really think that's a good idea?"

"No, of course not." Then I bit my lip. "Something Ander said is bothering me. He spoke about a prophecy, and Regan being chosen."

"The rantings of a lunatic," Gabriel dismissed.

Before I could ask more questions, Regan suddenly appeared in the doorway. "Hey!" she squealed when she saw me upright in bed.

She launched herself at me so hard, it took the breath out of my lungs. "Oof." Still, my arms wrapped around her, hugging her tightly as if I'd never let go.

"Be careful of your mother's injuries," Gabriel scolded.

"Oops. Sorry." She extracted herself from me, taking better stock of my condition. "You're looking great though."

"I'm feeling pretty good." And I honestly did. For the first time since this whole fiasco began, I felt like I wasn't looking over my shoulder. The threat of someone trying to kidnap Regan had disappeared.

She was safe.

That's when Regan burst into tears.

Gabriel quietly exited the room as my daughter apologized upside down and sideways about the entire situation. A part of me wanted to soothe that pain, knowing how much she'd been through.

I gave her a few minutes to grovel and deal with it first, allowing her space to realize the ramifications of her actions. She needed to know how serious our situation had become, especially moving forward.

But when she launched into her fifth "I'm sorry," I pulled her back to me, smelling the fruity fragrance of her shampoo. Leah must have brought Regan's favorite brand that she'd been using since middle school. Memories of the little life we'd built washed over me. Suddenly, all I could see was this wonderful child I'd raised from nothing, begging me for forgiveness.

I held her the way I used to as a young child. I assured her things would be fine, even though the future was a lot more uncertain with magic in the mix. Fear gripped me, but I reminded myself I was not alone. My mom, while not the most reliable person, obviously understood this new world. Jessie and her family also knew what was going on and would be in our corner, like always.

And I thought of how Gabriel had stayed by my bedside, watching over me.

As I hugged Regan close, a strong sense of hope overwhelmed me.

"It's okay, honey," I whispered. "We're gonna be okay."

THANK YOU FOR READING!

If you enjoyed this story, there's more in the *Magical Midlife Mom* series! Check out the next book:

MOM ON A QUEST

Please also consider **leaving an honest review** on Amazon for this book. Positive reviews help independent authors like me tremendously.

You can also keep up to date with all my writing adventures and snag two free short stories by subscribing to my newsletter at **dmfike.com**.

MAGIC MIDLIFE LIBRARIAN SERIES

Rosalind is adrift after a bitter divorce, but when she receives a letter from her estranged grandmother, she discovers she's the heir to a magical library. With an angry dragon on the premises and a killer gunning for her family, Rosalind will have to learn the ways of the fae quickly in order to survive.

BOOK 1: CURSE OF THE FAE LIBRARY

BOOK 2: SECRET OF THE FAE LIBRARY

BOOK 3: FATE OF THE FAE LIBRARY

MAGIC OF NASCI SERIES

"I do not recommend striking a whale corpse with lightning. You will regret it." – Ina, nature wizard-in-training

Ina is a rookie nature wizard, learning the ropes of elemental magic—fire, air, earth, and water. She can also wield lightning, setting her apart from the other followers of the goddess Nasci. If you like action-packed urban fantasy with just a hint of a slow-burn romance, you'll love reading about Ina's adventures in the Pacific Northwest's national forests.

BOOK 1: CHASING LIGHTNING

BOOK 2: BREATHING WATER

BOOK 3: RUNNING INTO FIRE

BOOK 4: SHATTERING EARTH

BOOK 5: SOARING IN AIR

BOOK 6: RISING SCORN

BOOK 7: GATHERING SWARM

BOOK 8: HOWLING STORM

BOOK 9: EXTENDING BRANCHES

ABOUT THE AUTHOR

DM Fike worked in the video game industry for over a decade, starting out as a project manager and eventually becoming a story writer for characters, plots, and missions. Born in Idaho's Magic Valley (you can't make this stuff up), DM Fike lived in Japan teaching English before calling Oregon home. She loves family, fantasy, and food (mostly in that order) and is on the constant look out for new co-op board games to play.

More places to keep in touch:

Website: dmfike.com

Email: dm@dmfike.com

Facebook: facebook.com/DMFikeAuthor

Amazon: amazon.com/author/dmfike

BookBub: bookbub.com/profile/dm-fike

Instagram: instagram.com/dm.fike/

GoodReads: goodreads.com/dmfike

A SPECIAL THANK YOU

This story has been supported by so many wonderful people. Jennifer Marshall, Sandra Schiller, and Jillian Diehl read early versions of this book and gave much needed feedback. Samantha Marshall provided constant encouragement of my writing efforts. I'm also extremely fortunate that Lori Diederich, my editor, fit me into her busy writing schedule (and you should check out her books under pen name Lori Drake).

A final shout-out always goes to my husband Jacob Fike. Without his encouragement and support, I never would have published novels in the first place. Love is indeed a choice we make every day.

Printed in Great Britain
by Amazon